PORTRAIT OF A WOMAN

Joseph Roccasalvo

Portrait of a Woman

SAN FRANCISCO   IGNATIUS PRESS

The lines from "After Long Silence" are reprinted with permission of Simon & Schuster, Inc. from *The Poems of W. B. Yeats: A New Edition,* edited by Richard J. Finneran, © 1933 by Macmillan Publishing Company, renewed 1961 by Bertha Georgie Yeats.

The lines from the poem "Peter Quince at the Clavier" by Wallace Stevens are taken from *Collected Poems of Wallace Stevens,* © 1923 and renewed in 1951 by Wallace Stevens. Reprinted by permission of Alfred A. Knopf, Inc.

Cover design by Riz Boncan Marsella
Cover art by Christopher J. Pelicano

© 1995 Joseph Roccasalvo
All rights reserved
Published 1995, Ignatius Press
ISBN 0–89870–545–2
Library of Congress catalogue number 94–73066
Printed in the United States of America

Se piacere sarà di colui a cui tutte
le cose vivono che la mia vita duri . . .
io spero dicer di lei quello che mai
non fue detto d'alcuna.

If it shall please Him who sustains all
things that my life continue . . . I hope to
write of her what has never before been
written of any woman.

Dante, La Vita Nuova

Acknowledgments

This novel would have been impossible without the help of the following scholars and their historical studies: Barry Rubin's *Istanbul Intrigues;* Susan Zuccotti's *The Italians and the Holocaust: Persecution, Rescue, Survival;* John Bierman's *Righteous Gentile: The Story of Raoul Wallenberg, Missing Hero of the Holocaust.* I have relied on their research for the opening section of chapter seven. I have drawn on the Hills brothers' biography, *Antonio Stradivari: His Life and Work (1644–1737),* for details about his peerless instruments and likewise for the composition of his varnish, which gives them their unmistakable sonority. Other sources, less of research than inspiration, were Mark Amory's collection *The Letters of Evelyn Waugh,* Thomas Merton's *Asian Journal,* and the selected poems of W. B. Yeats and Wallace Stevens.

Special thanks must go to my mother, Lucie, who pored over the text with her customary verve; to my sister, Sr. Joan Roccasalvo, C.S.J., for her faultless advice on all things musical; to my agent, George Ziegler, whose admonitory blue slips dispersed throughout the first draft had all the portentousness of flashing detours.

Cemil Hasan and Beatrice Stradivari are fictional. For candor's sake, it must be said that Mother Ambrose is derived from a cloistered nun to whom, under God, I am indebted for my hyphenated calling as priest-novelist. No other character is drawn from any person, living or dead.

Chapter One

It took twenty minutes to change engines at New Haven. Immediately after, Amtrak's Narragansett continued its afternoon run to Boston. Philip was pleased it was moving. With the power turned off, the frigid February air had seeped through the doors and windows. Now that the train was in motion, the heat from the vents circulated through the club car and warmed him.

The waiter moved up the aisle and paused at his seat to take his order. He decided to skip the meal. He had already eaten with Miles Gannen, his agent, after the interview. Philip was glad he had chosen the train rather than the air shuttle. Time gained from the flight home was invariably wasted getting to and from the airport, not to mention the wait on the runway to take off. He needed to be away from crowds. He had wearied of press conferences, book signings, and talk shows. Haggling over film rights was the most recent ordeal, and the horror of a paperback auction lay ahead. At least he was guaranteed four hours of solitude on the train with all the attendant joys of anonymity. After the glut of coverage about the Hollywood bid, he was grateful for the seclusion in the club car's limited seating.

The waiter, who brought the hot tea with milk, had brewed the Earl Grey strong. The scented steam rose from the cup. Philip sipped and inhaled as he watched the drab olive scenery rush past. The Rhode Island marina dazzled in the afternoon sun, while the streams near the tracks tumbled into falls despite the icy weather.

He set the cup down on the tray, closed his eyes, and replayed the morning. He had slipped from the apartment on Mt. Vernon Street without disturbing Lisa's sleep. He then took the next flight to La Guardia and took a taxi to NBC. Though Philip had been given the questions in advance, they were altered during the interview to allow a semblance of spontaneity. The conversation, on hindsight, had not gone well. Not only was he all talked out, but his morning instinct for brevity came off as curtness. Philip was sick of the book and tired of the hoop-la. "I'm a writer, not a salesman", he told his agent. "Let someone else hawk it to the public." But Miles managed to coax him into one last appearance.

The show was "Meet the Author". The host, Charles Bertell, had quizzed him with an enthusiasm designed to keep the nine o'clock audience awake. Reluctance to be on display along with Bertell's morning verve created a grudging mood in Philip. He struggled to be civil.

"Mr. Stratton, you've been touted as a potential literary lion—some say cub, given your age. You've been compared to the early Waugh, J. D. Salinger, Kingsley Amis. These are high marks for someone who's just thirty. Do you agree with the comparisons?"

"Only in that I've tried, like the authors you've mentioned, to write well. That my book is a best seller makes me doubt I've succeeded."

"Are you saying a smaller audience of readers would please you? Most writers would kill to get a book on the best seller list for ten consecutive weeks. *Love in the Torrid Zone* is the season's blockbuster. And now Leonard Cuckold wants to direct the film version."

"I think the name is Cukor."

"Yes, of course. But don't you find it exciting, I mean, to see characters you've created appear on the screen larger than life?"

2

"Mr. Bertell, I do not believe anything is larger than life. What matters to a writer is how faithfully his book is adapted. Hollywood is not notable for fidelity."

A pause, and then:

"I was wondering, Phil."

"Philip."

"Yes. It's been a year since the first novel came out. Do you plan a sequence like Lawrence Durrell's? For instance, something like *The Climate of Love Quartet;* the first book followed by a second, say, *Love in the Temperate Zone;* then a final one, *Love in the Frigid Zone.*"

"Quartets usually comprise four units."

"Of course. But you see my point."

"I think my weather image is all played out. I said what I knew about love in my first novel. With all the publicity and talk about deals, I've had no time for a new story. My attention has been divided."

Miles chided him later for the last remark. Over lunch, he rehearsed with Philip how hard and long they had worked to get him launched. But there was something in Philip's nature at odds with himself. He wanted to be left alone yet remain in the swim of things.

"So you can't say what the next novel is?" Bertell continued.

"No."

"What are you planning in the meantime?"

"While I wait for a theme, I'll write more poetry. Despite my recent success, I received in the past dozens of rejection slips. Fortunately, I can still remember disappointment."

As the train lurched at Providence Station, his memory was brought back to the present with a jolt. He would try to sleep, since he had two more hours of travel to South Station. It was sheer luxury to close his eyes without a doorbell or telephone ringing. This time, he was not obliged to remain in New York

3

and submit to the manic pace of that city, where jockeying for position was construed as initiative. Philip was glad he had made Cambridge his home. Where else did people carry Sophocles in Greek, whistle Vivaldi, or call events antipathetic? He loved Cambridge with the affection of a parent watching a child mature. Here people were maturing everywhere in buses, trains, and cafes. Philip preferred the population of students, for the epicenter guaranteeing literacy was a stone's throw away at Harvard.

Philip was not a Harvard man. He had graduated from Swarthmore in imitation of both his parents, who had met on campus and married after graduation. Philip Sr. had been an English major who chose graduate studies in business at Yale. Having graduated near the top of his class, he began work at Merrill Lynch first as an investment analyst in retirement funds, then in company mergers. Over the years, he and his wife had established trust funds for their two children. Philip Jr. was permitted to use the interest and a portion of the principal to finance his secondary education at Grotton and his undergraduate degree at Swarthmore; however, Philip's father insisted that graduate school should be his son's responsibility. His mother agreed publicly with her husband but privately proved an easy touch. As a successful illustrator of children's books, Doris Stratton had a comfortable income which she dispensed to both daughter and son. Philip was grateful for the generous checks that arrived the first and third Monday of every month. Along with a partial scholarship, they helped support his Masters degree in linguistics at the University of Chicago.

In 1985, Philip began his doctoral work at Harvard in English. Three years were enough to convince him his analytic powers were strong, but his imagination was stronger. Literary criticism competed with his first love, writing poetry. He would spend all his free time on versification when he wasn't researching for his graduate advisor. Philip turned to Yeats to keep his

4

imagination alive. Something about the Irish poet quickened his pulse. Clearly it was the rhythm of the lines, the studied diction, the intricate rhyme schemes that clinched ideas as each poem announced the universe had a sufficient reason for existence.

Philip tried his hand at odd verse forms like rime royal, ottava rima, the ballade. They resembled a delectable menu in an exotic restaurant. That was living, he thought, digesting experience and spewing it forth as poetry. Let others schooled in biology fret over in vitro fertilization and surrogate motherhood. Neither his ethics nor gender would shed any light. Nor would he waste his libido on shallow lovemaking. "I will keep my seed to myself and sire poems", he told Eric Bromley when they were both slightly drunk. "They will be word children, not love children."

Philip had no greater joy than to stumble upon the apt phrase, to hear after spinning the dial and trying countless combinations the felicitous click, the vault of literature opening. To what within? To noble ideas and passionate feeling. He would devote his life, he told Eric, to those ritual moments when human experience was enshrined in language. Here was perfection born of this world, the flesh made word. Romance, wealth, power were all secondary. To mediate life through poetry, that was his priestly errand in the world.

In recent years, he had been to bed with five women. Except for Lisa, all of them, like his thesis, competed with his writing. Philip warned during the first night together he would need to be at his computer in the morning. Afternoons, he would sit in Milano's cafe and gape into space in search of the perfect word. He explained himself to Eric in a moment of candor: "Sex is not the most intimate thing I do. Language is. For me words are as dense as bricks."

Philip had never attempted extended prose. He had his favorite stylists: Strachey and Waugh, Saki and Santayana. They were verbal craftsmen who set for him the boundaries of excellence. While he dared not try to surpass them, against their grace, economy, and wit he measured contemporary writers and found them largely unreadable. When pressed for an opinion after three bourbons, he would rail at the publishing houses, whose stacks of new releases were a vast conspiracy against grammar and good taste. He knew that his likes and dislikes followed strict criteria. Inhibited by perfectionism, Philip refrained from novel writing — until he met Lisa Roberts.

Lisa fell in love first with Philip's vocabulary, then with him. It was the pungent way he mixed words that made her thrill. She encouraged him to write a satire, part romance, part morality tale, all of it tongue in cheek. *Love in the Torrid Zone* resulted. It was her title. She was clever at christening with sassy names.

They met in 1988 in the February of Philip's final semester. Eric had thrown a party for the Cambridge Arts Group. A dozen or so members gathered bimonthly at his home to discuss each other's work, while each author sat voluntarily mute through the verbal battering. Eric was Petronius to the group, able because of inherited wealth, to play advocate.

To Eric's party Lisa Roberts had come, looking for unpublished talent. Her real name, Alicia Robertelli, she had changed to ensure ethnic neutrality. A green-eyed blond who had failed as a New York ballet dancer, Lisa found her proper stride in Boston. She was now the youngest and most promising editor at Little, Brown.

She and Philip were introduced at the party and they promptly hit it off. They spent the following weeks discovering what "it" was. Beginning a relationship under the duress of work was new for her. Since coming to Boston, she had been so intent on her career that she dismissed romance as an entanglement. But she sensed that Philip was exceptional. It became clear that her editing was as crucial to her as his writing was to him. Her commitment to work suited his days of solitary writing and literary gaping. So they found an apartment and moved in together. By now, she was used to his quirks and could negotiate distance. Drawn to Philip's good looks—the wavy brown hair and blue eyes, the face always fencing with an indiscreet but funny remark—the interest was more than sexual: it was commercial. Lisa had an ear for what was marketable in language. Better still, she had a nose for it. She was like someone sniffing for truffles. She had foraged before and knew the complex aroma.

With Lisa's encouragement, Philip's attempt at a novel had proceeded with remarkable rapidity. The sluices of prose had opened and let flow a steady stream of narrative and dialogue. His environment, together with his fixed routine, had helped. He had used the study of their apartment, situated in the back of a building on quiet Mt. Vernon Street, where no pedestrians or traffic rushed about. As he gazed into a garden of massive trees and pruned shrubs, he could write in an atmosphere of total serenity. After filling a dozen pages with careful penmanship, he would put them on his computer. Again he would sit for hours, umbilically tied to his machine in a state of infantile dependence until Lisa arrived to emancipate him. They first had dinner. Then over dessert she listened to a recitation from his most recent chapter. She respectfully criticized but mostly enthused, oohing and ahing at a witticism or a sly conjunction of words. She was an ideal audience of one, receptive and applauding, like a parent who dotes on a child's every move, however commonplace. Then they went to bed. Invariably, Philip broke his slumber by rising at odd hours to turn the computer on and change a word or a comma. Often he talked in his sleep, his imagination in one world, his body in another.

After breakfast next morning, they left each other at Little, Brown. Immediately, he slipped into his predictable schedule. Afternoons, there was always Milano's and the mass of students and workers who entered and exited to provide variety. Thus the book got written steadily, imperceptibly, with a modicum of pain.

Love in the Torrid Zone was a farce combining romance, black humor, and a dose of religious satire: the story of an upwardly mobile devil who, in his efforts to get placement in the highest echelon of Hell, tries to win his gold horns by corrupting religious figures. Appearing as a born-again Christian, he seduces a drum majorette in the Salvation Army. In the process, he is smitten with her superior, a lady general. Gradually this officer returns his passion till both are embroiled in a torrid love affair. When he learns she is pregnant, he escapes to his inferno but is ordered back to finish the assignment and dutifully ruin her. Consciously derivative, the novel poked fun at demonic possession in the context of a seduction comedy. It was as if pages of *The Scarlet Letter* got scrambled with *Rosemary's Baby*.

Finishing the book in a record ten weeks created more problems than it solved. Once the text of the book satisfied Philip, the question of where he should send it remained. He refused to take advantage of Lisa's clout at Little, Brown. He insisted on trying other houses to secure impartial judgment. So the hefty novel got posted.

Letters of rejection were swift in arriving, their contents burned in his memory:

"A little too reminiscent of *Rosemary's Baby*. The author should beware of plagiarizing and give credit where it's due."

"A fascinating, twisted tale. But the story hurtles at breakneck speed. Someone else may go for this more completely."

"*Love in the Torrid Zone* has hilarious moments, the characterizations of the born-again devil and oversexed preacher memorable. Still, this religious send-up is not for us."

"The plot tends to complexify with no cumulative integration of prior and subsequent epiphanies. This works against the reader. Thanks for sending it, though."

"The writing is strong but the plot unoriginal. The author should rescue the premise and rework it along Hawthornian lines."

The remarks were no less obtuse than what Philip received for his poetry. But poems were inexpensively mailed. It was costly to duplicate a novel and send it out. Whatever he saved during his graduate years had been spent on travel. Now that he no longer held his teaching fellowship, eating privileges at the Harvard Commons were rescinded. His meager funds were dwindling. Though Lisa's salary was adequate for support, his ego would not permit him to live off his girlfriend.

His parents' situation had also changed. Having opted for retirement after a thrombosis, his father had become more vigilant about the dispersal of money. Philip's mother still offered to send him bimonthly checks, but he would have felt demeaned to accept them. His parents' move to Florida and the purchase of a house in Key West had been a major investment. Philip refused to add to the burden. Meanwhile, the interim time of no new writing weighed heavily. His frustration peaked one evening when Lisa returned to find him sprawled on the rug with another rejection crumpled beside him. One look and she deciphered the scene. Later, when they sat at dinner, Philip was silent and played with his pasta. Lisa spoke without preface.

"I know we've discussed this a hundred times, Philip, but you have to let me submit it. What's wrong if I get it to our top editor? That's what Jasper Keating pays me for. To scare up new talent. No one knows we're involved. As far as they're concerned, you're another unknown looking for a break."

"The answer is no. If the book is to keep its integrity, it must sell itself. Otherwise, I'll never know."

"Never know what?"

"If my writing has what it takes."

His inflexibility exasperated her. But Lisa had made up her mind. She would deliver the book to Keating as a novel she had screened and found worthy of a second reading. Fortunately, she still retained the copy Philip had given her for correction. She needn't risk having him miss his own.

Keating did not read the novel immediately. He spent most weekends in Provincetown paging through manuscripts sent weeks earlier. He kept to the strict pecking order of first received, first read. Lisa noticed how Philip's novel lay in the corner of Jasper's desk and gathered dust. She would allude to it when the two conferred during the week.

"By the way, Jasper, did you get to that torrid book?" she asked, using humor to disguise her interest. But Keating was always distracted by some new piece demanding a decision.

"You can unload on me", she said, and nearly added, "so you'll get to Philip's novel." She knew Jasper's procedure. If the opening paragraphs hooked him, he would read the first page. If he turned the page, the book turned a corner. If he read the first chapter without checking his watch, he read the book entirely. And if he liked it enough to reread, he would phone Lisa before Monday to share his enthusiasm.

It was Saturday night when the crucial call came. She and Philip had returned from seeing a film. After they got home, Lisa made the mistake of playing her taped messages without realizing Philip was within earshot.

"Liz, call me!" came the buoyant voice. "The novel's a howl. I haven't laughed this hard since *Vile Bodies.* I think we've got a winner."

Philip turned to her. "What book is he referring to?"

Lisa was caught between Jasper's exuberance and what she knew would be Philip's anger. Her hesitance shaped his next question.

"You gave him the novel?"

"Yes."

"Knowing what my preference was?"

"Philip, I'm sorry. I just couldn't bear seeing you mope. I

had to do something. So I nudged it a little, that's all. Keating would never back a book he felt was unpromising. Anyway, I gave him the novel with no hype. Your writing did the rest. Obviously, it has what it takes."

The rapidity with which Philip composed the novel was no greater than its swift arrival on the best-seller list. The chain of events leading to this singular occurrence was every writer's dream, as each small success produced a subsequent larger one. First, Little, Brown accepted the novel. Keating had already received the go-ahead from Lisa, who praised the book for its strong writing and clever plot. But a third reader was consulted, one to whom Philip was a complete unknown. Jeb Russell was prized in the trade for his keen criticism. It was rare that any author won him completely, least of all a new one. He combed a first novel for juvenile errors in grammar, structure, and style, eager to go for the jugular. His dissent would have forestalled publication. Keating was looking for unanimity, and Jeb's opinion was to be the clincher. In his memo, his praise was unqualified. He placed Philip's talent squarely in the British comic tradition, while insisting Philip's idiom was "trenchantly American". He ended his remarks with the following: "*Torrid* is neither fussy nor labored. There's nothing worse than constipated laughs, and here the humor moves, if you'll pardon the alimentary image. A clear green. Go ahead."

Convinced by Keating that the book was being taken on its merits and not because of Lisa's intervention, Philip signed a contract. Keating promised an initial printing of twenty thousand copies along with advertising in the Boston papers. He sent a copy to the *New York Times Book Review* in the hope that his clout would gain a major reviewer. Meanwhile, word got passed among former Harvard colleagues. Lisa mailed notices to all Philip's former friends and associates. She knew that a book's sale, despite the widest publicity, was the result of word of mouth. It was the initial boost necessary. In addition, she listed all the students Philip had tutored as Teaching Fellow, and an announcement arrived in their mail.

What gave the novel its momentum was its timely satire of bogus religion sparked by headlines of scandal among TV evangelists. The book's publication elicited a brief but important notice in the *Times* by the arts critic, Aubrey Chanler:

> During these dog days of summer when the humidity is high and the breeze from the harbor offers no solace, a novel has appeared whose only connection with the sultry weather is the title. *Love in the Torrid Zone* has an infernal theme, but the language is brisk, the wit agile, the dialogue cool. For sheer quotability, the book rivals Shaw's terse style and Saki's pinched diction.
>
> The novel belongs to a fledgling author, Philip Stratton. In this reviewer's opinion, Little, Brown has launched a counterpart to Evelyn Waugh. Chapter for chapter, Stratton matches Waugh's riotous imagination without the latter's bullying manner. However dark the humor—and I warn you, it gets black—at the end of Stratton's tunnel is a flickering light.
>
> No effort to summarize the book can do it justice, for the twists and turns of the plot are numerous. But allow me to say that the author has done for religious hypocrisy what Waugh in *The Loved One* did for the mortuary business. He's cleared the decks.
>
> For those readers eager to observe what happens when evangelism is joined to seduction under the rubric of piety, I can recommend no book more highly.
>
> During this New York heat wave, *Love in the Torrid Zone* is a refreshing experience.

Chanler insisted that though the plot rose above the topical, its connection with the scurrilous news accounts gave it a peculiar mix of moralism and veiled gossip. It was a winning combination. The book was toted everywhere. It flattered Philip to take the Red Line to Harvard Square and watch someone across from him holding his novel and laughing.

"What's so funny?" he asked, playing dumb. And from the opposite seat came a free appraisal of his work as well as guesses about the TV evangelist after whom the main character was modeled. What made Philip even happier were the royalties that increased when the novel went into its second printing.

As the book caught on, offers came for public appearances. Boston College, Boston University, Harvard, MIT—all had book forums, and Philip was invited to display his literary wares. The opportunities were so numerous that Keating spoke of an agent-manager to arrange Philip's schedule. He suggested Miles Gannen, who had apprenticed at the William Morris Agency. Miles was bright, knowledgeable and, most of all, preternaturally patient. He met Philip's angry outbursts with long pauses that helped cool his client's combustible nature.

Keating further suggested a speech consultant who would teach Philip camera presence, for he had finally agreed to appear on "Meet the Author", the most coveted forum for writers. Miles had met the show's producer, Keith Barnes, who cautioned him about Philip's terseness. "Brevity's all right, but 'yes' and 'no' are out. When authors switch to clipped answers, viewers switch the channel."

Between forums and speech therapy, interviews and book signings, the flurry of activity had cut a large hole in his time. Philip was always preparing for an appearance or en route to one. He longed for Milano's, but his schedule left no time for gaping in search of flawless sentences and impeccable words.

His only new writing was a short poem, "The Linguists", whose free verse form was exceptional:

> Wordless, they spoke, two mutes
> Articulate with loud hands
> And the sound of fluent fingers

Making some private rejoinder.
Utterly unheard of words
Opened them, one to the other,
Under the subway warning,
Please Keep Hands Off Doors.

The last line was a plea for privacy. He wrote it during the interminable sessions with Albion Films as they haggled over his book. When the novel finally sold for half a million dollars, the deal nearly collapsed. After Albion had hired the screenwriter, Rob McDaniel, to do the film version, Philip insisted on retaining sole right to add dialogue to the script. McDaniel protested; Philip held his ground. Albion's concession cost him dearly. The penalty for breaking contract with McDaniel ran into the thousands.

The big-butter-and-egg mentality, the thinking in brassy print and brazen amounts exhausted Philip and succeeded in putting him on edge. Despite his earlier yen for recognition, Philip now craved solitude. Thus he imagined sitting alone in Amtrak's club car with the motor humming and the scenery whirling by as a form of nirvanic bliss.

The hostess's voice interrupted his tranquillity. The next stop was South Station. Lisa had wanted to pick him up, but he insisted on taxiing to the apartment alone. He anticipated a foul mood and did not want to punish her with it. He had promised to phone Little, Brown as soon as he got in. The train came to a halt. Philip exited on to the open-air platform and found a cab outside. It was only fifteen minutes to Mt. Vernon Street.

The day was frigid, the harsh Bostonian weather whipping his face. It was ten degrees colder than in New York, where the wind chill had been below zero. Thank God for his long johns, cashmere sweater and vest, and beaver ear muffs. He was bundled against the elements in his mobile outer shell. He paid the cabbie outside the brownstone and hurried up the steps. He wanted to run a hot bath, soak, and take a real nap. He saw that the light was lit on Lisa's tape machine, so he played the message. It was Eric saying he would come by that evening. Could the three of them go to dinner? "Yes", Philip replied mentally, for Eric was an island of sanity. Perhaps he could suggest a place where Philip might hide for a week or two. He needed to keep counsel with himself. He had done no writing for months and felt useless and empty. Was it possible, he thought, he had blown his literary wad on one book?

Eric honked the horn outside the brownstone. Within minutes, Philip joined him in the front seat.

"Where's Lisa? I thought she was coming."

"She came home frazzled from a day of arguing with Russell over a manuscript. Now she's saddled with a new one. She's the tie breaker. I took a quick look. It's another 'How To' book about sex. It reminds me of those dance manuals, where the steps are all laid out. Just mechanics, no flow. That's where we are today. Sometimes I hate the twentieth century. Lisa says I was a monk in a former life."

Philip directed Eric to turn off Charles Street in the direction of Cambridge.

"Where are we going?"

"To an Italian restaurant near Central Square. I ate there the night Keating called about the book. They serve only pasta and salad, and they have some excellent wines. Pasta and champagne, that's my pleasure: the pedestrian and the rarefied."

"You're in a funny mood. I thought you'd be undone after the TV bout. You sound awfully vital."

"I napped all afternoon to prepare for tonight. I need to be with a friend. I'm getting no sympathy from Lisa. She says I'm mourning my success, which makes no sense."

The traffic was light, so they arrived in fifteen minutes. Eric parked the car a block from the restaurant. It was called Cincìn, a trattoria employing all the stock clichés: red-checkered table-cloths, Chianti bottles with candles, Parmesan dispensers. The two friends chose to sit in a quiet corner.

As Philip had promised, the food was delicious. Fresh pasta, tossed at their table, and sparkling wine in an ice bucket restored Philip's trust in the world. His friendship with Eric completed the dinner. Presently, dessert was served. They both cut into the flaky cannoli, which oozed ricotta and citron. Meanwhile, Philip caught up on recent events in Eric's life. He and Vicki, his girlfriend, had ended a two-year relationship because of a disagreement about which state they should live in.

"I can't move to L.A. My roots are in New England. Anyhow, I hate the West Coast."

"I'm sorry for being so preoccupied with the novel. I never bothered to ask how you and Vicki were doing. Your break up happened weeks ago, and I'm just finding out. You seem calm about it, almost placid. From your face, one would never guess. No brooding or dark rings. Did you stay at the house on the Cape?"

"God, no. That's all I need is to have my parents breathing down my back. They were fond of Vicki and expected an engagement. No, I go to the Cape only when they've vacated and I have the place to myself."

Eric was at the demitasse stage. He was wringing oil from a zest of lemon into his espresso.

"To answer your question, I went to a monastery for a week."

Philip looked up incredulously. "Surely thou kiddest."

"I'm serious."

"Did you find the neurotic celibacy supportive? Not a healthy way to cope with sleeping alone. You need to go cold turkey till another woman catches your eye."

"You're embroidering, Philip. You have to visit the place

16

to see what I mean. It's ideal for sorting things out. Anyway, didn't you say, not sex, but words were the most intimate thing you do? Conversation with the nuns would prove your point."

"Nuns. I thought you said monastery."

"I should have said abbey. It's called Regina Pacis. The community has three hundred acres, and it's a short distance from Springfield. A mile down the road are hermitages separated from each other by a few hundred feet. They're cabins with wood burning stoves and fireplaces. You can stay there if you want to avoid the main guest house."

"Who supervises?"

"A group of cloistered Benedictines. Their original foundation was English. They sing the Office in Latin and the place has a medieval flavor to it. It fits in with your anti-modern mood. Why not go for a rest? You'd thrive. If it doesn't grab you, I'll drive you back. Try a weekend. You can stay longer if you like. I'll call the abbess and tell her you're a friend who needs time alone."

At first taken aback by the suggestion, Philip became less and less put off as he listened. His writer's instinct for novel experiences was being addressed.

"Must I participate in the services? After writing *Torrid,* my churchiness is nil."

"The nuns leave their guests alone. Unless you want to talk with them. One nun you might find interesting is Mother Ambrose. She's more up your alley than mine. I hope you don't mind, Philip. After dinner one evening, when she and I were talking, I mentioned you. You both have the same interest in poetry. She published a collection in England. I bought a copy at the gift shop and have it at home. It's called *Poems for Two Violins.* A perfect title, given her name before she entered. Beatrice Stradivari."

The biographical sketch and surname intrigued him. For the

first time in months, Philip felt his imagination racing, but he spoke with restraint.

"The idea of roaming the woods is appealing. Shades of Thoreau. But what do you do all day?"

"You can read. They have a library of classics. You can also help with the outdoor labor. A lake is on the property where you can go boating. It's ideal for clearing the head."

"You amaze me. I had no idea you were, as the colloquialism goes, 'into' religion. I thought you were a Quaker who dallied with Episcopalianism when you were feeling Proustian. Now I learn your deity's Roman Catholic." Laughing, Eric allowed his friend the last word. Philip liked clinching a conversation with a *bon mot,* and Eric enjoyed the performance.

"A cordial?" Philip asked.

"Fine with me."

"Anything special?"

"No, you order." Philip summoned the waiter.

"Can I get you something, sir?"

"Yes. For both of us. Benedictine, straight up."

The day after their dinner, Philip phoned Eric to ask him if he could borrow the poems.

"No problem. I won't get to them for awhile. I'm going to the Cape, now that my parents are away. I want to set up my easel and paint. Shall I leave the book off?"

"No. Leave it with your housekeeper. I'll come by late morning."

After picking the book up at Eric's, Philip took the train back to Charles Street, walked to Milano's, and ensconced himself in a corner. It was noon when he arrived and five when he left. He had pored through all the poems. Entranced by the language and the treatment of love, he forgot the time. By early evening, he knew several by heart.

During the marathon reading, he wondered what accounted

for his undivided attention. He knew his interest preceded the poems. Eric's description of Beatrice had piqued his curiosity. But there was more to it than that. However congenial Philip's relationship to Lisa, a part of his emotional life was on hold as if he were waiting for someone more compelling to fill it. Philip believed he had found that person within the boundaries of a book. His doctrine of recognition had been confirmed. He had several ways of talking about this revelation. He called it an act of alignment, a moment of plenitude, an event of pure affinity. They were abstractions for talking about someone who enters one's life with qualities making for perfect compatibility. "A relationship is like a garment you put on", Philip once said. "In the way it clings or covers the body, it's another skin. The significant other is like that. Experience and background combine for an ideal fit."

When Philip had tried his theory on Eric, his friend had chided him for a Platonism gone haywire. "She's part infatuation, part hallucination. She just doesn't exist. You'll only be disappointed and wake up alone." But Philip had held his ground. "When she and I make love", he continued, "I'll imagine transcending our bodies to experience the totality of being."

Over the years, he listed the attributes of women whose writings he most admired: the sensuality of Colette, the intellectualism of Virginia Woolf, the earthiness of Willa Cather, the spirituality of Saint Teresa. It began when as a teenager he had read *Anna Karenina* and felt Count Vronsky's bliss as he caught sight of Anna descending the staircase in her black velvet gown. Here was the essence of woman. Philip noted how Vronsky's eyes followed Anna around the room; how they watched and explored and recorded her every gesture. Like Vronsky, Philip had memorized her. He vowed he would repeat the experience with a living woman. But he wanted his incarnation to combine the attributes of lover and wife, mother and siren and goddess. In short, he wanted it all. "It's childish and perverse," Eric had said, "a kind of emotional idolatry." Philip listened but would not be budged. He had read enough primers in psychology to know his desire was the residue of unresolved infantilism. But the yearning persisted which no relationship had yet dislodged.

So here he was at Milano's reading the poetry of a woman whose youth had passed. He had inferred her from her artifacts and invested her with the multiple qualities of his imagination. He had no right to extrapolate from the poems, but something in the fluency of language, the delicacy of sentiment, the ease of rhyme and meter told him he had found what he was obscurely looking for. The revelation resembled the sparkling wine he and Eric had drunk at the trattoria. But here was no wine to dim his faculties, only the vinous substance of poetry dizzying him. Short of meeting the poet, he would memorize her work. As he turned to the poems, his enthusiasm made the effort easy.

They were largely antiphonal in composition. In the section entitled, "Notes for a *Vita Nuova*", they were presented in three movements: *Adagio, Cantabile,* and *Grave.* In the first, the beloved addresses the lover:

> I had passed by your face but once, yet who could guess
> That, with a momentary glance, it should so please
> Your eyes to grant me visions in my wakefulness,
> When you walked by at your ease.
>
> Now I am alone. I do not see the leaves rise
> And go drifting amid the stir of vagrant wind.
> I can but gaze upon your face with bewildered eyes—
> And young love has a thousand.

B.S.

In the second, the lover responds:

> When upon your face I held my gaze,
> I could not keep myself from wondering

Where you had gone to spend your winter days,
That you should be so lovely in the spring.

D.V.G.

The sequence ended with a sonnet of bereavement:

No longer will I share late summer days,
Walking with you beneath the pallid skies,
Nor look at you with warm and simple gaze,
Showing in ways of love, I have grown wise.
No more to feel the touch of fingertips,
And in my silence, hear you improvise
With genial laughter set upon your lips
And quiet love that waits within your eyes.

For now, alone, amid the shadowed hours,
I hear the western wind go drifting by,
Lamenting you who passed beneath the flowers
That shed their ample blossoms where you lie.
And though the summer sun both dawns and dies,
My sun has set, and it shall never rise.

B.S.

It was clear the initials at the end of the first and third poems belonged to Beatrice Stradivari. That she had chosen the *Vita Nuova*—the love sequence Dante Alighieri wrote to Beatrice Portinari—as the framework for her own declaration placed her poetry in the tradition of courtly love. The stock use of eyes as love's entry, the astonishment of recognition, the wistfulness and controlled eroticism were all part and parcel of the troubadour response enacted in twentieth-century verse.

In the presence of such refinement, Philip could not but marvel. Yet he realized he was deriving less and less satisfaction from the poems. The second set of initials had distracted him. He was intensely curious about the man who had initiated the love duet, and not a little envious. That Beatrice had joined nobility to deep sentiment won Philip's admiration, for the poetry was an expression of his own esthetic creed. But that such feelings had been wakened in her by a contemporary roused his competitive instinct. Who was D.V.G.? Perhaps no one at all. Perhaps Beatrice had used the initials simply to fill out the courtly love conceit. Down deep, he knew it was not the reason. Only a real person elicited such passion.

Philip shut the book and checked his watch. It was after five and he was running late. He had promised to join Lisa at the Ritz to celebrate the anniversary of their meeting at Eric's party. He raced up Mt. Vernon Street to the apartment. First things first. He had to call Eric at his parents' house on the Cape. He found the number in his address book.

"Eric, Philip. I want you to do something for me. Remember your suggestion about the abbey? Well, I want you to call the abbess. Tell her you have a friend who needs time away. No, I don't mind staying at the guesthouse. Yes, the weekend would be fine. You don't have to drive me, I'll take the bus. How long? I don't know. A few days. Well, I never said no to your suggestion. It suddenly took hold. Probably reading the poems. They've stirred the embers which I thought were out. Call if there's a problem."

Philip put the phone down. Purpose galvanized him. Something shackled for months was freed. He was on to the scent like a hound in pursuit. He got undressed and stepped into the shower. He recited the poems, sometimes recalling isolated lines here and there:

> So let the night discard the stars as dead
> And day withdraw the sun from out of sight.
> Small wonder, were this easy done as said,
> That I would rather live by candlelight.

One or two he remembered *in toto,* so he recited them several ways, softly at first, then loudly orating them into empty space.

Like Dante on the Ponte Vecchio, he announced her name, "Beatri-ce", but elongated the vowels and weighted the consonants.

Later that evening, after cocktails in the Ritz Bar, Lisa and Philip sat in the main dining room which overlooked the Public Gardens. They had just finished a salmon dinner. An empty Clicquot Rosé stood on its head in an ice bucket. Having polished it off with a dessert of chocolate mousse, they were now enjoying espresso and liqueurs. Lisa had ordered Grand Marnier, Philip B&B.

"That's new. You usually have cognac."

"I'm eager for a Benedictine with a kick." He laughed, enjoying the private joke.

"You've been chipper all evening", she said. "And the grim mood. Completely gone." Philip grinned. "Have you swallowed a cage of canaries?" Lisa continued. "You look as if your tongue is in both cheeks."

"I feel happy."

"I'd like to think I'm entirely to blame. But the beaming is too intense. Did you flirt in Milano's?"

He grinned again. "If you must know, I'm feeling gloriously literary. A book's coming on. It's not unlike a woman who's tried to get pregnant and finds out suddenly she is."

"I'm excited. In your case, what's responsible?"

"Too early to say. It needs time to gestate. That's why I'm taking time off. You don't mind?"

"Not at all", she replied, as she strained to sound neutral. "Did Eric invite you to the Cape?"

"He suggested it the other night. No, it's not the Cape." He paused and added:

"I'm going to an abbey. To a community of nuns. It's called Regina Pacis."

"Philip, is this a joke?" Her response was not dissimilar to his own when Eric had mentioned the abbey.

23

"I'm quite serious."

"But you could go to a dozen places round New England. You spoke of an inn near Bar Harbor. But an abbey. It sounds bizarre. Are you working on a sequel to *Torrid?* Philip, are you telling me everything?"

"It's not very nice to get suspicious on our anniversary. If you want to confirm, call Eric at the Cape. He made the suggestion."

She looked baffled. She believed him, and yet she could not relinquish her intuition that something else was afoot. But Philip's candor and his invitation to test it made her doubt herself.

"When do you leave?"

"Tomorrow."

"How long will you stay?"

"I haven't decided."

She reached for his hand as though she were losing him. In the months of living together, she had come to rely on him. What began as a relationship that was sexual and commercial had become a vital dependency. She had tried keeping herself in brackets, but each day had widened them till Philip was settled within. If possession were nine-tenths of the law, so, she argued, was emotional closeness. She and Philip belonged to each other. She would have flinched at the expression months ago, but that's what she felt now. Had she been right in thinking it was mutual? If so, why was she denied entrance? She could feel a motive, compelling yet withheld, and it affected how she heard him. As the idiom went, Philip was up to something, and being up to it meant getting on with it. His brief answers suggested he didn't want her pressing him for details. She could hear a wall being erected, brick by brick, shutting her out, and she felt frightened. Sensing her anxiety, Philip reached for her hand. The action soothed her, and she dismissed her voices as so many perjured witnesses.

Philip gave her cordial to her and lifted his own. She held it and waited, as though she were ignorant of what came next. He clinked her glass, then tasted the binary liqueur. Philip allowed it to roll over his tongue. He did not notice her watching. Having closed his eyes, he was too absorbed in discerning where the Benedictine began and ended.

Chapter Two

Philip took the late afternoon train to Springfield and arrived after four. As he waited for a car from Regina Pacis to pick him up, he watched the snow outside. Earlier it had fallen in a blizzard of flakes, now it was dwindling to light powder. He had been waiting in the arrivals area when Sister Ursula came. Despite Philip's ignorance of Catholic monasticism, she was unmistakable in her black Benedictine habit, veil, and scapular. She greeted him warmly, and he followed her to the abbey's station wagon. The conversation to the monastery was largely informational about the history of the foundation, the community's works, the hospitality to those who visited the place. Sister Ursula did not ask about Philip's book or his recent celebrity. She spoke with him simply as a guest. He wondered why she did not probe. Was it because secular books were forbidden in the cloister? Could it be that news of *Torrid* had not yet penetrated the abbey's precincts? Or was it the contagious satire against which the nuns were safely immunized? Still, this woman's comments suggested she knew more about him than she admitted. It was in the way she addressed his writer's vocation without ever saying so.

"We have many artists who come to stay with us, Mr. Stratton. The majority aren't Catholic, but they're looking for a retreat away from the stresses of their work; a time to examine their lives or rethink a project. We all need to stand apart, Mr. Stratton. Even Our Lord took time to be alone."

The allusion was new to Philip. He was not used to the interjection of religion into casual conversation. It was as if he had landed in a country where he was ignorant of the basic vocabulary.

"I'm not that familiar with scripture, Sister", Philip confessed. "My Sunday school background is rather thin."

"Well, then, perhaps your stay at the abbey will add bulk." There was no rebuke in her voice. She said it with such directness that it made Philip laugh. It pleased him to be in the company of someone who took hold of a metaphor and embellished it humorously. This woman is smart, he said to himself. There's a sureness with people. She's been around the block more than once. He smiled at the cliché and imagined watching Sister Ursula go around the block.

In twenty minutes they arrived at the abbey's winding road. As they drove past the gate, Philip noticed a large sign that hung from a stake. It announced ABBEY OF REGINA PACIS. The roadway up to the house was planted with pine and fir trees on both sides. The snow that had fallen the night before weighed down the branches so that their outlines were barely perceptible. As the sun set, the glare became uncomfortably bright. Philip reached for his sunglasses and put them on. It was an act not only to protect his eyes but to shield himself from the unexpected. He needed to be behind something when he arrived.

Sister Ursula stopped the car at the front door of a wooden and stucco house. "This is Saint Thomas More", she said. "Our two guesthouses are named after saints. We use this one for male retreatants. Saint Teresa's for women is on the other side of the road."

They both left the car. She helped Philip retrieve his bag from the trunk and walked him into the cozy interior of the house. "Your room is upstairs. It's first on the right at the top of the stairs. Saint John the Evangelist is on the door. Another writer."

So she does know, Philip thought. "Thank you. It should be

easy to find. One last question, Sister Ursula. I hope I'm not impertinent for asking, but is there a reason why you're a Sister and not a Mother?" As he finished the sentence, he caught the double meaning too late and blushed. Seeing his embarrassment, she smiled but went on with perfect naturalness: "In my case, Mr. Stratton, it's because I haven't made final vows. I hope to in another year. Have a fruitful stay." She gave him a small bow and left.

Philip climbed the creaking stairs to the second floor and found his room. It was no more than a cubicle, nine by five. The appointments were visible at a single glance: a crucifix on the wall, a sink, a desk and lamp, a small closet, a platform bed, whose mattress looked more like a straw pallet. He cranked the window open. The view from the back of the retreat house looked out on a large poplar blanketed with snow, while the Berkshires in the distance were visible in the twilight. The air had turned frigid. Philip cranked the window closed and turned his attention to unpacking his suitcase. He placed his toiletries on the rack above the sink and deposited his clothes in the closet's one drawer. Tired after the train ride, he decided to lie down. The bed was firm to the point of hardness but not uncomfortably so. A shelf to his right displayed some books: a New Testament, the Rule of Saint Benedict, the Psalms. He closed his eyes and dozed for what seemed seconds. A bell tolled in the distance—for Vespers—but he ignored it. He did not open his eyes till after five, when he heard someone descending the stairs. He sat up, rubbed his eyes, and walked to the sink to splash his face. He noticed the daily order on the door. Dinner in fifteen minutes. He changed into flannels and a sweater, combed his hair into place, and walked down to the first floor. He noticed that the dining table was set for three but no one was around. Someone had stacked the fireplace with wood and lit it. A large fire roared behind the grating. It spat and crackled as the resinous wood caught flame. Philip chose a rocker close by. He set it at an angle so he could watch the fire and observe anyone who entered the room. The house was silent except for the roaring blaze. The fire is company enough, Philip thought. He closed his eyes and enjoyed the cozy warmth.

At around six, two men entered from the front door, chatting amiably as they shook the snow from their boots. One was dressed in a black habit; the other, a young man in his mid-twenties, in overalls. They removed their parkas and hung them on the clothes rack to the left of the door. Philip stood up and turned in their direction as they walked toward him.

"You must be Philip Stratton. I'm Father Walter Stewart. This is Wayne Johnston." They both shook Philip's hand. "We usually use first names. Do you prefer Philip or Phil?"

"Philip."

Father Stewart was a man in his late fifties, largely bald except for a fringe of dark hair. His features were too large for his face, and his ears protruded at a conspicuous angle. He had laborer's hands with thick, unmanicured nails that were clipped but not filed. He spoke briskly as if he were chairing a business meeting and wished to clear away the preliminaries.

His companion, Wayne, was a lanky young man who, in another setting, might have been addicted to T-shirts and blue jeans. He had warm brown eyes which blinked thoughtfully. His hair fell over his forehead so that he wore perpetual bangs.

The two men took their customary places at table as Philip followed. Father Stewart stood at the head, Wayne to his left. Philip took the remaining chair. He then noticed a name card next to his napkin. As Philip pulled his chair out to sit down, he saw that the other two were standing with heads bowed for grace before meals. He reddened at his *faux pas,* but his companions had their eyes closed and failed to notice.

"Bless us, O Lord, and these your gifts which we are about to receive from your bounty. Bless Wayne as he decides about seminary. Bless our guest, Philip, during his stay, the community of Regina Pacis, our friends and benefactors. Through Christ, Our Lord. Amen." Once grace ended, they sat for the evening meal.

The table was set with a crusty bread and creamy butter that looked freshly churned. A pitcher of milk, a carafe of wine, and three beers stood alongside awaiting selection. While Father Stewart and Wayne made small talk about snow and snowplows, Philip could hear the footsteps of someone in the kitchen.

"Is another guest joining us?" Philip asked during a lull in the conversation.

"No. It's the Guest Mistress in the kitchen. She'll be serving table tonight."

"Whose turn this week?" Wayne asked.

"Sister Vera's. After dinner, Mother Ambrose will come to help her return the dishes to the abbey kitchen."

"Mother Ambrose", Philip said, startled by the name.

"Do you know her?" the priest asked.

"Only from her poems."

"You mean the volume on sale at the abbey store", Wayne said. Philip nodded.

"I'm not a poetry man myself", Father Stewart added, "but I'm told Mother has quite a following in the area. She'll be pressed to get back after dinner, Philip. But if you like, you can ask to speak with her in parlor this week. She's a busy lady, but she may find time."

Sister Vera oversaw the table as if she were the maître d' at a Michelin-starred restaurant. She was small and plump with a round beaming face that easily laughed. In a former age, one might have called her jolly. The dinner she served was in the monastic tradition: vegetables from the garden and milk from the barn; potatoes and mixed beans; a cheese casserole; deep-dish apple pie with sliced cheddar on the side. Philip struggled to attend to the chit chat about the building campaign, the extension community, the postulants coming in a week, but his

31

mind wandered. Mother Ambrose's imminent arrival had usurped his awareness. When she finally came, it was during a second round of coffee, when Philip's patience with abbey gossip had waned. She entered from the front door, dusting off the snow that had collected on her voluminous shawl. Philip's first impression was of firelight reflected on her face, a mix of brilliance and shadow as she approached the table.

"Good evening, Mother", Father Stewart and Wayne said in unison. The priest continued with an introduction:

"This is our guest, Philip Stratton."

She paused to observe who was being introduced. She turned toward him and with a glance seemed to grasp his entirety.

"It's a pleasure to have you as part of our community, Philip. If I can do anything to make your stay comfortable, please ask."

Her accent was impossible to place. At first it sounded British, but there was a liquid quality to her diction that suggested a Mediterranean lilt. She is immensely attractive, Philip thought; in fact, still beautiful. She had that delicate skin typical of a woman who during a lifetime views the sun guardedly. Of more than average height, she had superb carriage, what the French call *"un port de tête."* Her presence and the graceful way she moved in her Benedictine habit announced the born aristocrat. She wore it with the delectation and pride with which some women wear Chanel. Philip's silence in the presence of an intriguing personality ran the risk of appearing rude. Wayne rescued the situation.

"Mother, Philip's an admirer of your poems."

"Ah", she said, as she waited for him to declare himself without help.

Philip responded on cue. "A friend of mine, Eric Bromley, gave me a copy of *Poems for Two Violins* after his visit to the abbey. I read them in a single sitting."

The light in her eyes flashed momentarily and modulated. She spoke with measured words like a poet making each one

32

count. "I have learned to value most the appraisal of another writer", she said. "I should like to hear you comment further." She smiled and moved briskly from the dining area into the kitchen.

Father Stewart and Wayne took her absence as a signal to end dinner with a closing grace. They all rose and stood at their places.

"We give you thanks, Lord, for the gifts of food, friendship, and fellowship. We are grateful, too, for those writers who feed the spirit with living words. We make this prayer through Christ, Our Lord. Amen."

Father Stewart turned to Philip: "You're welcome to join us for night prayer. Compline's at eight. It's held in the chapel to the left of the abbey. Otherwise, I'll see you at breakfast."

"That reminds me. After Compline, I have to go and check on the temperature in the barn", Wayne added. "Philip, my room is three doors down from yours. St. Joseph's. If you need anything, knock."

Philip thanked them both. He was eager to return to his room and retrieve his notebook. He felt a strong desire to sit in front of the fireplace and make an entry in the journal he had packed. He took the stairs in threes, grabbed his notebook, and returned to the rocker. He put another log on the fire and watched it catch flame. He turned to a blank page and stared into space in the way he did at Milano's. He was about to write when he heard the clatter of dishes behind him. Mother Ambrose was at the door with her arms holding a large tray. She was alone. Sister Vera had left.

"I'll get the door, Mother", he said without being told to assist. "Could you use some help carrying that back?"

"Thank you, Philip. It isn't necessary. It appears you were settled in for a night of composition." She noticed the book and pen he had left on the dining table when he walked to the door.

"Mother, may we talk again soon?"

"Yes, I should like that. I will leave a message for you at breakfast. Meanwhile, have a restful sleep. Good night, Philip." He closed the door behind her, returned to his seat, and began to write. His mood was exhilaration. It so focused him that he wrote with almost no corrections:

I imagine her on a massive stage in a baroque theater. Sconces on the wall, frescoes on the ceiling, chandeliers at intervals. Flowers are tossed at her feet after the final scene of Swan Lake. *Or the last act of* Medea. *Or the death duet from* Thaïs. *Thunderous applause and relentless cries of "brava" demand another bow. She obliges her audience and slips from behind the curtain. She curtsies deeply and crosses her arms at the breast, pressing her heart with gratitude. She is an artiste in the grand manner. Her skin resembles Parian marble held to sunlight. Her slightly almond-shaped brown eyes suggest a Slavic ancestor. Her pupils dilate and the blue vein at the brow quivers whenever she's thinking. But it is the Gioconda smile that transfigures her. It reveals both clarity and mystery.*

This woman understands. "What", you ask, "does she understand?" "Everything." In her case, the word is more than a transitive verb encompassing persons and objects. It is a state of being, visible in her smallest gesture. For she has been there, wherever "there" is. And yet to worldliness she conjoins innocence. The combination confounds me, it is so rare. My reaction to her is the same as to her poetry: I must know her. I must learn her secret. Here is the theme for a novel. What would it be like to meet a woman who understood life entirely, someone who grasps the whole when I cannot see the part, who knows where it begins and ends while I cannot tell where I stand? In whatever way and to whatever degree, she and I will claim each other. For in one meeting, I have seen the possibility in her eyes, heard it with my mind. Between us, the recognition is instantaneous.

Philip put the notebook down and looked at his watch. It was seven forty-five. Recalling Father Stewart's invitation to join the community for Compline, he decided to go. It would provide him with an opportunity to see Mother Ambrose in another setting. He went upstairs to his room and put on his hooded jacket. Rapidly he descended the stairs, opened the front door, and braved the cold outside. The temperature was below freezing, but the night air was calm with no perceptible wind to punish his face. The stars were in full array, the moon brilliant in its first quarter. As he walked, the dry snow crunched underfoot. He passed the high wooden wall of the monastery that partitioned the nuns from the outside. The porticoed chapel was to the right of the monastic garden. He entered through a side door. The chapel was in complete darkness except for candles that flickered before the statue of the Virgin. Philip looked around. At first it appeared he was alone. Then, as his pupils dilated, he saw two hunched figures. Father Stewart knelt at a prie-dieu alongside Wayne. Both were on the left side of the chapel. Philip sat in the corner, where he could observe the ritual without participating. In the semidarkness, he saw the vases of ferns and flowers etched in soft light. The sanctuary light hung from the ceiling, while a small flame flickered within. A nun appeared with a long taper, which she used to light the candles on the altar. The cloister area behind the sanctuary was hidden from view, the curtain drawn completely. Promptly at eight, as the chapel bell tolled, the curtain drew back, revealing choir stalls to the left and right, the abbess' chair in the center.

Reverend Mother entered first, then the nuns in twos according to seniority. They bowed synchronously to the altar and to the abbess until the stalls on both sides filled. A pitch pipe sounded a note. With quavering voice, not untypical of a woman in her seventies, the abbess sang the opening antiphon. The Latin verses of the psalm alternated, first one side singing, then the other. Philip picked up the psalter and made a vain attempt to find the relevant passage, but surrendered his effort because of darkness and unfamiliarity. He strained to see where Mother Ambrose was. They all looked alike, these nuns, in their duplicate veils and habits. The black serge enveloped their

35

limbs and faces. He sighted her to the immediate left of the abbess. He had hoped to watch her react, but it was impossible. So he closed his eyes and listened.

The singing went on for half an hour and ended with the communal chanting of the *Salve Regina.* The nuns exited in the same way as they had entered, bowing to both altar and abbess. Again the curtain protecting their inner sanctum was drawn. A few minutes of silent prayer followed. Father Stewart and Wayne left their prie-dieux, genuflected, and walked to the door. Philip exited shortly after. Outside, no discussion followed, just a brief "good night".

Philip walked to Saint Thomas More alone. He entered the house, left his jacket on a chair, and sat down on the rocker. He picked up his journal and pen that lay on the seat. The fire had reduced itself to smoldering embers. He put on another log and felt satisfied when it caught flame. He then reread the first entry he had written before Compline. His reaction was vehemently negative. It struck him as exaggerated, presumptuous, emotionally indulgent. How could he compose such tripe when the critics had hailed him for his irony? And now he was wallowing in sentimentalism. Why these projections about a relative stranger? Am I so desperate, he thought, to be swept off my feet? She's a nun, remember? The poetry you read in Cambridge was written decades ago when she was young, available, and far from this nunnery. Philip was on the verge of ripping out the page and discarding it when suddenly he saw its value. It did not matter if what he wrote was fanciful. It was, first and foremost, an act of imagination. If Mother Ambrose were not as he described her, he would make her so. The woman he had asked to see was the occasion, not the cause, of whatever he would write. Her life was grist for his imaginative mill. How he shaped her in his mind's eye was everything. He would hear her story and heighten it exponentially. If the Beatrice Stradivari of his wildest dreams never existed, he would refashion her image and likeness.

He was pleased with his decision. But as he remembered her presence, he realized that something in her manner resisted manipulation. Like her country of birth, she might be conquered but would finish by conquering the conquerors, the adage, *victi victores,* proven true. She was imperious in the way she spoke and walked, the way she commanded a situation. She was the kind of woman, he thought, who would wait at a door till her escort opened it, sure of herself, convinced of her inner worth. Philip had read of literary characters like her. After an initial nudge into action, they would take flight with a life of their own. They would draw on authorial inspiration but would resist being ordered about. Philip had experienced this once when he was writing *Torrid.* It was in his misguided effort to be kind to one of his characters, the Salvation Army majorette. In an early draft, he had pitied her, and for one brief scene she defended herself against the bullying of the main protagonist. But she resisted his efforts at a kinder portrayal than her personality warranted. With Beatrice, too, he knew he could no more press her to act out of character than make a Stradivarius play a brittle sound. All right, if it was presumptuous to fashion her after his own image, he would become the amanuensis of her spirit. He shut his eyes and imagined her fifty years back. All he could formulate were basic questions. What was the color of her hair? What clothes did she wear? Did she have lovers? Who were they? Who was D.V.G.?

He opened his eyes and looked at the logs on the fire. It was nine forty-five and he was getting sleepy. In his mind he could still hear the Gregorian chant of the Compline, the nuns' voices climbing, soaring, hovering, descending. He had been awed, more now as he recalled it in retrospect. The darkness punctuated by candle flame, the glimmering sanctuary lamp, the intimate stillness—the cloister was a powerhouse, he could feel it. Sister Ursula was no slouch, nor for all her jauntiness was Sister Vera. And then Mother Ambrose. He had met this Beatrice,

37

not on the Ponte Vecchio: no feverish glances across a bridge, no Dantean eyes lowered at the sight of majesty. He had looked into her face, had spoken ordinary words to a mortal woman, and she had responded. He turned toward the front door. Wayne entered in a confetti of snow.

"Philip, you're still up. Our guests are usually out by now. The fresh air acts like a sedative. I'm about to make some tea. Would you like a cup?"

"Yes, thank you. Earl Grey, if you've got it."

Wayne disappeared into the kitchen. Philip could hear the faucet running. In minutes the electric kettle was whistling. Wayne returned with two cups on a tray. He had brought milk and honey so Philip could mix the tea to his liking.

"I'll get sugar if you like."

"This is fine. Wayne, at the risk of sounding cynical, is everyone always so nice here?"

"You mean considerate. I thought the same thing when I came nine months ago. Now I know it's normal. Anything else amounts to creeping inhumanity. I don't think I could backslide into my old ways. The nuns are great at reinforcing new attitudes. I usually talk to Mother Naomi. She's our resident Hebraicist. With her help, I found my own vision of things."

"I gather you've chosen the priesthood. I got that impression from what Father Stewart said at dinner."

"Yes. I'm entering the seminary in the fall. A buried vocation. Mother Naomi's good at unearthing things. She was an archaeologist before she entered."

"Archaeologist? And Sister Ursula before she came?"

"A lawyer."

"And Sister Vera?"

"A pharmaceutical chemist."

"Doesn't anyone simple enter here?"

Wayne laughed at the phraseology. "Well, what can I say? They've brought their talents, and each one is special. Entering

38

doesn't mean giving them up. They become instruments of their Benedictine calling."

"But they're virtually behind bars," Philip objected, "or symbolic bars anyway. In a cloister, you can't go on excavations or be in a court of law or work in a lab when you've let this kind of life interfere."

"In a way you're right except for the interference part. Their talents are used, but not always directly. It's hard to explain. They're swerved. It took Mother Naomi's digging to help me find myself. It's amazing what she's helped me uncover. Nothing gets lost. That's the impression I have after almost a year."

"And Mother Ambrose?"

"I don't really know her. Each of us is encouraged to know one nun well and the others more generally."

"She's seeing me tomorrow. She said she'd leave a message at breakfast, telling me the time and place."

"Count yourself lucky. I don't remember her ever acting that fast. She's usually kept busy with visitors from abroad."

Philip could not resist asking. "Any of them have the initials D.V.G.? If he stayed in the men's quarters, you might recall."

Wayne thought for a moment. "Six months ago, we did put up a guest for the anniversary of Mother's monastic profession. A man from Switzerland. His name was von Galli, but I don't remember his first name. He was very distinguished. Older than Mother. I'd say his late seventies. But all her guests that day were fascinating. It was like a session at the U.N. I helped serve dinner. It was remarkable to see her hold court. She moved from one language to the other. I counted six along with Turkish."

"How did she know Turkish?"

"She'd been married to a man from Istanbul. The scuttlebutt I got was that he was a Muslim by the name of Hasan. The name was on her Silver Jubilee card. I gave them to all her guests. It said: 'Mother Ambrose Stradivari Hasan, O.S.B., rejoicing in twenty-five years of monastic profession'." Wayne paused as he watched Philip digest each piece of information.

"Why are you eager for details? Is that the writer's instinct? Father Stewart said you were an author. I don't read much fiction — I prefer history — so excuse my ignorance. Are you well-known?"

"At the moment, yes."

"That explains it. You're interested in character. And Mother Ambrose is quite a character. I asked her once why she became a Benedictine so late in life. 'Wayne,' she said, 'it was either enter or remain a gypsy.'"

"What did she mean?"

"I'll venture a guess from my own journey. Like most of us, I think she was looking for a center, something around which her identity could cluster. She found it in a life dedicated to God."

"Most people, Wayne, are content to find it in a specific person and profession. Freud put it succinctly, *lieben und arbeiten,* love and work. From my observations, you find either one or the other. With a little luck, you sometimes stumble on both. I'm currently one of the lucky ones."

Wayne did not answer immediately. His smile suggested that Philip might have missed something.

"I thought that way before I came to the abbey", he finally replied. "I used to measure my choices in length, breadth, and height."

"And what did you find here?"

"Depth." He looked at his watch. It was almost midnight.

"Philip, it's late. I promised myself I would make it to Lauds in the morning. Sorry to cut this off. I know we'll continue it another night."

"I'm sure we will."

They both trudged up the noisy steps. Philip deposited his

40

clothes on the floor, fell into bed, and was asleep. His last waking thought was of Mother Ambrose supplanting the Mona Lisa at the Louvre.

The cold room woke him the next morning. He had left his window open a few inches. The February air was frigid and sent a sharp chill through him. He cranked the window closed, stepped out of his pajamas, and put on his bathrobe. Opening the door, he walked to the bathroom at the end of the hall and was pleased to find it free. The hot shower felt good. He decided to skip shaving since he had shaved the day before and his chin felt raw. He dried himself, put on his bathrobe, and went back to his room. He quickly dressed, brushed back his hair, and was downstairs in minutes. The same arrangement prevailed, but the table was set for breakfast. As he walked past his assigned place, he noticed a small envelope propped against his coffee cup. His name was on the envelope. He picked it up and with a knife sliced it open.

Saturday, 25 February 1989

Philip:

I am able to see you in parlor this morning from ten o'clock until midday. If the time is not congenial, tell Sister Vera who will inform me. Otherwise, I shall expect you.

Mother Ambrose, O.S.B.

The handwriting was generous with wide loops, strong stems, and dramatic capitals. For all the embellishment, each word was perfectly legible. He reread the brief message. Of course he would be free. He was free to see her now. His day at the monastery had no agenda. All he had planned was keeping his diary, reading, and walking in the woods. He checked his watch. It was already eight and time for breakfast. Father

Stewart and Wayne, he guessed, would enter punctually from their spiritual exercises. As he was thinking of them, both walked through the door. Sister Vera he could hear from the sounds in the kitchen.

"Good morning, Philip", Father Stewart and Wayne said in sequence. They both came to table where Philip stood for grace. After they were seated, Wayne launched into talk about his chores.

"Good thing I went to the barn last night. It dropped below zero. The cows and chickens needed the extra heaters." Sister Vera came in with steaming oatmeal, eggs and bacon, corn muffins. Stimulated by the aroma of coffee, Philip's stomach rumbled. He helped himself first to the oatmeal.

"Did you sleep well your first night here?" the priest asked.

"Yes, very. It was chilly in my room. I forgot how cold it gets in the suburbs." After the oatmeal, Philip drew liberally from the platter of eggs, bacon, and muffins. The rustic environment had sharpened his appetite.

"What are you planning today, Philip?" Father Stewart asked.

"Not much. I'm open to suggestions." He was on the verge of saying he planned to meet Mother Ambrose but withheld the information. How and when they would see each other had become a private affair.

The priest got up and went to the mantelpiece where he removed a sheet of paper from a folder. "This is a map of the area", he said as he returned to his seat. "You can find your way to the cabins, lake, and barns. The road leads to the hill where we hope to build the new abbey. You'll see that the foundation is already laid with boulders and stones from the grounds. It will be a marked contrast to the house the community lives in. The present abbey belonged to the Montclair family who gave it to the Benedictines rather than sell it. They wanted to preserve the ecology."

Philip thanked him for the map. "And you're welcome to

come to the services in chapel. Did you like Compline last night?" He did not wait for Philip's answer but ran on. "You'll have to excuse what could be taken for rudeness. Neither Wayne nor I talk afterward. We practice the Great Silence and break it only for emergencies."

Wayne and Philip looked at each other and smiled conspiratorially. "It will take awhile for me to accommodate myself to your customs", Philip said. "As for Compline, I did feel a sense of connectedness. I find that unusual since I don't know you well and my Latin's rusty. Yet every word was felt. I could guess at the meaning from the voices as they reached into the darkness for I don't know what. The world I come from thrives on noise. Last night was a kind of DMZ."

"That's the first time I've ever heard the chapel called a demilitarized zone", Father Stewart said. He enjoyed Philip's description while noting the sympathetic reaction to Compline.

They said grace to close the meal. Sister Vera came in to collect the dishes. Philip helped her stack them. While Wayne and Father Stewart talked near the door, she turned to him: "Philip, any message for Mother Ambrose?"

"Yes, Sister. I'll meet her as suggested."

After everyone had left, Philip moved to the rocker to sit and think. He liked Wayne. He was frank and intelligent, and his sincerity was a refreshing change from the movie moguls Philip had dealt with during the year. He hoped their evening conversations would move beyond monasticism. He wanted to learn more about Mother Ambrose. As for Father Stewart, without dismissing him out of hand, neither could he say he liked the man. He seemed limited in his interests, a fact symbolized by his clerical garb which had not altered once. He reminded Philip of his father who ate, drank, and slept business. A bone of contention between them had been Philip's commitment to poetry. "You can't live on what they pay for sonnets", his father had said. What sparked the criticism was Philip's revulsion to

43

high finance, which he equated with megabuck mergers and cutthroat deals. He wanted nothing to do with his father's world. Philip Sr. had taken his son's rejection personally, and when their relationship wasn't icy, it proceeded pro forma. It thawed when *Torrid* became a best-seller and the Hollywood bids multiplied. The elder Philip had approached his son with parental advice which drew them closer. Till then, Philip had accepted losing his father behind the *Wall Street Journal.* He had a similar problem finding the man behind Father Stewart's cassock. Nor did the priest's conversation help. He selected his topics within limits and gave a judicious commentary as if he were being taped and assessed. He exhibited not a shred of spontaneity. Yet Philip admitted the priest, like his father, was solicitous, a quality he appreciated as a newcomer.

A half hour later, Philip found himself outside, ambling along the abbey road. He decided to walk to the highway and back to kill the hour before his appointment. It was below zero, but the brilliant sunshine, absence of wind, and avenue of trees made it feel warmer. His stomach growled nervously, a visceral response that always preceded his visits with someone of rank or personal importance. Apart from the diarrhetic effect his breakfast coffee had had on him, the prospect of time with Mother Ambrose further agitated his insides. He had never been alone with a nun before, let alone a woman of her accomplishments. He already knew too much and too little about her. That, together with his musings, had blurred the boundaries of where her reality began and ended. He looked at his watch. He had a half hour before he was expected in parlor. So he started up the road while his stomach rumbled. He asked himself why he was jumpy. Suppose, he thought, Mother Ambrose had read a copy of *Torrid* and disapproved of his satire. Would they get into a wrangle about religion? That wasn't possible. Even during the cursory meeting at dinner, he had decided that here was a woman of latitude and longitude. Her poems were proof this was the case. No, his nervousness came from excitement at the prospect of her company. It would be an event from which a story might spring, that much he guessed. It's a time of genesis, he told himself solemnly.

Philip walked past Saint Thomas More in the direction of the abbey. As he approached, he saw the main door open and a nun exiting. From where he stood, all he could see was a vague profile. When she turned to walk down the few steps to the road, he confirmed it was Mother Ambrose. She wore her shawl over her cloak. Catching Philip's eye as he walked closer, she greeted him in her lilting English.

"Mother," he said, "I thought we were meeting inside."

"It's such a glorious morning, Philip, I thought you might enjoy walking on the grounds. Does it suit you? We can still use the parlor."

"No, no, it's fine."

"We can take the main road to the entrance gate. It veers to the right away from the highway and curves to the lake. It's all beautifully plowed thanks to Wayne. It should be easy going."

"I walked in that direction earlier, Mother. You'd hardly know the temperature was freezing, the air is so still."

Philip moved to her left as she took the lead. He watched her breath, when she exhaled, hanging in the air. The cold had reddened her complexion so that her cheeks seem artificially rouged. She stepped carefully on the roadway, looking down every so often to avoid an icy patch. She initiated the conversation.

"Are you enjoying your stay?"

"So far, yes. Father Stewart and Wayne have been helpful in making me feel at home. Frankly, I'm just happy to sit in the rocker staring at the fire. I love the quiet, especially the lack of interruptions. My life has been so jammed. This is a welcome change."

"It's important for writers to have a place where the spirit can be restored. I hope Regina Pacis functions for you in that way."

"Mother, have you read my recent novel?"

"I began it before you arrived, Philip. I'm close to finishing it. When your friend, Eric, visited last week, he spoke of your talent for writing. He mentioned your novel and how the critics received it. But he also said you were harried from all the publicity. I suggested that he invite you here for a rest. When I learned from Sister Ursula you were coming, I thought I would look for your book. I was surprised the library had it, but we often get review copies. Our librarian may have thought it was a treatise on charity in a tropical climate."

Philip laughed and asked: "What do you think of it?" She paused before answering. Philip said: "You needn't edit your feelings. After months of rejection slips, I'm used to bluntness."

"It's very clever, Philip, and moves trippingly along. It has the quality of all good storytelling. It makes you want to turn the page. Most of all, it demonstrates your gift for words. But I'm not so sure it's always satire. The best balances humor with criticism. From what I've read so far, you don't consistently join the two. Sometimes you attack all religion rather than just its insincere forms, as if piety itself were suspect. Consequently, the humor gets lost and what remains sounds abusive. I don't think nastiness is in your nature."

Her remarks did not sting him. He had to admit they were bull's-eye and expressed a more perceptive reading than any literary critic had offered. He had asked for her candor and she had given it.

"You know," she added, "for all the comedy — and I must confess I laughed more than once — what it lacks is reverence. But to possess that, you have to have felt the real thing. Perhaps that's why you're here at Regina Pacis. Part of a depth education."

"You're the second person to use the word 'depth'. Wayne spoke of it last night."

46

"It's an important word, Philip. In time, it may find its place in your vocabulary. Not explicitly, I hope. There's nothing worse than depth that announces itself. But, like background music, your audience will hear it without trying. It's a context like this road, which provides us with the chance to walk and talk."

After they had reached the highway, he followed her as she turned on to a path leading to the lake. The trees, tall and massive, so blocked the sun, that they walked in the shadow. Although there was no wind, it felt much colder. She pulled her shawl closer. The silence between them was not uncomfortable. It was as if she were giving him time to absorb her meaning. She turned to him.

"I've shared my opinion about your book. I would like to hear your comment on *Poems for Two Violins.*" Her request did not surprise him, for he had expected her to ask.

"I found them riveting. At first I thought you were writing a new *Vita Nuova*. Instead of Dante addressing poetry to Beatrice, now, I thought, Beatrice is doing the reverse. It wasn't till I saw the different initials at the end of the poems that I realized the book was co-authored. I should have paid attention to the title. Two violins mean just that, two instruments. I was curious about who the second was. . . . I mean what kind it was."

"You mean whose initials they were?"

"Yes."

"You know, Philip, inquisitiveness advances knowledge, but from my experience, it often amounts to vain curiosity." Philip realized she had come uncomfortably close to reading his mind.

"The initials were tantalizing. I couldn't help asking who D.V.G. was. Surely I'm not the first to read the poems and wonder who your interlocutor was. I suppose I'm no more curious about you than you are about me. How else to explain why you looked for my novel before you met me."

She smiled at the retort. "So there you have it. We are

47

interested in each other because, despite the differences in age and experience, we feel an affinity. It's the chemistry of recognition. To answer your question, his name was Darius von Galli."

"You must have cared for him deeply. Your poems are intense."

"They were written long ago, Philip, when I was young and filled with romantic yearning. It was the fervor of a heart with no direction. I remember Darius more fondly now. He died recently. I was able to say good-bye some months ago."

By now they had walked to the gazebo. Philip entered after her. A small stove stood in the corner with logs and newspapers stacked alongside.

"Shall I build a fire?"

"Yes. But before you do, you must come and see the lake. Look, a goose with her goslings."

Philip went over and peered through the window. He scanned the shimmering water. Pieces of ice floated aimlessly, some caught in the tall grasses. He could hear the geese squawking as they raised and lowered their bills in search of food.

Mother Ambrose settled herself near the stove while Philip built a fire. The dry logs caught flame with the help of the newspapers. Philip sat to her right. His view was partially of her, partially of the mountains. They seemed compatible images.

"So, tell me about yourself. One learns only so much from an author's book."

"I'm thirty, born and raised in Boston. Private schooling: Swarthmore, University of Chicago, Harvard. Religious background, Congregational. A short stint with Sunday school and emancipated from church at a young age. Father, a businessman; mother, an artist. I have a younger sister, Susan, who married last year. Her husband's finishing law school. She's pregnant, expecting in October. She wants a large family. I expect she'll procreate furiously while I write prolifically. Two stabs at immortality. Hobbies? When I'm not writing, I take trips. A trust fund from my parents allows me to travel. Now I rely on royalties to get me abroad."

"Where were you last?"

"Greece, two summers ago. I took the boat from the port of Piraeus to an island in the Cyclades. I left everything behind: family, dissertation, graduate professors. Just took my poetry and went." Philip noticed that her face had gone pale.

"Mother, is anything the matter?"

"Which island in the Cyclades?"

"Paros."

"You, Philip, of all people. Tell me about Paros. About the church and the windmill."

"You've lived there?"

"No, but tell me what it was like."

"I slept on the second floor of a taverna overlooking Homer's wine-dark sea. I have a poem about it which I'll show you. The room cost me a few dollars a night. The floor was Parian marble, the walls whitewashed. I slept on a bed with a straw mattress. I shaved under a vine trellis with a broken mirror hanging from a string so I could see my lips and chin. I showered under a hose and avoided the lascivious gaze of a toothless girl by the name of Aphrodite. She was the landlady's granddaughter. I took breakfast by the sea, eating honeyed pastry and fresh yogurt, and drank thick black coffee, whose caffeine would have wired an elephant. I watched the fishermen hauling in their nets as I wrote my journal. I swam near the promontory, lunched on olives, feta cheese, and a heady retsina wine. The peasant bread was so crusty my jaws ached from chewing. I wrote postcards or shopped for Penguin editions in the best stocked bookstore in the world. I threaded my way through the sinuous streets, lost my direction, and finally found an exit out of the maze. Then back to the taverna, slipping past Aphrodite for a nap in my room. Rose, showered, dressed. A late dinner of shish kebab and salad with more honey-drenched pastry. Then

49

ouzo as a nightcap. I watched the families strolling along the street and breathed the salty air till my eyes were heavy. I pulled my legs up the flight of stairs to my room. I dropped into bed, drugged by the air, and slept to the pounding of the surf. I could spend a lifetime like that."

During his recitation, she had closed her eyes. Her face lit up at an image here, a felicitous phrase there. When the reminiscence had ended, she opened them.

"It sounds enchanting", she said. "Another Circean isle."

She gave him her Gioconda smile and paused to think for a moment. The vein at her brow quivered.

"And the windmill?"

"You have to climb the cliff. It stands like a solitary witness from another age towering over the water. It once generated electricity. Now it turns listlessly in the wind. Down from the windmill, there's a small beach house on the same parcel of land. No one lives there. Shall I take you someday, Mother?"

"You have in your imagination."

"You never visited?"

"No. But someone I loved died there."

"Who?"

"My husband, Cemil."

"He was lucky to have known you." The nostalgia in his voice matched her own.

"Are you jealous?" Again she had aimed bull's-eye.

"In a way, yes. I wish I could have been with you. You see, I want to know everything about you."

"My dear child", she said, her eyes growing moist as she clasped his hand. The sleeve of her habit folded back, and she saw the time. "We will need to return. Lunch will be in twenty minutes."

Philip did not want their morning to end. He wanted this woman to himself. He wanted to be wrapped in her appreciation, her understanding. He wanted possession with none of her

50

memories as competitors. How could she speak of returning when in two hours they had come so far? At first he had stepped cautiously along her shoreline, testing the water. Now, having felt her depth, he wanted to take the plunge. It was the only depth he knew.

She stood up and he followed suit. She walked to the gazebo door and waited as he opened it. She pulled her shawl around her and turned to him. "When may I see it?"

"What, Mother?"

"The poem you wrote in Paros."

"I'll copy it this afternoon and give it to you at dinner."

"Thank you, Philip. I should like that. Do you mind if we walk silently up the road? The Angelus bell has rung." Religion again intruded to keep her at bay.

"Of course not, Mother."

Chapter Three

Philip had arrived from his walk after leaving her at the abbey door. She had said simply, but with warmth in her voice, "Thank you, Philip." He blurted "thank you" in return. Flustered, he wanted to express more than gratitude. He needed to do something tactile but was ignorant what it should be. How did one show affection to a cloistered nun?

He walked back to Saint Thomas More feeling alternately dejected and exhilarated. The dining table was set for three; Philip had no desire to share anyone's company. He left a note on Wayne's plate saying he was tired and planned to stay in his room. What concerned him most was the blank page in front of him. So he sat at his desk, staring out at the snow-laden trees, trying to remember a poem from another era. He moved to the bed and let his mind drift to Paros in the hope that the verses might come. Suddenly he remembered the opening line and the poem began to flow. He reached for his pen.

Oracle by the Sea

I come to the Sea, a suppliant from mankind,
To appease the inmost fever of my heart and mind.
And though I am caught in the sea's hypnotic trance,
Held by her swaying waters' sensuous dance,
There wanders beyond the waves my pilgrim cry,
Bidding the mouth of the sea to prophesy,
Disclosing there her dark, insatiable dream,
Where black, chaotic waters rise supreme.
Here I have come to wander, here to brood
Amid the darkness of my solitude,

For only the sea can come to set me free
From the loneliness of immortality.
These are the luminous waters of wakening
That bring me a freedom only the sea can bring.
And now her swells, her frenzied tides unfold,
And in her towering darkness, I behold
The waves like cymbals ring, then louder ring;
The sound of the siren wind keeps beckoning:
And I am lost in the wine-dark mystery
Of the wild, narcotic music of the sea.

Philip inscribed at the top, "For Mother Ambrose, O.S.B.".
As he went to sign it, he could not decide what complimentary
close to use. Considering what they had just shared, his name
alone seemed detached and distant.

"Respectfully" and "Sincerely yours" were stiff and formal.
After all, he wasn't sending out a resume or requesting a grant.
Should he sign it "Affectionately"? He weighed the word.
Admiration was closer to what he felt. He was about to write,
"With esteem", but that too sounded stilted. He put down his
pen in frustration. Why was there no word for what existed
between romantic love and friendship? He needed a phrase that
resonated, one without sexual innuendo. He could think of
nothing. Reluctantly, he settled for, "With affection". Philip
signed his first name and dated the poem: "February 25, Regina
Pacis".

He reread the text. What would an accomplished poet like
Mother Ambrose think? Would she find the poem's turbulent
mood adolescent? Once she received it, he would want her
immediate reaction. If only he could have access to her on a
regular basis. But that was impossible, for the cloister was there
to intervene.

He thought about their conversation. He had so many questions since returning from their walk. Why had Cemil died
alone on Paros? Where was she at the time? Even if the love

poems hailed from a time prior to her marriage, why had Cemil permitted publication? Wasn't he jealous that they were addressed to another man?

Philip opened his journal. He printed the word, STRADI-VARIUS, and started fiddling with the letters. After trying them in various combinations, he settled on one, a proper name, Daria Virtuss. With its double esses, the surname seemed odd, but he liked it. The Latin word for power, *virtus,* which peered out at him, was evocative. Philip asked himself what name he would use to translate Beatrice. He recalled some lines from Wordsworth: "Bliss was it in that dawn to be alive, but to be young was very Heaven!" It was another eureka. She would be Daria to her family, Bliss to her friends. He would write about an imaginary relationship with a woman named Bliss, starting from the first time he saw her. She was twenty-two, he twenty-four. Just as Dante saw Beatrice on the Ponte Vecchio, he had seen Bliss crossing the Charles River into Cambridge. Philip checked his watch. It was a little before two. He had the afternoon to explore his theme. His intent would be to imagine the early years of Beatrice Stradivari and transpose them into a story of young love. He chose Cambridge for his composition of place.

I took my racer out this morning [he began]. *I biked around a two-mile stretch of the Charles River. It's mid-October, and the leaves are at the height of their brilliance. I was out of breath, so I decided to walk my bike across the bridge from the Business School toward Harvard Square. I was eager to sit in my favorite cafe, the Bistro Français, and have a croissant and espresso. As I walked my bike, I was enjoying the crisp fall air, the smell of the river, the Georgian façades. I was at peace with myself in a harmony more given than earned. Everything was balanced: my checkbook, my thesis, my libido. That was all to change with a glance.*

I thought I was crossing the bridge alone but I was wrong. I looked over and saw her. She was across the street about ten paces ahead, walking, it seemed, with an imperturbable air. Perhaps it was the erect way she carried herself or the graceful manner with which she moved. Perhaps it was her clothes which, for all their casualness, suggested an eye for color and style. Whatever the reasons, I picked up speed.

She stopped at the light, and I took the opportunity to cross the street. I remained behind her so she did not see me following. When the light changed, she walked toward the Cafe Pamplona and crossed to Saint Paul's Church. The steeple bells announced to the faithful that Mass was about to begin. She had already entered the interior of the Church. I rushed up the steps and saw her kneel and enter a middle pew. I took a seat two rows behind near a marble pillar. For the moment, all I could see was the back of her head and her abundant hair swept up in a curl. She turned and reached for a hymnal. It was then I caught her face, for she looked up with a glance in my direction. Lowering her eyes, she turned again. She had not seen me, but I saw her. A shiver of pleasure passed through me and my pulse quickened. My palms were moist, and tingling immobilized my fingers. I clenched my fists to keep the blood circulating. Then I returned to contemplating her neck and the tendrils of hair at the nape.

The service began but I remember little of the ritual. I watched from behind, transfixed. I noticed how intently she listened or knelt, her posture motionless, her hands clasped reverently, her head looking straight before her. I watched her receive the host and return to her pew. She walked with deliberation from the altar, her eyes communing with what tabernacled within. Her face still haunts me: the dark eyes, skin the color of apple blossom, the forehead and finely-arched brows, the cheekbones and shapely mouth. She had stepped from a Tuscan fresco.

When the last hymn was sung and the church began emptying, I watched her rise and move from the pew. I stood half hiding behind a column, then walked along the aisle to the back of the church so she would not see me. Stopping to greet a friend, she smiled graciously. She embraced her and turned to go out of doors. Again I followed her but was forced to move at the pace of the crowd. I panicked when I could not find her among the parishioners as they chatted before leaving. Then at a distance I saw her turn a corner. I hurried after her, but my efforts were in vain. She had vanished. I craned my neck this way and that. Not a trace. I consoled myself with the thought that in a week she would reappear at the ten o'clock service. But the doubts that assailed me were stronger. Suppose she were a tourist visiting Cambridge, or a former Radcliffe student visiting a friend. Suppose I never saw her again.

Dejected, I walked back to my digs. I avoided talking to my roommates and shut the door behind me. The yearning I felt was now a palpable ache. What possessed me was this woman whom I had just discovered and just as suddenly lost. I decided to write a poem and describe my condition.

> Now you have gone to live far from this place,
> Where, among myriad faces, you are but a face,
> And left my heart a sea that will not tire
> Of all the ebb and flow of lost desire.
> This pain may pass, yet I cannot forget
> You in my wakefulness. And when I let
> The vision of your constant face depart,
> My mind's soft hammer beat
> Waits eager to repeat
> The bloodless crucifixion of my heart.

Considering my confused state, I was amazed at the rapidity of composition. The language, rhyme, and meter came effortlessly, so focused was the experience. But the poem was a mixed blessing. It eased and heightened the pain of my loss of bliss.

Philip stopped writing. As he reread the journal, he thought he heard someone knocking. He listened again. Another knock. He got up and opened the door to find Wayne standing in the hallway.

"Philip, sorry to disturb you, but there's a call for you. You can take it in the kitchen."

"Who is it?"

"A woman."

Philip thanked Wayne and hurried downstairs. His mind

imagined it was Mother Ambrose planning to tell him they might meet after dinner. He was eager to give her "Oracle", perhaps even have a chance to read it to her. Once in the kitchen, it took him some moments to discover where the phone was. He spotted it behind the door. Nervously, he picked up the receiver.

"Hello."

"Philip?"

"Mother?"

"Excuse me. May I please speak to Philip Stratton?"

"Lisa."

"Philip, I thought I was on the phone with a stranger. Was that you?"

"Yes."

"Why did you say 'Mother'? Were you expecting a call from home? Philip . . . Philip, are you there?"

"I'm here. I thought you were someone else."

"Did your agent call you? He phoned me from his Boston office to get your number. I suppose Miles will ring you later. The poor man's barraged with clients. I was on the phone with him for fifteen minutes. Ten were spent waiting for him to escape his conference line."

"If Miles plans to call me, why are you phoning?"

"I thought I'd drive you back to Boston."

"Why should I do that?"

"Philip, let's start over. When Miles and I spoke, he said he was on his way back from L.A. and would stop off in Boston. He needs to speak with you Wednesday before his meeting in New York with Albion. They're supposed to discuss *Torrid.* While you have the right to add or subtract dialogue, they have a say about the overall plot. They want to make some changes. I thought I'd drive you to make your meeting with Miles easier."

"I just got here. I've begun work on a new book, and I'm eager to get more done."

"You can do that in the apartment. What makes staying at an abbey so important?"

"My source of inspiration is here."

"You're being deliberately vague. I feel like I'm back at the Ritz, guessing whether you're telling me everything."

"Lisa, stop trying to flush me out. I'm working on a novel about violins. Don't ask me to explain. You know I can't say what I'm doing till I've done it. Now that I'm feeling inventive, I want to keep at it."

"But Miles says he needs you to decide about Albion. If you don't monitor them now, they'll plan a different film and call it *Torrid*. You said yourself Hollywood's not known for fidelity."

"When they show me a clear outline, we'll talk shop."

"Then there's no point in picking you up."

"No."

There was a long pause on Lisa's end. She had been fishing for information and for some show of affection. Her bait caught neither.

"You could at least say you missed me."

"I could."

"Why don't you? I've missed you."

"Because I'm too caught up in my imagination to miss anyone."

"Or caught up with whoever's there."

"What's that supposed to mean?"

"If I knew, it would make it easier."

"Make what easier? Lisa, stop it. Suspicion doesn't suit you. Anyhow, it's totally off base. Reserve it for a trip when I'm alone on a Caribbean cruise. Then you'll have grounds for suspicion. But not at an abbey of nuns."

There was another pause. He had stymied her with his reasoning, which made her doubt herself. Still, she could not relinquish the feeling that something lurked in the background.

"We're tying up the line. Miles may be trying to get me. If he insists on my returning, I'll have him ring you about my arrival. We'll meet at the bus depot. All right?"

"All right."

"Take care." Click.

Within a half hour, Miles Gannen called. Philip had been in his room reworking his journal when Wayne knocked to announce the second caller. The substance of the conversation was as Lisa had said. It was imperative for him to leave. He objected strenuously, but against Miles' quiet intransigence, Philip was powerless. No amount of irony could shake the professional resolve. He would go the next day.

Miles' call had come around the same time the bell sounded for Vespers. Philip had volleyed with his agent on the phone for twenty minutes. By the time he broke off, he was too upset to go to chapel. So he went upstairs, shaved, showered, and dressed, then sat at his desk rereading the last poem. He was not satisfied with the closing lines. He wondered if the phrase "bloodless crucifixion" was as dubious as it was startling. That he should have chosen a Christian image to express romantic yearning was a novelty. Had contact with the abbey infiltrated his vocabulary? He tried some alternate lines: "My mind's soft hammer beat / With gradual deceit / Nails shut the coffin lid upon my heart." No, they weren't right. He decided to retain the previous lines.

He looked at his watch. It was after six. He went downstairs and joined Wayne and Father Stewart who had just begun dinner. To Philip's taste, the conversation was more provincial than usual: a discussion of the bishop's visit the following week. Philip sat silent as he heard about protocol for a visiting prelate. His mind was on Mother Ambrose. Sister Vera had sole responsibility for supper that night.

"Are you okay?" Wayne asked, aware Philip had stayed in his room all afternoon.

"Saddened I have to leave tomorrow."

60

"Why so soon?"

"I hope it's not critical", Father Stewart said.

"No. Just literary business. My agent convinced me it's unavoidable."

Those were Philip's last words despite the repartee of his companions who respected his silence. When, after supper, they had cleared the table and Sister Vera was stacking the dishes to take back to the monastery, Philip approached her.

"Sister, this is something I promised to Mother Ambrose." He handed her a sealed envelope.

"Mother will be pleased. She said she looked forward to receiving your poem."

"She did?" His somber mood lifted under the clear light of her interest.

"Sister, would you tell Mother I have to leave tomorrow for Boston. I was wondering if I could see her after breakfast."

"Philip, we have solemn Mass Sunday mornings. But she might be able to see you after lunch. What time are you leaving?"

"Wayne said something about driving me to the bus so I'm there by three. I have an hour after lunch."

"I'll tell Mother."

Philip helped her to the door. "Sister, one last favor. Does the abbey have any books on music?"

"Yes. Would you like me to find you something?"

"Yes. On violin-making, especially the masters, Amati and Guarneri."

"And Stradivari?"

Philip blushed. "Him especially."

"I'll check the library and give you what we have after Compline. Will you be in chapel?"

"Yes."

The Compline service duplicated the one Philip had seen his first night at the abbey. Father Stewart and Wayne occupied their customary prie-dieux. The nuns processed in, bowed, and went to their choir stalls. Reverend Mother gave the note and the voices soared and descended in unison. But Philip was too distracted to focus his attention on hearing anything. At first he craned this way and that to discern Mother Ambrose's presence. He could find her nowhere. Perhaps he had missed her. In the dim candlelight it was possible she had merged into the sea of black. He looked again. She wasn't there. What had happened? First, she was absent from dinner, and now Compline. Was she staying away to punish him? That was ridiculous. It was maddening, nonetheless, for his imagination was going in contradictory directions. He decided that after the service, despite the Great Silence, he would ask Sister Vera. He picked up the hymnal to distract himself and flipped to the end of Compline. He followed the English words of the closing hymn: "To thee do we cry, poor banished children of Eve, to thee do we send up our sighs, mourning and weeping in this vale of tears."

The last notes faded. Father Stewart and Wayne rose from their kneelers and genuflected, while the nuns, two by two, exited from the sanctuary. Philip watched Sister Vera return and extinguish the candles. The chapel would have been in darkness were it not for the sanctuary lamp that glimmered in its central position. Philip continued to sit in the back. The scent of candle wax, the flowers and pine wood, together with the flicker of the sanctuary lamp were all beguiling. Finally, he saw her approaching. They moved to the exit where they spoke in whispers.

"I found two books. I hope they're helpful."

"Thank you. Sister, I need to ask you about Mother Ambrose. She was absent from dinner and Compline. Is she all right?"

"A bit of a head cold, Philip. She decided to take an early sleep. She said she will see you at one as you suggested. Come to the abbey door, and you can visit in the first parlor. Good night, Philip."

"Good night."

He left the chapel and walked back to the house. It was perfectly still. Wayne had already turned in, exhausted, no doubt, from his relentless work on the grounds. It was a congenial circumstance. Philip wanted to sit alone near the fire and examine the books Sister Vera had given him. First he put two logs on the gleaming coals and in minutes watched them blaze. He pulled the rocker close and sat with both books on his lap. The first was *The Violin,* a history of violin-making and musical performance. But the second book interested him more, a life of Antonio Stradivari by the Hill brothers. He skipped the preface and read the opening chapters devoted to Stradivari's ancestry, his workshop in Cremona, his two marriages. He read about Amati and Guarneri's violins and the more powerful tone of a Strad, which was achieved by its "secret", the varnish, whose formula had disappeared. Philip read on and on as if he were poring through a thriller. The character of the Stradivarius began to merge with the personality of Mother Ambrose till the two seemed interchangeable. The fire died and was twice relit. Philip went to the kitchen and made himself some tea and returned to continue reading. It was entrancing to sit by the fireplace and hear the small explosions of resinous wood while he learned of Mother Ambrose's forebears. As best he could make out, her paternal grandparents (Libero and Giovanna) had four children: Clelia, Anita, Italo, and Mario. But whose daughter was she?

It was three in the morning when he put the book down. The logs had been reduced to embers, which he doused with the remaining tea. He removed his shoes before walking up the stairs to keep them from creaking. Once in his room, he pulled off his clothes and dropped into bed. His last waking thought was of Mother Ambrose as the young Bliss. She had just finished the last movement of Beethoven's Violin Concerto, and the audience had risen to its feet in sustained applause.

63

When Philip woke the next morning, it was after eleven. Though he had missed solemn Mass, he knew if he moved quickly he could shower, shave, and be ready for lunch. It was his last meal with Father Stewart and Wayne. In twenty minutes he packed his overnight bag and walked downstairs. Lunch had begun.

"Sorry I'm late", he apologized. "I stayed up reading. I guess I got carried away."

"I have the same problem", Father Stewart added. "Books on the spiritual life absorb me completely."

"The book I was reading, Father, was spiritual in another direction. It was about violins. Sister Vera scared up two from the library. Is it possible to leave them with you, Wayne? I won't see her before I leave."

"No problem. I'll return them after I get you to the bus. By the way, Philip, are we still meeting at two? It will take forty-five minutes to drive to the station. You'll have to buy your ticket before boarding. Unless you have one."

"No, I only bought a one-way. I thought my girlfriend would pick me up, but we made other arrangements." Philip kept looking at his watch. Father Stewart noticed it.

"Are you late for something, Philip?"

"I'm meeting Mother Ambrose at one. Just a little concerned. She was absent from Compline last night."

"I hadn't noticed. You have good eyes."

"I bet it's another cold", Wayne said. "Last year, she had a cough that went on for weeks. She's still not used to our New England dampness. All those years of living in a southern climate, I suppose. And the abbey's a draft palace."

Lunch dragged on. Philip peeked at his watch when no one was looking. He tried to appear interested in the discussion but with little success. All he could think of was varnish and violins. Distracting him further was his journal entry on Bliss. He was absorbed in competing sagas, the one in his head and the one surrounding him. Finally, compassionately, grace ended the meal. Father Stewart wished him a safe journey and invited him back: "Everyone who comes here is part of the abbey. But the benefits, Philip, are not felt unless the exposure is longer. Two and half days are hardly enough." There was mild censure in his words.

"I promise next time to expose myself longer", Philip said with complete gravity. The priest missed the wit as Philip knew he would. They shook hands. After Wayne and Father Stewart left, Philip ran upstairs, got his jacket and gloves, and was out the door. He had one hour, and there was so much to say before he left her.

They sat opposite each other in the small parlor. They were close yet separated by the grille, which divided the space into sitting areas. She was clearly before him, her face undistorted, but the bars made him react with hostility. Would it always be like this, something between them: her age and history, her Benedictine calling?

When he looked closely he could see she was nursing a cold. Her eyes were irritated, the nostrils red. Pallor replaced the flush in her cheeks. She was still beautiful, he thought, with the kind of fragile loveliness that makes a man reach for a woman to hold and protect her. He could do nothing behind the cloistral bars. But from whom would he protect her? From her Savior God? He quieted his mind to allow for conversation.

"Mother, I was bothered by your absence from dinner last night and again at Compline. Sister Vera said it was a cold. I hope not a bad one."

"At my age, there are no good colds. While I love it here, I shall never become acclimated to the dampness. I'm southern at heart. I miss the cobalt skies of the *mezzogiorno.* I should have been more cautious yesterday. It happened when we left the gazebo. A chill shot through me. It was nothing a jigger of brandy wouldn't have helped."

65

"I'm responsible. I shouldn't have kept you out so long. I hate being unable to help."

"You did last night."

"I'm sorry, Mother. I don't follow."

"Your poem was the distraction I needed. I read it several times."

"Then you liked it?"

"Yes."

"I felt anxious passing it on. I wasn't sure how you'd react."

"Let me allay your anxiety. It's the poem of a young man celebrating the mystery of the sea and his merger with it. By the end, the sea is a God-image in feminine form. The diction still needs some work, but the music of the lines makes the poem flow. I can hear the influence of Yeats. Still, the voice is your own. The most intriguing thing is that, for all the upheaval, the poem is written in couplets. The tight rhyme scheme is played off against the unbridled images. It creates poetic tension and may reflect something in you, perhaps the desire to let go and find perfect communion while simultaneously keeping control. But I needn't psychologize. A poem is a world of its own."

She was bull's-eye again in her praise and reservation. He listened with alertness, trying to memorize her sentences. He needed to recall them like phrases from a musical piece. Everything she said had resonance. But would her words have possessed sonority if he were not already attached? He set the question aside as he continued: "Mother I'm grateful for the candor. So few people know how to criticize with mind and heart. Either they go for the jugular or they sentimentalize. There's a totality in the way you come at things. It's like the amplitude of a violin."

She smiled at the simile. "I see you've been reading. Sister Vera told me she brought you some books on the Cremonese masters. Sincere curiosity, I hope."

She shifted in her chair and pulled the woolen shawl around her. The cold, which had settled in her face, made her eyes shine. The enigmatic smile played about the lips. It was compounded, he realized, not just of genial irony. It projected affection and respect. And she showed her feelings in the only way she could, given her station in life, through an appreciation of all that he was. Appreciation, that was her word for love. It surrounded and cosseted him. Her presence filled the space as a Strad would a concert hall with its vivacity and brilliance.

"Mother, I said before I wanted to know you. You see, I would like to collect your memoirs. And if that's not possible, imagine you in my mind's eye as someone I'd known and (he stopped at the word 'loved' finding it too strong a declaration) . . . and esteemed. How else can I share the years I've missed? Learning about your genealogy is one way." She studied Philip's face and was touched by his earnestness.

"It's curiosity," he continued, "but it's based on admiration, not control."

"Then you have questions?"

"Only if you permit them."

"If they were not agreeable, I would not allow them."

He took a long breath, exhaled slowly, and began.

"From the reading I've done, I'm not clear about your parentage. For instance, whose daughter you are, Italo Stradivari's or Mario's."

"Neither. My grandfather, Libero Stradivari, married Giovanna Podesta. He sired four children, two boys and two girls, and a third son out of wedlock. This son was Ernesto, who was my father. In Florence Ernesto met and married my mother, Pierina Sforza. I was named after Beatrice of Dante's *Divine Comedy*. I had two sisters, Francesca and Daniela. The first is dead, the second is unmarried and lives in Rome. My uncles and aunts had no heirs who survived. Daniela and I are the last of the Stradivaris. What will outlive us are Antonio's instruments. They are the only progeny."

"Did he make many?"

"Some say sixteen hundred. About eight hundred violins have been confirmed. Others exist, all imitations."

"Have you ever owned one?"

She hesitated before answering. "Not a violin. Of all the plucked instruments Antonio made, it is believed two guitars survived. But there was a third my grandfather gave to my father. It was there to sell in case we needed money. My father was a successful businessman, so he kept it as an heirloom. The tone was remarkable like all Strad instruments. How does one describe it? But words are useless. In structure and design, Antonio understood all the parts of an instrument. He filled the pores of the wood to protect it from oxidation, yet the wood still rings. His varnish formed a delicate skin.

"You know, Philip, it is common knowledge among violin makers that if varnish is applied thinly, the instrument vibrates too freely; thickly, and the tone is deadened. If the consistency is hard, the sound is metallic; if soft, the tone is veiled. Antonio's varnish represents the ideal. It has defied all attempts at discovery. They call it 'the secret' of Stradivari. But it is the human element in what is better called the violin's mystery. Better still, its mysticism. It will always elude us, for the results seem beyond human ability. It's like the genius of sanctity, grace building on nature. Excuse my didacticism, but I believe grace the only counterpart."

"Has that happened to you?"

"If you mean that my life was transformed, yes. After Cemil's death, I traveled all over, revisiting cities where I had formerly lived. I came to Amherst where my sister, Francesca, had a house. We went out one afternoon and drove to Windsor. I happened to see a long road leading through the woods. We drove up. It was not an abbey then, just an old estate in disrepair. We roamed the grounds. I found the house, the barns, the lake entrancing. I knew I would live there some day."

"What happened to Cemil?"

"He was killed escaping from the Nazis. He had been hiding on the island of Paros where they captured him. He was shot near the windmill."

"Were you in Greece?"

"Yes. Cemil had left me in Salonika. I was pregnant at the time. My plan was to have him join me in Athens before returning to Cremona. It never happened. If he had, I would not have come to the States, and I would not be speaking to you."

"And your son?"

"Halil. He had your gift for words. He died in an accident in Switzerland. He lost his footing and was pulled over a cliff by his backpack. I had just received a postcard from Zermatt the day before the news came. It was my last word from him. With his death I was left alone."

"Mother, your life is such a crisscrossing of events. When I leave you I go with more questions than I came. If only we could sit without interruption, you could tell me the whole story." He wanted to add: You see, it's not just the content which grips. It's the refinement in your choice of words. It makes the story resonate. It creates such coloration that when I go you ring in my ears. He interrupted his thoughts.

"What I can't understand, Mother, is why your vows and Rule haven't stifled you. For all the constraints, you seem free. Freer than most of the people I know."

"Benedictine life, Philip, is like Antonio's craftsmanship. What is just good spruce and maple becomes in the hands of the master a unique instrument. But someone still needs to play, someone mature enough to make it sing."

"But you did that in your poetry. You had the demands of rhyme and meter, metaphor and verse form. You sat alone,

69

hour after hour, listening to your voices and composing. Wasn't that enough?"

"After my husband died, I wanted roots for Halil and myself. I had lived in so many countries, babbled in so many tongues, I didn't know where home was. I was tired of being a gypsy. I was hungry for a center, for something constant in my life. I found it later in the peace of this abbey."

Her energy was waning, but she continued in another vein. "Philip, what will you do when you return?"

"My agent called yesterday. I need to speak with him before he meets with the people from Albion. They've bought *Torrid.* I have to make sure they don't botch the film script. I would much rather learn about Benedictine life, most of all, you. As I've said, I wish I had all of your story."

"In time, Philip." She paused and then: "We shall stay in touch by letter won't we? It would please me to write you. I think it would benefit us both."

"Yes. It helps me to know you care. I've wondered why."

"To say you're gifted, Philip, is to repeat what's obvious. But it needs guidance. I can provide that. It's not the only reason. Your resemblance to Halil — or what Halil might have been — is striking. In your way you resurrect his possibilities. I feel that you and I have been brought together. Part of a plan."

She reached into her voluminous pocket and brought out a brilliantly dyed cloth. It was folded into a square. Without explanation, she handed it to Philip.

"Something in gratitude for your poem."

"Mother, how thoughtful." He hesitated to undo the folds.

"You may open it."

Within was a medallion of silver and enamel. On one side was a Celtic cross, on the other, the chiseled features of a Christian saint. Philip could not make out the name written in uncial letters. He looked to her for help.

"It's one of the Twelve. Saint Philip. In the fourth Gospel, his request to be shown the Father is recorded along with Our Lord's answer. He is the apostle who had to learn recognition."

Philip removed the medal and silver chain and put it around his neck. "Mother, thank you." He felt stymied in showing his affection. Again the grille kept him at arm's length. Reading his thoughts, she rescued him by looking at her watch.

"You should return to the house if Wayne is to drive you. Last night's snow may have created drifts on the way into town. It will take longer to reach your destination." She stood so that there would be no lingering.

"I'm glad we value each other's poems, Philip. It's a form of recognition. God bless you", and she vanished behind the cloister door.

The drive to the station had been virtually in silence. Wayne did not press Philip for conversation but left him to his thoughts. It was Philip who initiated the exchange.

"You were right, Wayne. She's a regal spirit. Now I know what *noblesse oblige* means."

Wayne smiled. "You're more on target than you realize. I never told you all the details about her twenty-fifth anniversary. After the consecration ceremony, she walked back to Saint Thomas More to be with her guests. She wore two rings. On her right hand, the silver band of religious espousal; on her left, a scarab given her by Cemil for their marriage. It belonged to the only female pharaoh of Egypt, Queen Hatshepsut. Mother wore it just for the afternoon. Now it hangs on Our Lady's statue in the cloister. It's worth a fortune."

"How did Cemil get it?"

"A Turk gave it to him to thank him for helping Jews escape from the Nazis. Cemil gave it to his wife in gratitude for helping him do the same. It became her wedding ring."

"Was Mother active in the resistance?"

"Yes, but she never talks about it. Once I heard her say she'd helped von Galli escape into Switzerland. He dedicated his memoir to her. You'll probably find it in Widener. Its called *After Long Silence.*" Philip made a mental memo. He would go to Harvard's library and search out von Galli's book. If he could not spend uninterrupted time with Mother Ambrose, he would research her life by consulting those who knew her. If necessary, he would even fly to Rome and meet her sister.

Before he left, Philip gave Wayne a check to present to the Guest Mistress. It was a generous amount to cover his stay at the abbey. He meant the sum more as a donation than as a payment. Finally, he thanked Wayne and wished him well on his candidacy for the priesthood.

Philip arrived late in Boston. The highway, for all the plowing and salting, was treacherous. The bus had moved at a sluggish pace. Once off, he grabbed his bag from the luggage compartment and moved toward the lounge. It was easy to spot Lisa's face as he came through the door.

"I'm glad to see you", she said as she broke from the crowd to greet him. They embraced each other and walked arm in arm to her car a block away. Philip threw his bag in the back and sat in the front. The traffic was light as the car moved through the icy streets.

"I owe you an apology, Lisa. I was short with you on the phone when you called at the abbey. I shouldn't have been. Basically, I was angry I had to return to Boston. I can't even count on a mini-break without an interruption. I resent Albion for it."

"You'll have to endure it. They bought the rights for a heap. You can't blame them for wanting control over their property."

"I have a hunch the distortions you mentioned on the phone are a reality. I have to tell you, I'm not in the mood for compromise. Either they go with the book or else."

"Or else what? You know the sale depended on their having some say. They made a concession by getting rid of their scriptwriter. They'll expect you to accommodate, too."

"You mean compromise."

"Philip, I can feel one of your integrity attacks coming on. You can be so unbudgeable. It's only a movie."

"Yes, and based on a book which I want respected. Didn't you suggest on the phone I should stand firm so they wouldn't distort the story? Now you sound like part of their team. Whose side are you on? Or was the call just to get me back?"

"I won't argue the first hour you're home."

"It's not a question of argument. It's a matter of consistency. And you talk of murkiness. You're no limpid pool."

"All right," she said as she turned up Mt. Vernon, "so I argued a point I had no stake in to get you home. I missed you. Anyway, Miles was the one who convinced you it was important. I'm glad he did. I had this feeling you were slipping away I don't know where."

"So you're relieved because you now have an eye on me, is that it?"

They were in front of the brownstone. She had turned off the ignition and headlights. Her eyes had become moist as she fought back tears.

"I feel like we're back at the Ritz with you in the shadows."

"Writers live a shadowy existence. I can't bare my imagination to ease your fears. You of all people should know how a writer works. Why do you want to compete with images in my mind? Whatever characters I cultivate aren't real. They're conflations. I'm writing fiction, Lisa, not a memoir."

Philip's self-defense consoled her. She got out of the car while he reached in the back for his bag. He followed her to the front door. They walked in silence up the stairs to the first landing. She turned the key in the lock, opened the door, and put on the foyer light. The coffee table was littered with manuscripts she was reading, some finished, others pending, all awaiting her judgment.

She turned to him. "What time do you have to meet Miles?"

"Seven-thirty."

She looked at her watch. The hands said after five. "We have two hours." He knew what she meant. Lisa always spoke of available time when she wanted to be intimate. He had been chaste for seventy-two hours. The only woman he had pursued was imaginary, and she had vanished around a corner. Philip looked at her. With her blonde hair loose on her shoulders, she looked alluring. He heard the resinous crackle of sexuality.

"Shall I take off my face?" she asked.

"It isn't necessary." Leaving her, he went to their four-poster and lay on the crumpled sheets. He kicked off his shoes and called to her. She entered the room and moved to the foot of the bed. With his elbows, he inched his way down till his legs were hanging off. Suddenly he locked them about her waist.

"Philip, what are you doing?"

He disregarded her question, tightened his hold, and pulled her toward him. She protested, laughing, and pushed him away. He maintained his grip.

"It's a new technique."

She fell forward on top of him. Gently, he pulled her to his level till they were face to face. He put his arms around her, kissed her, and with his fingers combed the hair from her eyes.

"It makes me happy to feel you close", she said.

"Yes, it's bliss for me, too." But as he said it, his face saddened. She noted the change as if he had lost someone.

"What's wrong? Did I say something?" He shook his head.

"It's not you."

When again they had turned to the preliminaries of love, he thought he heard a cloister door closing softly behind him.

Chapter Four

He was sitting in his agent's office on Commonwealth Avenue. Miles had just handed him an unsealed envelope, which he received with a shudder of displeasure. He took out the sheet of stationery. His eyes moved warily from the word, ALBION, at the top of the page to the salutation.

Dear Mr. Gannen:
  To prepare for the meeting with our writers and chiefs of staff, I am sending you an amended treatment of *Love in the Torrid Zone.* We have made what we feel are minor changes without altering the intent of Mr. Stratton's book. We have respected his contract, which lets him decide on all additional dialogue; however, we have maintained the right to modify the plot in order to maximize our audience.
  This letter is meant to acquaint you with the story's new direction. We changed the locale from the Salvation Army to the Garden of Eden. We left the nudity and retained the temptation scene, but decided to have Eve eat the apple while Adam doesn't.
  We kept the story simple. The basic thrust is Eve's effort to seduce Adam. After several attempts, it ends successfully with their joint expulsion from Paradise. We rejected an earlier title, *Easy Come, Easy Go,* as too trendy. Our current title, *Just One Bite,* will replace *Torrid.*
  You will note we are incorporating a large dollop of Genesis. It's important to keep the gist of the original if the film is to have a wide patronage.
  Our theological writer, T. K. Hill, whose big idea this

was, is available to discuss any further refinements of plot.

Cordially,
J. Richard Savage

"Philip . . . Philip!"

"What?"

"Philip, wake up! You're supposed to meet Miles in a half hour. It's almost seven."

Lisa was shaking him in an effort to return him to consciousness. He opened his eyes and focused her face as her words registered. He felt a surge of relief when he realized he had only been dreaming. Bolstered by the knowledge he could still avert disaster, Philip dressed quickly and moved to the bathroom. He splashed and dried his face, then combed his hair. Lisa was waiting with his scarf and parka.

"Shall we eat when you get back?"

"Don't wait for me, Lisa. Miles always talks business over food. If dinner is light, I can expect the worst. He hates giving me indigestion. If the food's substantial, Albion has behaved. Wish me a full menu."

They embraced and kissed at the door. Outside, he took her car and drove to Copley Square. In twenty minutes he was parked in front of his agent's office on Commonwealth.

Philip had seen his agent the previous week when they had met for lunch after Philip's appearance on TV. Being together was a rare occurrence. Their professional dealings were largely by phone, occasionally by letter. Miles was not easy to reach, since he was often in transit from L.A. to London. When he did return to New York, he was inaccessible for days. His phone line hummed with a growing clientele.

They were now sitting at Ninotchka's on Newbury Street.

At first observation, Philip could never tell what Miles was thinking. His agent's face was not completely open. He had grown a thick barrel moustache, which overhung his upper lip and partially hid his mouth. The reserved brown eyes had a cautious, thoughtful look. For all his frenetic involvement in gala openings and first-night parties, testimonial luncheons and awards dinners, Miles remained a private man who, as the cliché goes, never showed his hand till the end. So when it came to guessing what Albion had in store, Philip's criterion was dinner. This evening, it wasn't working. Miles had ordered moderately: an omelette, hash browns, a salad. Philip matched the simple fare with a burger and beer. Anxiety had lowered his appetite.

Miles' customary remarks about hardcover books and paperback sales prefaced their talk. Philip accepted the pace and in no way hurried it. At some point, his agent would become personal.

"What did you do at the abbey?" Miles asked. "My phone call didn't give me a chance to find out."

"I've started a novel. It's a Boy-Meets-Girl story about the love of a man and a woman caught in the generation gap. It's also about violins. There's even the hint of a thriller involving varnish."

Miles laughed. Philip was testing his interest with selected details.

"It sounds rich. But then, I like fruitcake. Just remember, Philip, people eat it once a year. So I hope you're writing something for general consumption." He paused and asked: "Why an abbey?"

"I'll answer you the way I did Lisa. My inspiration is there."

"Is the novel a sequel to *Torrid?*"

"Lisa asked that, too. Am I so predictable?"

"As an agent, I've got some idea how my clients work. It could be that you're taking up the slack in a new book because themes in *Torrid* aren't resolved."

"You've said the magic word. Have you resolved things with Albion? Or must I measure my dreams by the Richter Scale? I had a nightmare before I came."

"Things are reasonably secure. They're planning to stay quite close to the story. Closer than I've seen with most adaptations. Your rejection of their writer made it clear you meant business. So we've almost won the battle."

"Sounds like a Pyrrhic victory. I keep hearing those weasel words, 'reasonably', 'quite', 'almost'. Do we have it our way or not?"

"For a writer who likes ambiguity, Philip, you want it black and white in real life. Most of the time, I work with gray. Albion's no exception."

" 'If thou art neither hot nor cold I will vomit thee forth.' Didn't someone famous say that? Anyhow, I'm braced for the worst. What are the damages?"

"They're nervous about two potentially libelous characters. It may not be possible to disguise them on the screen. The Salvation Army comes in for heavy knocks, not to mention feminists. It's an explosive package. They're afraid of picketers. They want you to soften the material. They're not telling you how. In that sense, you're still in control."

As he listened, Philip wondered if reality had taken on the trappings of his dream.

"They want me to soften the material. Did they say to what consistency? Satire is hard-edged. Am I supposed to turn the plot to mush?"

"That's more black and white talk. They're giving you two choices: either you submit a new treatment or their writers will. In each case, you have the final say. But they warned me the process can't go on indefinitely."

"I'm not in the mood to go back to *Torrid*. I've started something else. My mind's on varnish and violins. I have research at Widener, and I may need to go to Rome. Let them submit the treatments. You screen them. When you think you have something acceptable, let's talk about it."

"Anything else?"

"Tell them the only work I'll do on *Torrid* is tighten it."

"You mean cut it. I could do a variorum edition of the scripts sitting on my shelf. I always know your most recent version. It comes back shorter."

"By the end of my life, my novels will be in *haiku*. Writers today waste words. The best seller list reminds me of a landfill."

"Philip, we've had this conversation." Miles was finishing his black coffee. His last question coincided with the dregs: "About Albion. Is this how you want to proceed?"

"Yes. One last thing. The advance. Do we have to return it?"

"No. So long as you agree to a treatment. Remember, it can't go on forever."

They both stood up. Miles called for the check and paid with a credit card. Before they parted, he assured Philip of a satisfactory arrangement and asked for his cooperation.

As Philip drove back to the brownstone, it began to snow, softly at first, then heavily. By the time he parked the car, entered the apartment, undressed, and got into bed, it was after twelve. Lisa did not hear him. Meanwhile, Philip lay awake staring at the snow beyond the window, and hearing, as he watched, the nuns in their choir stalls keeping their midnight vigil.

While the Red Line train crossed the Charles River, Philip failed to notice the boats docked in the marina. He never tired of the view, but this time the book he carried distracted him. He was glad he had found it in Widener. Earlier, his heart had thumped as he neared the stacks to which the card catalogue directed him. Scanning the volumes, his eyes slowed as they reached the right call number. The book was on the shelf. As he slipped it from its assigned place, he felt like an archeologist finding an artifact for which he had dug for weeks. His pleasure was so intense he clutched the prize as he walked downstairs to the library's cavernous foyer. Once outside, he took the steps in threes to the Yard. He walked briskly to Harvard Station, paid his fare, and boarded a waiting train. He found a secluded corner where he opened the book. He turned the title page and read the dedication: "For Bea". Under her name were the words:

> Bodily decrepitude is wisdom; young
> We loved each other and were ignorant.

> W. B. Yeats

Philip recognized the poem, "After Long Silence", which Darius had chosen for his title.

It was ten minutes to Charles Street. He got off and descended the stairs in the direction of Milano's. Since it was mid-morning, the breakfast crowd had dispersed. Philip had his choice of corners where he could write, undisturbed, or divert himself watching those who entered and exited. He went to the counter, bought a cappuccino, and returned to his table. He removed his journal from his shoulder bag and opened to the page where he had made his last entry. He had been intent on writing the whole afternoon, for Darius' book had become a rival text which goaded him on. Only after he had completed his requisite twelve hundred words would he read the memoir to reward himself.

Philip examined the last lines he had penned in his journal: " . . . the poem was a mixed blessing. It eased and heightened the pain of my loss of bliss." The pun was obvious, but it made him smile. He lifted his eyes from the page and stared ahead. In minutes, the room lost immediacy and fell to the side of his eyes as he slid into his hallucinatory state. His mind clicked into place as he recalled the plot. His authorial "I" needed to meet the young Bliss if the story were to progress. But how? She had vanished around a corner without a trace. His mind shifted to the back of the church, to the parishioners thronging after Mass. Suddenly he saw Bliss greet her friend. That was it. This friend would advance the plot. Philip began to write:

I woke late morning after a restless night of sleep. My first class was not till five, so I got dressed and walked over to the bistro for breakfast. By the time I arrived, the place was filled with students taking lunch. I found a corner for my books. Running into someone I knew was likely in restaurants around the Square, for the same people used them day after day. I bought a croissant and French coffee and returned to my corner. As I cut diagonally across the room, I noticed a classmate from my seminar sitting with a woman who, though her back was to me, looked familiar. I moved closer. She resembled the person to whom Bliss had spoken on Sunday. I didn't know my classmate. But if saying hello would put me in contact with someone who knew Bliss, I didn't mind appearing foolish.

I left my jacket and books and walked with my coffee toward the two of them.

"Hi", I said, trying to sound casual, "aren't you in my James seminar?" Clumsily, I reached for some pressing question to suggest why I'd walked over.

"Is Haskell giving out the seminar topics today? He was pretty vague last time." We exchanged first names as he confirmed the Haskell assignment. Then Bill introduced his companion Deborah, who was a grad student in one of his other classes. He invited me to join them, so I brought my jacket and books over. After a lame discussion of James's merits — we talked academics for fifteen minutes — I thought it was time to hone in.

"You know, Deborah, I'm sure I've seen you before." Pregnant pause. "I remember. Yesterday at the ten-thirty Mass at Saint Paul's. You were in the back. I was trying to get through the crowd. You were talking to one of your girlfriends."

"Yes", she said. "Daria and I usually meet before Mass. We missed each other. I got there late."

"Is Daria a grad student in English?" I asked, as I adjusted to the new name. (Imagine, I thought, both of us in the same program. But she couldn't be; I would have noticed by now.)

"No, Daria's a musician. She's first year at the Boston Conservatory studying violin. She's here from London doing the advanced program." Deborah looked over and smiled at Bill. My interest had given me away. We were all aware of my little ruse.

Deborah suggested, "Since you go to the same Mass, at Saint Paul's maybe we could all meet there next Sunday."

"Yes, I'd like that", I said, trying to control my eagerness.

"Fine", Bill said. "After, we can come here for breakfast." I heard him vaguely, for I was still processing Sunday. My heart had dropped. Sunday was eons away. I had to know more about her before the weekend.

"As a foreigner", I asked, "does Daria have a sponsor?"

Her reply pulled me up short: "Philip, I'm not sure I know what you're asking." I stammered. "I . . . I was just wondering if she had a . . ."

"A boyfriend? Not that I know of. When she isn't in class, she spends all her time practicing. She said something about a debut next year. She's already putting together a program." They both stood up.

"Sorry we have to leave", Bill said, "but Deborah and I have a class. I'll see you at the James seminar."

"See you next week, Philip", she said.

How I got through the next five days was miraculous. I threw myself into my studies with a diligence unknown to me. When the Daria mood came on, I went to the gym and exercised till my body ached from pressing weights, swimming laps, running track—anything to help me fall into bed exhausted. I hated waking in the middle of the night with her image on my mind and fixing on it till the early hours of morning. Unrested, I got up to face the grim day alone. The drips and drabs of time trickled into days. This is crazy, I told myself. I haven't even met her. All I really know is the gait and arched head and the mysterious piety. How could she bewitch me this way? It's all in my imagination. I, who prided myself on being cautious, on never giving all the heart, was ranting like a "lapsed Romantic".

It happened. I've met Daria. Somehow I got through Mass alongside her. I remember little of the service. Even the sermon is a complete blur. I kept looking over at her face to study her reactions. Brunch at the bistro was equally a trial. I wanted Bill and Deborah to leave so Daria and I could be alone. I wanted our talk to range freely. Instead, I was stuck with trivial remarks about literature and music. I tried being intelligent, amusing, cosmopolitan by putting my best foot forward, but it got stuck in my mouth. The blissful part came when I left to escort Daria back to her apartment. I wasn't surprised to learn where she lived. Joy Street on Beacon Hill.

On the way, she spoke of herself: an only child; family home in Mayfair off Grosvenor Square; a year at New College before she decided on the violin. She has such a sweet voice with that trained diction of the British public schools. On most it sounds artificial and snobbish. On her it's like chimes at noon. When she mentioned Oxford, I said:

"Someday, when I visit, we'll meet under the Bridge of Sighs."

"Shades of Dante and Beatrice", she said.

"Yes, but no loitering with intent. And I won't recycle my feelings in sonnets."

She laughed. "You're very funny when you're arch."

"Is that a compliment?" I asked.

"Yes. When it isn't, I'll tell you."

We had arrived at her door. I wanted to be impetuous and ask to come up. I knew the timing was off. She had physically excited me, and though my mind cautioned one thing, my body was flushed by another. The sun rises and the sun sets, I repeated to myself, like a mantra for chastity.

"Will I see you again?" I asked.

"Yes, I would like that . . . Philip, you're not a Catholic, are you?"

"No."

"And as a rule, you don't go to Mass."

"No. Was I obvious?"

"Yes. You looked to see what to do next. Catholics always know."

"Something else you can teach me."

I looked at her. What I wanted to be taught was what her lips felt like. Normally, I know how to get instruction. But her innocence was *like a medieval grille cutting me off from the other side. I didn't have to decide what to do. She took the initiative and pressed my hand warmly in hers. I lifted it to my mouth and kissed it. It's the first time I've ever done that. I must be reading too much James. But the quaint gesture pleased her. Daria paused, smiled, and vanished behind the door.*

Philip looked up. His contemplative withdrawal was being challenged. The voices around him had become loud and intrusive. Milano's had filled with customers who were waiting in line to pick up lunch. They had arrived en masse: secretaries from the Hill, workmen from the avenue, real estate agents and antique dealers from the shops, all chatting effusively and putting in their orders. Their accents were as different as those at Hong Kong's arrival lounge. Philip tried to retrieve his hallucinatory state but was forced to grant more awareness to the crowd milling about than to the stationary images of his mind.

The intrusion so irritated him that he began wielding his mental switchblade. Didn't these midday masticators see what he was doing? Didn't they realize their strident tone had interrupted his characters, whose voices could not compete? It was a question of literary courtesy. Philip turned his glare on two tables which were especially irksome. A mahogany-skinned Jamaican talked to his woman companion in a patois broken only by her tittering. Three Moroccans at coughing distance blew smoke rings in his direction, while a cleaver of cold air sliced into him each time the front door opened. The garbled language, encircling smoke, and frigid blasts sent shock waves through his system. The formidable alliance had succeeded in halting him.

It took several minutes to recall where he was and to regain his composure. He was not in the hushed precincts of Widener where people spoke in whispers. This was a cafe, a public oasis. The rule was clear: adjust or get out. Philip knew he was beaten. His inner voices conceded, the white flag was raised. If

84

he stayed, his characters would be held hostage. Better, he thought, to retreat to the apartment where he could claim sanctuary.

Philip packed his fountain pen, ink, and journal. He stood up and put on his parka and beret. Nothing lost, he thought. Milano's had served its purpose. He had met his goal of required words. Outside, he made a left on Charles Street to Mt. Vernon and strode up the sharp incline. Afraid of slipping on the encrusted ice, he moved to the cobbled street, for the sidewalks were poorly salted. He passed Louisberg Square, willing his legs up the last hundred yards till he reached the brownstone. The weather was blustery and made every step an ordeal. He marshaled his energy and raced up the stairs to the apartment. Once inside, he put on the kettle. Despite his goosedown coat, he was shivering. It was nothing Earl Grey couldn't fix. He defrosted in minutes and sat in front of his computer to type from his journal. He entered all the pages he had written at the abbey and Milano's. He made initial changes to tighten the prose, following his rule: Every Word Must Count. He excised adjectives and intensified verbs, retaining an adverb if no unitary form of the verb existed. He saved the material on a diskette he called the "Bliss Text" and printed it, leaving a copy in his desk drawer. He decided to go back to Milano's where he was sure the crowds had thinned. It was after three and Philip felt he had earned the right to von Galli's memoir. He was especially eager for those sections that spoke of Mother Ambrose. He hoped they might feed his imagination and suggest how Daria would mature. Once on the street, he strode cautiously down the incline to Charles. No longer derailed from his purpose, Philip felt joyous and confident.

Though she worked just up the block, it was unusual for Lisa to return to the apartment during office hours. She never took lunch at home. Either she ate with fellow editors or scheduled lunch with agents. Rarely, and only by mutual consent, did she meet Philip at Milano's for a quick sandwich. She made it a point never to intrude on his cafe territory. Only once, when Philip was hell-bent on completing the final chapter of *Torrid,* did she visit him without prior warning. The scene was permanently etched in her memory.

She found him in his accustomed corner, his eyes staring glassily ahead. He had been there since nine that morning. His cafe table was a litter of coffee cups. She walked over in a gingerly manner, expecting that her effort to surprise him would be met by spontaneous delight.

"Philip", she said, pulling up a chair, "I was just passing by and thought I'd pop in. I was wondering what you were up to."

"Paragraph two."

"Really. I thought by now you would have written more than that."

"Interruptions do not conduce to writing."

She kept his clipped answers from stinging by focusing on his harried face. It was devoid of any expression.

"You've been sitting here over four hours. Couldn't you use a break from your writing?"

"Your visit has already broken it."

She tried not to hear. "Then why not relax with some lunch? You ate nothing this morning. You're probably famished."

"Not for food."

"For what."

"To be left alone."

"There's no need to be rude, Philip. I'd leave if I thought being here didn't help."

"It doesn't help.".

"Then you'd like me to go?"

"Yes."

"You could at least be polite about it."

"Please, will you go?"

Angered by his treatment, Lisa had regretted her courtesy call for hours after. On his side, Philip had resented her "popping in", when she knew he was meeting a self-imposed deadline. Though he apologized later, he had discouraged her from setting a precedent.

This Thursday afternoon, she had no intention of dropping by Milano's. Another errand, quite pedestrian, called her from her office. She had lost the key to her briefcase. The keys had come in a set of three on a leather string. She was certain Philip had put the remaining two in a safe place. Lisa had left her locked briefcase in her office. Returning from lunch, she found she was without a key. She was loathe to force the lock, but she needed immediate access to the manuscript Keating had assigned her as tie breaker.

Entering the apartment, she first checked for messages on her answering machine. Finding none, she went to Philip's study and opened the desk drawer. It was a chaos of office materials: scotch tape, calligraphic pens, ruler, clips, rubber bands, staplers in different sizes, bottles of colored ink. She remembered he had put the keys in an envelope with the word "briefcase" on it, but she could not find it amid the disorder. While rummaging through the drawer, she saw Philip's loose-leaf notebook, the one in which he kept whatever he was writing. It was forbidden terrain, but it roused her curiosity. She picked up the book, lifting the cover haltingly, had second thoughts, and closed it. She did not return it to the drawer but left it on top of the desk. Meanwhile, Philip's words, the night of their return from the abbey, came back to haunt her. She could still hear him as if he were standing opposite: "I can't bare my imagination to ease your fears. Whatever characters I culti-vate aren't real; they're conflations. I'm writing fiction, Lisa, not a memoir." Her need now to test those assertions was overwhelming. She silenced her conscience, lifted the blue cover, and scanned the pages.

At first observation, it appeared to be a journal. The dates, penciled in, corresponded to Philip's stay at the abbey, the most recent to the previous day. She was about to close the book and return it to the drawer when she noticed the name Bliss. She looked closer. Phrases jumped from the pages as she pieced the story together: his following Bliss to church, losing her outside, composing poetry in her honor, finding her through the help of friends, escorting her home—it was a memoir that had all the ring of realism. She felt it in the intensity of language. Her worst suspicions had come true. Philip was in love with another woman and had used the abbey to deceive her. Cold fear gripped her and she began to shake. With difficulty she regained control. Though it was mid-afternoon and Philip was at Milano's, the possibility remained he might return any time. He occasionally walked back to pick up messages or to use the phone. If she intended to act, it had to be now.

She removed the journal and turned on Philip's copier, which he kept on the file cabinet. She duplicated each page, making sure the print was dark. She wanted every word legible. After finishing, she put the originals in the binder and replaced the book. She then turned her attention to finding the key. She had not inspected one drawer. She was in luck; the envelope was there. Hurriedly, she left the apartment for the privacy of her office. Keating's assignment could wait.

When Philip entered Milano's the second time, he sensed the alteration of mood. The cafe was filled with unemployed poets and playwrights who had settled in for the price of an espresso. Enjoying the buzz of fellowship out of the cold, they lingered for hours over a table, the rental the cheapest in town. A compressed log blazed in the fireplace and enhanced the chummy atmosphere. Philip bought a cappuccino and sat in the rear. He opened *After Long Silence,* paused at the dedication, and moved to the preface. His reading coincided with a perceptible quickening of pulse.

As an inveterate writer of travelogues, composing a memoir should make me jubilant. What could gratify more than reliving past exploits in the safety of my easy chair? But the prospect of returning in print to times gone by leaves me uneasy. Three years ago, I chose to relinquish public life for the shores of Como. Since then, never once did I regret my retirement. It was beatific to step from the glare of publicity into the cool shade of anonymity.

For decades, my books were the subject of constant appraisal: dissected by historians avaricious for facts; examined by biographers in search of a dubious motive; revered by religionists extolling my natural piety; scrutinized by students, whose clumsy theses slipped incontinently from their fingers. I would gladly have hidden in the Amazon, but deforestation curtailed the hope of invisibility. I even thought of returning to India where the populace is all-embracing; of becoming a pale speck in a brown sea. But I can barely endure my present aches without having to tolerate a dysfunctional colon. I am of an age when luxuries are viewed as necessities.

You may ask: "If your mood was to avoid the public at all costs, why did you concede to a memoir?" I answer sincerely when I say my friends requested it. As the Americans among them put it, "It's time to set the record straight."

As I advance in years, my capacity for remembering has diminished. If retention of appointments has become impossible without secretary or daily planner, how much more the past, which recedes like a pond under an aggressive sun. Before my memory becomes a wasteland, I shall complete this record while some greenery remains.

I cannot deny outside encouragement. But the willingness to set aside reluctance has little to do with the benevolent pressure of friends or the mounting loss of memory. Nor was I persuaded by an enviable advance. The dictum about the heart having reasons which reason cannot understand is relevant. Yet Pascal's words do not entirely fit the case. I have never espoused a romanticism that turns exclusively to feeling for an explanation. Nor in this matter am I partial to reason. A union of mind and heart issuing in fidelity is responsible, along with the effort to remain faithful despite the inroads of time. What have we but words to confound the Law of Change? How else to remind the world? The perfection of art to which Horace aspired nineteen centuries ago is my ambition today: to erect a monument "more lasting than bronze".

Here I must make an act of faith as mysterious as any creed. On trips to the United States and to that hub of industry, New York, I have visited second-hand bookstores. I have seen the counters piled high with residual books marked down to a pittance of their former price. Thousands of trees felled to make paper to print books with a shelf life of scarcely a week. Sic transit gloria libri. *A preface is no place to reflect on the bookstore as mortuary; and while religions function admirably to remind us of death and the vanity of human wishes, nothing is more likely to produce writer's block than a meditation on transience that begins too soon.*

Sufficient for the day is the Black Hole in space. It seems to be increasing so that all entities, language included, must elect to pass through its dark vortex. Nonetheless, an urgency in the human spirit hopes against hope. Despite overwhelming odds, we take up the five smooth stones of words with the expectation that by one pelting Goliath will topple and truth stand firm forever. I tremble still to face vicious critics and a fickle public, though confident of the outcome.

Every life has moments of exquisite timing when, with cyclic precision under a gracious star, someone enters to benefit our being or rescue it from forces that would impair it. We meet such a person and talk for hours, astonished at perceptions which reinforce our own but which spring from a life so different as to have issued from another planet. How is it, we ask, that radical difference should produce such radical sameness? Is this a foretaste of our ancestral home, of the Primordial One whence all of us derive? Do individuals exist who regularly traffic near the Source? I answer only for myself. I have met such a one, and it is she who is responsible for this memoir. Not that she has encouraged it, or that she has knowledge of it. But you, my reader, shall not be ignorant.

If, in recounting my story, you recall once when you turned a corner and came upon a luminous peak in a forest of somber pine, then you know how it was when as a young man I chanced on her. Since I owe her my life, this memoir is my parting gift. Its writing is sufficient to dislodge me from my alpine security.

How wide and deep and high is the love of a woman, how incalculable the consequence. Hers has enfolded me wherever I am. And in the hour of death, as some Christians turn to the Virgin for solace, so in my mind's eye shall I reach for her hand, that in its clasp I may be eased into eternity.

A final counsel to you, my reader, as you move through this reminiscence: the words of a Zen monk who, when asked about mindfulness on entering the path of meditation, answered:

> *If you will now consent*
> *To let your mind and heart walk hand in hand,*
> *Then, come bewilderment,*
> *You need but close your eyes to understand.*
>
> *D.V.G.*

Philip finished the preface and put the book down. Moved by von Galli's words, he needed to take stock of them. Humorous at first, they became, in turn, urbane, wistful, world-weary, resigned as the preface ended on a note of romantic fervor. Without having met him, Philip could imagine Darius in his mind's eye, a Santayana-like esthete in a high, starched collar with waxed moustache and pomaded hair, ambling with a cane or sitting indolently in a deck chair; critical of a world he no longer relished, yet constrained by loyalty to deal with it; at times, mildly misanthropic, yet longing for the companionship of the one person who had anchored him, whose presence had been his safe harbor. Both the vehemence of von Galli's words and their exorbitance made Philip grasp how the young Beatrice could command such total allegiance. But calling on her at the hour of death seemed like idolatry—except that she had become his central icon, the portrait of a woman in whom all women were epitomized. Philip's envy of von Galli gave way to gratitude. What his youth had deprived him of sharing he now experienced vicariously. More disposed now to Darius, Philip could feel the memoir stretching his sympathies.

Philip returned to the book and flipped through it at random, checking chapter headings and scanning pages. At one point, the words, "resistance" and "escape" leaped from the print. Philip tried finding them, and after several attempts, succeeded. They occurred at the beginning of chapter three, "Tranquillity Revisited". His eyes settled on the key paragraph:

More astonishing still is that I now live on the shores of Como. This area was popular with the Milanese aristocracy until World War II when scores of us in the resistance hid from the Fascists in the villages around the lake district. We thought that, whenever necessary, we could cross without detection into Switzerland. As I learned later, the transit was nothing less than a via dolorosa. Bea and I were locked together in our flight like the lovers in A Farewell to Arms *who fled across the border on a stormy night. Our escape was similar, but only after days of eluding Fascists.*

Here my memory does not fail. How easy to summon up that grim adventure when death was our constant companion. We were outlaws with a price on our heads. Shunted from place to place, we finally took refuge in Sorico on the western shore of Como. It surprised no one that the independent populace was the center of partisan activity. Mussolini, who loathed the lake district, was forced back to it as the Allies marched north. He had made a last ditch effort at Salò on Lake Garda. The entire region swarmed with Fascist troops. What was worse, refugees, wounded soldiers, and prisoners of war clogged the roads which the spring rains had made impassable. Bea and I took advantage of the pandemonium by concealing ourselves in a wagon, one of hundreds, it seemed, moving north. Outside Sorico, the Fascists stopped the convoy of trucks and the wagon train behind it. Soldiers on crutches, blitzed men and women, orphaned children were all forced into the piazza beside the lake. Identity papers were checked, and partisans who had mixed with the crowd were flushed out and shot. Bea and I slipped away during the turmoil.

For a week of rainy days and nights we hid in a barn that had sheltered partisans before us. But Mussolini's soldiers, who canvassed the area, were inching closer. We decided to take our chances and run. In short stages, we traveled south to Como, then west to Lake Maggiore. We moved in a straight line, zigzagging only when we suspected a Fascist patrol was near. After two weeks traveling on foot, exhausted from lack of food and rest, we sighted the lake. In the dead of night, we inflated a dinghy and rowed around the eastern shore, staying close to a line of pollarded plane trees. We evacuated the life raft at a suspicious sight or sound and just as quickly reentered it when normalcy returned. We were spotted once by a land patrol that shot at us from the shore. Fortunately, a storm had come up which, for all its violence, rescued us. Rather than move in pursuit and risk drowning, the soldiers left us at the mercy of the lake.

The sky had turned a menacing black while a massive squall moved southward down Maggiore. Forked lightning flashed over the mountains while winds of ferocious velocity churned the depths. We were besieged on all sides as hail pummeled us from above. Bea bailed out the boat while I struggled with the oars to keep us from overturning. At one point, my efforts proved too strenuous. Leaning far to the right, I toppled over. How she saved me by heaving and hauling as I clung to an oar confounds me still at this distance in time. When the winds had calmed as suddenly as they arose and we were in Swiss waters approaching Ascona, she collapsed from fatigue. You now understand why, after the war, Maggiore was the last place I would go on holiday, let alone live. The memories were graphically painful. Sorico on Como was an exception. There, till the Fascists came, hidden in a farmhouse, I was blissfully at peace. Bea was at my side.

Philip put the book down. As a result of the pages he had read, the preface no longer seemed exaggerated. It was true. Darius owed Beatrice his life. She was, like her namesake, a source of salvation. Philip was about to read more but checked the time. He was shocked to find it was almost six. Lisa would be home from the office and starting dinner. They usually prepared their meal together as they chatted about their work day. Not being there to greet her when she arrived was rare. It was the nicest aspect of their routines that his was malleable and could adjust to hers, which was fixed. He felt happy, for his day had been fruitful in many directions. He had made a sizeable entry in his journal, had read critical passages in von Galli's memoir, and his imagination had already begun to rework them. If only he could have more days like this when mind and body felt integral and the world cooperated. He looked around. Milano's had changed. A crowd of diners supplanted the afternoon luncheon set. With more stressful faces, they stood in line, waiting to choose from the steaming buffet. The entrees made Philip salivate, and he looked forward to dinner with Lisa. He would uncork a special bottle from their wine rack. If the memoir had widened his sympathies, it also made him appreciative. He bundled himself against the cold and left for the street. With his batteries charged from the day of work, he walked briskly up the incline to the brownstone. Once inside, he took the stairs in twos to the first floor. As he reached for the keys in his pocket, he noticed an envelope stuck to the door. Was the super complaining about garbage bags? Cantankerous man, Philip thought. But the super always used note paper with an adhesive strip on the back. Philip removed the letter and opened the door. Odder still was the dark apartment. He switched on the light and checked the answering machine. Zero messages. Where was she? He tossed his coat on the couch, putting the book on top, and opened the letter. It was Lisa's handwriting.

March 2

Philip:

I've decided I need time away from you. Frankly, I can't stand a liar. I believed you about the abbey, a novel in the works, new characters. The only character that's new is you. You've shown a side to yourself I didn't know existed. Though I silenced my doubts and took you at

94

your word, you deceived me. As I say, I can't stand a liar. Do you expect me to sit amiably across from you when I know your feelings are with her? If you need help with dinner, call Bliss or Daria or whatever her name is.

Eric is back at his house, so I'm staying with Vicki. Her number is unlisted. I've taken clothes for tomorrow and the weekend, but I'll need to return to the apartment. Don't alter your schedule at Milano's. It helps to know you're not home.

Lisa

Philip went to his desk drawer, removed the loose-leaf binder, and opened it. His habit was to leave his last typed page on top. It was now in numerical order. In her haste, Lisa had forgotten his peculiar arrangement and put the pages in sequence. He replaced the binder, returned to the living room, and sat in an easy chair to sort out his feelings. It was galling to know the unthinkable had happened. Lisa's doubts had caused her to violate her agreement never to go through a work in progress without his permission.

He picked up her letter. The more he examined it, the more his moods shifted from anger to guilt to frustration. If he wanted her back, he had to prove her wrong. But how could he convince her that the woman in his diary did not exist? Would she believe his model was a cloistered nun in her sixties? Would she then accuse him of emotional infidelity? No matter how he presented his case, it appeared she would find it untenable and have the last word.

He crumpled her letter and tossed it in the corner. He had boxed himself into a hole from which he could see no exit. Another novelist would appreciate the predicament. Not Lisa. For all her years of editing, she had not yet accepted the imagination as a free agent.

It was almost seven. Philip had eaten nothing since early

afternoon and his stomach growled. First he would phone Eric. He needed to share his dilemma and ask for advice. He would also ask for Vicki's number. He dialed Eric's home. No answer. He brought the cordless phone to the kitchen. While he made supper, he dialed Eric at fifteen minute intervals. Still no answer. Then he recalled it was Thursday. Eric was at the Cape and would remain there through the weekend. Philip realized there was nothing to do but eat, read, and go to bed. He consoled himself with the thought that Monday morning he would wait for Lisa. Since she needed clothes, she had to return to the apartment early. If he could speak to her, she was bound to understand. He would need to be judicious in his words. After all, as he never tired of saying, language was everything.

Chapter Five

Although it was still an early hour, Philip was in bed by eleven. Ordinarily on Fridays, he accompanied Lisa to a film or to Symphony Hall. Afterward, they sat with drinks, chatting in the Copley Lounge. It was their way of capping off the week; of reacquainting themselves with past interests and impending goals. Dating was the mainstay of their relationship, and Friday's excursion was often a preliminary to making love by the fireplace. During winter, Philip made sure the hearth was crisscrossed with logs. He and Lisa would lie on the rug before the blaze under an eiderdown. The coverlet would be kicked off when the fire and body heat became intense. Now without her, he felt abandoned. As he lay in bed, the only sound was from the radio and someone singing, "It Had to Be You". He glanced at Lisa's side of the bed, reached for her pillow, and pulled it under the sheet, pressing it close. With the singer still crooning, he fell asleep.

He woke in the middle of the night with a start. The radio was on while a lugubrious baritone was singing, "Sometimes I Feel Like a Motherless Child". Repeated innumerable times, the melancholy words and the poignancy of the voice were intolerable. He put on his reading light, reached for the volume knob, and turned the radio off. The music had gone right through him. He sat up in bed and gaped into space. The apartment was completely still. Lisa's pillow lay on his lap, its goosedown contents twisted out of shape. He closed his eyes to induce drowsiness, but the song's refrain mentally repeated itself. So he got up and shuffled to the kitchen. Something sweet, he thought, might make him sleepy. He boiled water, added a raspberry tea bag, and sweetened it with honey. He filled a mug, moved to the easy chair, and sat before the fireplace. His mind flashed back to the abbey and Saint Thomas More House. He saw himself before the fireplace as Mother Ambrose carried the dinner plates to the front door. The scene synchronized with the memory of the baritone singing, "a long way from ho-o-ome, a long way from home". He was wide awake now and suffused with melancholy. He looked over at the coffee table stacked with the books he kept within reach: Yeats' *Collected Poems;* Waugh's *A Handful of Dust;* Santayana's *Persons and Places.* On top was von Galli's *After Long Silence.* The broken night of sleep, he thought, would yet prove purposeful. He removed the memoir and flipped through it, finally settling on chapter two, called "Early Years". He began to read:

Bea was still unwell. Since my farewell meeting with her in Milano, her condition had not improved; on the contrary, it was worse. Because she viewed medicine as an imprecise art and drugs as a sign of defeat, she turned for help to natural remedies: mentholated steam and eucalyptus drops, nasal washes and herbal teas, heat lamps and mustard packs. Nothing worked. The congestion persisted along with a hacking cough and a low-grade fever. The wheezing alarmed her parents most. The sound resembled the bellows of a church organ pumped by foot. The family physician, Dr. Gaetano Lenghi, had examined her the previous month and given her a clean bill of health. But that was before she started coughing. Despite her protests, her parents scheduled Dr. Lenghi to see her again. It would come as no surprise if she were told she had pneumonia and were properly confined. In fact, it was inevitable, for she knew the symptoms by heart. She had been there, times without number, though each relapse became more serious. Last year's had been her worst to date. Her lungs were her undoing. Though she loved Cremona, she abhorred the dank weather which lingered through March and April. Her hands developed chilblains, her lips cold sores. Even when spring came officially, the glacial air waited behind doors in perpetual ambush.

If I close my eyes, I can indulge my imagination by turning to a warmer clime. My memory wanders to the mezzogiorno, *to a steamer leaving Sorrento. I am twenty-eight at the time. I can see the boat cut a furrow of foam through the Bay of Naples as it cruises toward Capri's grottoes, cliffs, and vertical coastline. After her implacable bout with bronchitis, I am eager for Bea to come here for a little* dolce far niente. *Meanwhile, I have taken the first boat out, handed my valise to the porter on the dock, drunk Campari in a bar, and taxied to the village of Anacapri. As the cab circles up, I note with pleasure the stairways flanked by juniper and myrtle, inhale the orange blossom and jasmine, hear the steeple bells toll from the rope and the donkeys bray at the twitch—all this as I near La Sconzonata.*

La Sconzonata, how Bea loved the name of her family villa: "The Carefree One." This was her nest perched high on a cliff with its garden of azalea, oleander, and wisteria, and its swimming pool fed by a natural spring. Both overlooked the inlet of Marina Piccola. The villa was L-shaped, its interior fitted with blue tiles, its patio trellised with vines interspersed with white morning glories.

"Oh," I still hear her say, "to climb again to Anacapri and feel the sun beat down. In one afternoon, it would dry my lungs. At La Sconzonata there are no pills or pacifiers, thermal wraps or humidifiers. Only the cobalt sky and the solar heat of the Mediterranean. And for food, fish from the day's catch, a liter of wine, and the dark bread of the meridiale."

Beatrice traveled alone to the villa in May of 1938. Her parents planned to come in early June. Five months before in December, we had met in Cremona during the bicentennial of Stradivari's death. It had been a weekend of concerts, all happening simultaneously in selected quarters of the city. In her house on the Via Ceresole, Beethoven's quartets were performed on priceless instruments which had arrived with their owners from around the world: the Greffuhle and Ole Bull violins; the Medici viola and Marylebone cello. She was scheduled to play after dinner on the final evening of the festival. I remember the occasion for two reasons: It was her debut using the family's Stradivari guitar; it was the evening we first met.

The night of the recital was taxing. She had practiced solidly for weeks with this one performance in mind. Having taken lessons for ten years, Beatrice was an accomplished guitarist. But this was no ordinary event. As a Stradivari, she was called on to celebrate her forebear in a solo recital, and she was to use one of Antonio's prestigious instruments. The foyer of her house had been cleared and fifty chairs assembled on each side of the tapestried hall with an aisle in between. By seven-thirty, most of the guests had arrived, and the audience was buzzing with expectation. Four seats to the right were kept vacant for her parents and sisters, Daniela and Francesca.

For three weeks she had used only the guitar. Yet, for all the hours handling the instrument, she was still in awe of it. Dating from 1665, this family heirloom was a masterpiece in every element: in the wood, the varnish, the exquisite marquetry. She touched and cradled it like a young mother her first child. The back of one maple piece had flames slanting from left to right with a sheen resembling silk. The top was of spruce, the sound hole cut out in an intricate rosette. The decoration of the back was a double row of purfling and, in between, a design of ivory lozenges and circles. The sides were etched in arabesque foliage alternating with rampant lions. For all the ornamentation, the guitar possessed sobriety, finesse, and elegance. It had a crystalline sound brilliant on the lower register, and a sonority long associated with Antonio's name. As Beatrice held the guitar, she knew it was meant to be played. It was only as memorable as its sound.

During her hours of practice, the guitar presented problems. It was six-stringed rather than twelve, the gut strings producing a sound that was soft, smooth, and long on resonance. It met the demands of the first part of her recital, four sonatas by Domenico Scarlatti. Her choices, less spirited than a program of Bach, were more notable for harmony than counterpoint. Beatrice knew she had to play the sonatas with élan if they were to remain animated. So she emphasized a half note here, an eighth note there to give vivacity to the music. The guitar's size and structure supported her efforts.

But the remaining half of the recital made her anxious. After the intermission, she had selected "Echoes of Spain" by Isaac Albéniz. In choosing his music, she wanted to inform her audience that she had arrived. "Look," she seemed to be saying, "I'm inaugurating my first

Iberian program, and you know how Albéniz requires miraculous technique." By letting the Spanish composer occupy a paramount place, she hoped to close with a tour de force and thus announce her advanced repertoire.

Beatrice loved the instrument, which was longer and in some respects smaller than a modern guitar. Lithe and curvaceous, it was a Botticelli as compared to a Rubens. But artistic comparisons were impertinent. What concerned her was whether the guitar would transcend its limitations. Would it dramatize the fire and eloquence of Albéniz?

She felt jittery now behind the makeshift curtain. Peering out at the audience, she realized it had so filled up, that the crowd was standing in the aisles. The concert was scheduled for eight. Fifteen minutes remained. Earlier in the day, workmen had set up the stage with a chair and music stand on an elevated platform. Somehow, despite her nervousness, she had dressed herself in her blue-shadowed silk with matching shoes. An aquamarine necklace belonging to her mother sparkled on her neck. Her auburn hair was swept back and tied high while whisps curled at the nape. The creamy complexion and high cheekbones, the eyes and face tensed in thought made her striking to see.

Once, when we discussed her debut, Bea told me that her mother had come behind the curtain to encourage her.

"Darling, you know the program inside out. You will do beautifully."

"But Mama, my fingers are like stone. I can't go out there. I'll embarrass you all."

"Nonsense!" her father had added from behind, as he joined his wife and daughter. "You'll play splendidly. You always rise to the occasion, blessed one. Pierina, look at the program. The calligraphy is admirable. Bea, you are in lights." Ernesto gave copies to both of them. Beatrice saw her name on the cover in gold embossed letters.

It was now after eight. Bea's father signaled that he was ready to begin. She nodded her confirmation. He walked in front of the curtain and received sustained applause. He raised his hand for quiet.

"Ladies and gentlemen, honored dignitaries, friends and neighbors: it is with pleasure that I welcome you on the occasion of this bicentennial.

My wife and daughters are pleased to host you for the final celebration of our great ancestor, Antonio Stradivari. His incomparable instruments have graced the stage for decades. Pierina and I are proud to give you our daughter, Beatrice, who will perform on Antonio's guitar, one of three by his own hand. Without further ado, let the recital begin."

The curtain was drawn. Beatrice stood in the middle of the stage, curtsied to the audience, and sat in the central chair as the applause subsided. Through the quiet, Beatrice felt the crowd wrapping her in benevolence. They were wishing her well; she had only to comply. She knew their faces, had known most of them from her childhood years. One face she did not know — my own. I stood to the far left for want of a chair. She took two breaths and exhaled slowly. She stroked her fingers, strummed twice to ensure tuning, and began.

Beatrice's initial playing was slightly hesitant. Even when she dominated the Scarlatti, it lacked bravura. I felt she was too judicious, that she had not let go. Still, the music was notable for its clarity, her playing fluent and polished. There was brilliance in the F Minor Sonata though it sounded a bit driven. The inexorable feel may have reflected the pressure from an audience of relatives and friends. Yet she communicated surprise to Scarlatti's intricate concoctions. The program deserved the enthusiastic press she received during the intermission.

But it was in the second half that Beatrice shone. Albéniz's Iberian miniatures she performed evocatively, thanks to the guitar which fully cooperated. Her playing was muted in the first song, "Córdoba", the virtuosity hidden in her concern for atmosphere. The effect was haunting as she expressed the Iberian mood of yearning and wistfulness.

In "Sevilla" and "Majorca", she took advantage of the foyer's acoustics by playing robustly. Of Albéniz's songs, she kept the most fiery till last. Her performance of "Asturias" was electrifying. In the driving, ostinato rhythms of the outermost section, she gave the impression of a guitarist caught in turbulence while playing on the city walls. A storm of clapping arose and encircled her: "Brava, brava! Encore, encore!" they yelled. "Beatrice, Beatrice, Beatrice", they repeated as they stamped their feet in unison. Twice they called her back, twice she acceded, first to play Scarlatti's Sonata in G Major, then "Malagueña" by Lecuona. She would have continued playing had her father not *intervened. She curtsied deeply and acknowledged the thunderous applause, the audience on its feet, the flowers strewn about her. Beatrice moved behind the curtain to savor her success. A champagne reception followed in the family's baroque dining room.*

Admirers and well-wishers besieged her, toasting her unique performance. Beatrice found herself rooted to one spot. When she tried to move, more people surrounded her. She was flushed by the excitement of so much attention and goodwill. Her cheeks were rouged from high spirits and her eyes shone with joy. She seemed lovelier than ever.

It was difficult for me to approach her. She was the adorable figure dispensing satisfaction to her devotees by a word here, a hand clasp there. I wanted to intrude on the ceremony and speak with her. But how could I? She was constantly surrounded. I was at a disadvantage, a stranger to her family and a newcomer to Cremona. But I was set on meeting her before she retired to some remote precinct of the house.

At one point, Beatrice excused herself, leaving her parents to entertain friends while she disappeared through a door. I moved to the spot, assuming she would reenter in the way she exited. I surmised correctly. In ten minutes she returned. She had freshened her face and removed the ribbon so that her hair hung on her shoulders. As she came through the door and moved toward her parents, I accosted her.

"Please, Signorina," I said, "would you stop for a moment so I might speak with you?" I addressed her with such earnestness, she found the request irresistible.

"Do we know each other? I don't recall meeting you. Are you a friend of my parents?"

"No, I am no one you know. But tonight, after hearing you play, I was someone who wanted to know you. Your music was like a javelin through my spirit. Please forgive what must sound exaggerated, but I had to meet the person who could make such music." I stood in front of her while my frame blocked her view. As long as we stayed in that position, her presence would be mine.

At first, Beatrice found my words disconcerting. She could have excused herself by saying that her family and friends were waiting, but my deep interest fixed her to the spot. Besides, I knew she found me physically pleasing.

103

"I'm glad you enjoyed the concert", she said. "Are you a musician, too?"

"No, a writer. My father is a banker in Zurich and wants me to follow his profession. But I have a mind of my own."

"Do you have a name of your own?" She smiled while her face registered genial irony.

"Forgive me, Signorina. My name is Darius von Galli. I am happy to meet you."

'You already know my name. But you may call me Bea. My family and friends do." That she had given me something intimate, a name of endearment, pleased me. I relaxed a little. She had accepted my presence despite the way I ensnared her into conversation.

"Darius," she continued, "I wouldn't be surprised if my parents were craning their necks to see where I've vanished. I'll need to get back."

"I understand perfectly. But could we meet tomorrow? For tea, perhaps? I'm staying in a small room at the Palazzo Hotel. Now that the festival is over, I will leave the following day." Again the intense interest made her attentive. My politeness left her free to choose, but my sincerity proved irresistible.

"I'll have to see. It's been a demanding night, and it's not over."

"Of course. How selfish of me. You will need to rest through the morning. By the afternoon you may want to vary your day. It would please me to see you again."

While looking for some sign of encouragement, I removed a personal card from my wallet. On one side was my Zurich address; on the other, I wrote the hotel's phone number. She received the card without promising anything and put it in her pocket. As she shifted her position, she noticed her parents were still where she had left them. Her mother's eyes were surveying the room.

"I must go, Darius. My mother..."

"Yes, I quite understand. Good night, Bea. And thank you for the beautiful concert. I look forward to seeing you."

I stepped aside and the room, formerly blocked to her view, reappeared. She walked toward her mother who looked disturbed. I can still hear Bea imitating the maternal voice when she repeated the conversation:

"Bea, darling, where were you? You're not ill from the excitement?"

"No, Mama, I'm sorry for taking so long. It's hard to move without being stopped."

"Was it that young man?"

"Yes."

"He must be a visitor to Cremona. I've never seen him before. Do you know him?"

"No, Mama, I don't. I have a feeling I shall."

"Bea," her father interrupted, "the mayor wants to thank you before he leaves. Not to see him would be very bad form."

"Yes, Papa", she said. But as they crossed the room, she told me she could not refrain from looking back to where we had stood, and feeling as she looked a twinge of disappointment that I had vacated the room.

I called Bea late the next morning and urged her to come to tea. I was thrilled when she called back and confirmed. With her mother it was otherwise.

"Bea, why are you going out? Is it that young man who called earlier?"

"Yes, Mama. He asked me to tea and I accepted."

"But you know nothing about him."

"I know he likes tea."

"Your father would not approve of your eating with a stranger."

"Mama, please don't treat me like a nun. I'm almost nineteen. After last night, can't I enjoy a little diversion?"

"Of course, darling. But you will be noticed at the hotel. People who heard you play are bound to see you."

"It's only tea, Mama. If I were trying to hide something, I wouldn't be sitting at the Palazzo in the middle of the afternoon."

"Shall I come by and pick you up?"

"Thank you, Mama, it isn't necessary."

I met her in the hotel lobby and gave her a corsage which she wore on her wrist. Beatrice exhibited a schoolgirl freshness in her blouse, plaid skirt, and matching jacket. Pale from the rigors of the concert, her fragile look appealed to me. She seemed more accessible now, less an object on a pedestal, more likely to draw on my instincts as well as

105

my inexhaustible reserves of awe. I was dressed in a dark blue suit, starched collar, and blue tie. For all my aversion to the profession, I looked like a banker.

It was an afternoon of gushing: the two of us seeking intimacy to keep pace with the onrush of desire. We talked and laughed at our leisure. In three hours we consumed the sandwiches, scones, pastries, and two pots of tea. The high point of the afternoon was neither the ambiance nor the service but my right hand settling on her own. It was the first time I had touched her. She blushed but made no attempt to disengage.

"Someone might be watching", she said.

"I cannot tell. You're all that I'm watching." I let go of her hand to keep from embarrassing her. "Bea, do you believe in love at first look?"

"At first sight."

"Yes, that expression. I very much believe in it."

"I know you do."

"You do also. I saw how you looked for me as you crossed the room with your father. Is that not so?"

"Yes."

"Then you do care."

"Darius, we scarcely know each other. All we know is that we're mutually attracted. But wood and varnish don't make a great instrument. They need a craftsman to relate the parts. Neither of us is that far."

"That can be remedied. We will craft our relationship, each of us contributing parts. I will write you. Promise you will write in return." She nodded.

"I need to hear you say it."

"I'll try."

So began my epistolary courtship with letters sent twice a week. I kept drafts to bolster my memory.

27 December 1937

Dear Beatrice,

Is it over a week since our tea? Like a monk in a cloister, I feel I have renounced you forever.

106

Good luck on the concert in Milan. Forget your teacher's crabbed words. I'm certain you will play immaculately.

I plug away at a piece on the Protestant Reformer, Zwingli. Hope to have the Catholic cantons of Lucerne, Zug, Schwyz, Uri, and Unterwalden descend on Zurich and kill him off with his banner in hand.

Beatrice, please discover you are discontented in my absence. My happiness is halved without you.

xxx
Darius

2 January 1938

Dearest Beatrice,

I am restless and cranky and need your presence to augur a good year. If you have a free morning during your stay in Milan, can you breakfast with me? Any day is fine. In fact, any meal will do. My calendar is filled with government officials, but none that I would not happily shun. This assumes you still want to see me. I have a job as a reporter for a local newspaper and shall be on assignment. Please say yes. I will comport myself honorably, you have my word.

Love,
Darius

Beatrice replied by postcard:
Darius,

I thought I would see you here in Milan because Papa agreed to it before we left for Cremona. But by the time we arrived he was so dyspeptic from the mule train he recanted.

Beatrice

12 January 1938

Darling Beatrice,

I woke up late this morning and asked myself what you were doing. In fact, I question myself about you all day long when I am not scheduled to meet in conference with editors who play truant. What I think about is your hair when you sleep, how it must cascade over the linen. How provocative that sounds. I am only guessing.

I feel so distant from you. I cannot hope to write for two weeks.

All my love,
Darius

1 February 1938

Dearest Beatrice,

I suppose you are working on a new repertoire and snapping strings in the process. I am told Paganini's "Variations" from Rossini's Mosè in Egitto was composed for the fourth string. Some say Paganini broke his upper strings during a performance, apologized to the audience, braced himself, and began the Moses Fantasy, which he intended all the time. Others say he endured months of incarceration with a one-stringed violin as his sole diversion. Well, it is one better than my journalist's pen, and I know you would make music on no string at all.

You will be receiving a copy of Zwingli. Don't read it. Wait for my piece on Strad instruments which you inspired. All my love to you, blessed one.

xxxxxx
Darius

12 February 1938

Dear Beatrice,

Another letter from you this morning. I would like to show my gratitude by penning four pages of anecdotes of my last twelve hours. It isn't necessary if I see you in person. I need to go to Milan for a conference. Can we succeed in meeting where last time we failed? I dare not get my hopes up, but please say yes.

Missing you,
Darius

Dearest Beatrice,

Did we meet in Milan, or is it my journalist's mind embroidering to prove a story? That marvel of white marble, the Duomo, bristling with belfries, gables, and statuary—did we kiss in front as the sun set? I keep looking for duplicate stubs to verify you were there. Thank you, thank you for a memorable time.

It is not in your nature to be mendacious. I know how you felt about misleading your parents in order to meet me. Next time you will be stronger and tell them outright.

It was wonderful to amble about the heart of the city, arm in arm, and watch the Milanese on the terraces of the big cafes. I would love to dress you from the fashionable shops along the Corso Venezia; choose antiques with you on the Via Monte Napoleone. The tea at the Caffè Alemagna brought us back to our beginnings. If there be a heaven, I can think of nothing more blissful than walking with you in the Parco Sempione.

You had a slight cough before you left the station. I feared you might have caught a chill in the gardens. Please, please take care of yourself. I will phone you March 4th at the usual hour. I need to be sure you are thriving.

Six days from now, darling heart, I shall hear your voice. I think of nothing else.

Lovingly,
Darius

Beatrice remembered my pain when I called during her incipient stage of bronchitis. I was desperate, for she had failed to respond to my letter. When she answered the phone, I barely recognized her voice. Her rasping frightened me. She tried to be reassuring but without success.

4 March 1938

Darling Beatrice,

If I was sad leaving you at the Milan station, I got sadder after hearing you on the phone. I want you to know how pained

I am not to be with you. Blessed one, you were so sweet to me during that glorious day in Milan. I loved it all and looked forward to repeating it. I always want to be at your side. It is madness to proceed with business as usual while you are bedridden. I need to know you are healing.

If I risk irritating your parents by sending flowers, that is a risk I take. Since I cannot be present, the roses stand proxy for me. Do, do get well, dear heart.

Love,
Darius

By April she had convalesced successfully. There was a break in our letter writing, but my flowers continued together with phone calls of encouragement and cards of endearment. After a medical checkup in early May, she was told her lungs were clear. Her parents suggested that she go to Capri for a holiday. When she wrote me of her plans, I cabled to say I had to see her. She agreed to a visit but asked that our rendezvous not be viewed as a tryst. Her words bothered me. I assumed that her caution was the aftermath of illness, and that her mood would soften once we were together. This interpretation strengthened my resolve to go. I arrived a week before her and stayed at a modest pensione. I wrote her from there:

2 May 1938

Beatrice,

It is a morning of intoxicating freshness. I have opened the terrace doors to find the birds singing, the sun high, the waters of the marina glinting with sunlight. I returned for my sunglasses to dim the brilliance.

The air is a composite of floral scents and citrus, each competing for dominance. I have inhaled and swallowed the deliciousness.

I am taking breakfast in the courtyard at a table near the fountain. Another enchanting sound is the water from the jet riding over the lip into the basin below. A tricolored cockatoo to my left inhabits a cage. His eyes are open but he is motionless, as mesmerized as I by the conjunction of smell and light and sound.

Am I composing a brochure? It's just that Capri in the morning is flush with life. I am choked by the beauty and need to siphon it off. If you were here, there would be no overspill.

I came in advance and thought I would spend the time distracted by the island's delights. Don't misunderstand. I hoped to trick myself into forgetting this yearning for your presence. A vain hope. No artificial light, however brilliant, compensates for the sun. Beatrice, you are my central light. When I feel cold and desolate, you so warm my spirit that the sap rises and it's spring all over. During twenty-six years, I have lived through winters of discontent. Never again. I now reside in the deep south of your caring.

You are my companion along the way, whose musical gift I revere. Though we will part by necessity—I to explore some land, you to thrill others by your playing—we will return to each other, wherever and whenever. Home for me, Beatrice, is where you are. That is why I feel so restless. You are not here. I left half myself in Cremona and dragged the remnant to Capri. But when you arrive I shall be whole.

Did I tell you? That evening in December as you stood, stage center, I recalled the words of a poem by Stevens, true for me then as now:

> And thus it is that what I feel,
> Here in this room, desiring you,
> Thinking of your blue-shadowed silk,
> Is music.

I love you!
Darius

In mid-May, Beatrice arrived. We met on the quay and kissed each other affectionately. Careful to respect her wishes, I retained my room within walking distance of La Sconzonata. Beatrice visited me without questioning the arrangement, coming as though chaperoned from her separate location. Since it was my first visit to Capri, she acted as tour guide. She accompanied me to all the sights, tiring sometimes but never bowing to fatigue, Diana framed against classical ruins.

III

Our week together passed swiftly. On some days we rented a motorboat from the marina and sped along the coastline honeycombed with caves under tropical vegetation. We paused at cliffs plunging vertically into the sea, their surfaces fringed with asphodel, acanthus, and myrtle. We stopped at the Blue Grotto to watch the shimmering light enter by refraction through the water while she and I took on a ghostly silver. On other days, we remained landlocked to explore the island's shadowy streets. We threaded our way through gardens and villas, stopping where the houses formed terraces with flat, oriental roofs, or ambled through the public parks that opened on panoramas of Mount Tiberius and the Tyrrhenian Sea. After a day of sightseeing, we straggled to the piazza and sat in the Caffè Caso. We drank Carpano or the local wine, and knew the cocktail hour was ending when we saw each other better in the cafe's light than in the gathering dusk outside. One night, before we left for dinner, I asked her to linger.

"Bea, you know what I have been thinking. You received my last letter."

"Yes. Your words touched me, but their intensity is frightening. You've lived longer so you're more focused on what you want. I don't know my heart that well. The only thing I want is my music."

"What I will say may alarm you further. What I suggest you do when you find some solitary time is to consider the thought of marrying me. I will not encourage you because I know our life together would be harder for you and more pleasant for me. I am impatient and edgy and often antisocial, a person of fluid schedule and no routine. I have one living relative, my father, who lives in the world of finance. My only commitment is to writing. This means for weeks throughout the year, I shall be on assignment. You may join me if you have a taste for high adventure. We could travel any time and put up anywhere. You need not make up your mind, Bea, or even respond. Please don't be anxious. Just let my offer swim about."

I clasped her hand and helped her with her chair. Arm in arm, we walked to Grottino's where we ate roasted fish. We listened to the itinerant singers and watched the souvenir photographers brandishing their cameras. Later, I escorted her to La Sconzonata and dutifully kissed her before retiring to my hotel.

112

As the days passed, instead of dining out we shopped for produce and cooked at the villa. One evening, toward the middle of my visit, I expressed my feelings. We were finishing dinner and the wine had loosened my tongue. The prospect of leaving her that night was too painful.

"Bea, you know everything about me", I said under the vine trellis. "I'm already naked before you. Let bodies do what souls have done already. I want us to make it complete." With the sky and sea as witness, I would have taken her on the spot.

"I want the same completeness", she replied. "I'm not made of stone. But not this way, Darius."

"But when, if not now?"

"Soon, but not yet."

Thus, at La Sconzonata she swerved our ardor into antiphonal poems, she beginning with, "I had passed by your face but once"; I with, "When upon your face I held my gaze". By transposing our needs into verse, she began assembling a body of poetry which later became Poems for Two Violins.

When in June, before her parents came, I had left the villa, my yearning for her became intolerable. I began a letter from Zurich, but a call to military service brought me to Lugano. After a week of settling in, I wrote her:

8 July 1938

Dearest Beatrice,

I arrived in Lugano yesterday and finally have a chance to write. Our real work has not yet started though we are occupied throughout the day. Tomorrow, I plan a trip into town to buy stationery, ink, and nibs.

The troops are a decent lot drawn from the local cantons. At first it was a babble of regional dialects. We have been asked to stick to French or German. In deference to the Italian Ticino, the commander made a trilingual speech to the assembly the other morning, apologizing for everything: barracks, showers, bedding. He said, "All we want is a little indulgence which age gives to youth in return for the respect youth gives to *age." I'm not in my dotage exactly, but being twenty-eight is a plus.*

The infantry courses are telescoped into a short period, a year's worth in twelve weeks. They include endless drills and exercises, not to mention international law, sanitation control, and use of firearms. So far I've dug one trench, crawled under barbed wire, and been gassed. The difficult maneuvers begin in a week.

On the 15th, I have a brief leave of twenty-four hours. I wondered if we could meet in Milan at the Duomo around noon. This is very short notice, and I understand if you cannot come. But I could not let the chance slip by without trying. I remember our holiday in Capri con tanto piacere. *I miss you beyond words.*

D.

Beatrice received the letter, but she later told me she was reluctant to answer. Since leaving Capri, she had mulled over my offer of marriage. The more she thought about it, the more fretful she became. Two weeks passed and still she did not write to explain her silence. I tried calling, but she had instructed the housekeeper to say she was out. One morning, I phoned twice and left word I would try again. Years later, Bea told me her mother had intervened, calling her aside.

"But Mama, I don't want to talk to him."

"You're not being fair, Bea. I said from the beginning he seemed too tenacious. But your praise accustomed me to his name. You cannot cultivate friendships and lop them off without explanation. When Mr. von Galli phones, you will take the call and deal with him directly."

"Mama, do I have to? I'm sure there will be harsh words."

"There will be nothing of the sort. You have him dangling by a thread, Bea. He has a right to know if you want him as a friend. I had a premonition this would happen as a result of all those letters. It's remarkable how persistent he is. It's nine months since your concert. Well, some men are like that. When he phones, you are to take the call in your father's study."

"Yes, Mama."

She went into the study and exited later with a promise from me that I would pressure her no more.

"Well, Mama, it's done. I told him he was making me unhappy and that my music was suffering. I think I hurt his feelings."

"I'm sure you're exaggerating. You merely told him the manner of his attention was not desirable."

So my writing and phoning stopped. A card and birthday greeting were my sole attempts to maintain contact. Even these efforts were aborted when war was declared in June of 1940, and Italy sided with the German Madman. If I had tried to write, Beatrice would never have known. The mails were censored or destroyed, and foreign letters roused suspicion. Where once they had flowed, now they trickled. Finally, they ceased.

Philip looked up from the book and noticed that the fire had begun to die. Pushing the ottoman away, he stood up as the book dropped from his lap. He walked over to stoke the logs and added another. When he returned to his chair, he retrieved the book and saw he had lost his place. He flipped to the end of the second chapter:

Bea heard her father approaching the dining room as she finished her caffè latte. He spoke from the threshold.

"Bea, have you brought your bags downstairs? The car will be here shortly."

"Yes Papa", she answered sleepily. It was five-thirty in the morning, an ungodly hour to be awake. It was her mother's turn to question her.

"Did you pack the guitar securely, Bea? It's a long trip."

"It's near the door, Mama, if you want to check it."

Beatrice moved to an overstuffed chair in the drawing room. Yawning, she struggled to keep her eyes open. She and her parents were waiting for the limousine that would drive them to the station. They had to catch the train to Milan and change in Rome for the one to Bari. From there an overnight ferry would take them to Dubrovnik. If all went smoothly, they would be unpacking at the hotel in twenty-four hours. To simplify the trip, Daniela and Francesca were staying with their maternal aunt. Being exempted from the trip suited their mood perfectly.

They were not eager to exchange hiking plans in Switzerland for a trip to Yugoslavia.

Dubrovnik's Arts Council was sponsoring a summer festival for young musicians as part of a campaign to bolster tourism. Beatrice's playing at the bicentennial had caught the attention of some visiting luminaries. Her performance was noted, her name inscribed in memory. When the invitation came, asking her to repeat her concert in the Rector's Palace, her parents encouraged her to accept. The opportunity to leave Cremona could not have been better timed. Though Beatrice felt relieved that my letters and calls had stopped, she had to admit that the relief had its price. She missed the intensity of being first in someone's life. The sense of loss made her rethink her decision, and she felt she had acted hastily. My infatuation with her was matched by her longing. It became acute when she remembered La Sconzonata and our days of companionable sharing. She shuffled about the house, sighing at meals and staring into space. When the invitation to Dubrovnik came—for the Arts Council wanted a Stradivari on the program—Pierina urged her daughter to accept.

"You will be launched in the musical world, Bea. Who knows who will hear you or where it will lead? You would be foolish to pass it up."

"Does Papa agree?"

"Yes, but neither of us will press you. Still, we feel the trip will do you good and take your mind off this." Pierina wanted to say "off Mr. von Galli", but Beatrice grasped her meaning.

Since the performance in Dubrovnik was to be a repetition of her December concert, she needed only to refurbish the Scarlatti and Albéniz. But loneliness had lowered her stamina while the thought of practicing repelled her. To fire her interest, her father intervened with lyrical descriptions of the city; its atmosphere pulsing with life; its cloudless days, cool nights, and delicious alfresco cuisine. Through her mother's coaxing and her father's cajoling, she gradually changed her mind. Going would be a distraction, she told herself. Above all, the Arts Council desired her. It wasn't romance, but it was desire, nonetheless.

"I would like to accept", she announced two days after the letter

116

came. So Ernesto reserved three seats on the train and made an advance booking at the hotel.

The trip was tedious. Exhausted from all the emotional churning, Beatrice slept most of the way. It wasn't till they left Bari and were on the overnight ferry that she got her second wind. Her parents were asleep when she climbed to the top deck to watch the boat ploughing through the dark Adriatic waters. Thanks to the moonlight, she discerned a sliver of coastline on the other side. When the salt air had tranquilized her and her yawns became more frequent, she joined her parents below. The pulsing sound of the motor was a welcome cadence. Her mind, a muddle of images, simplified as she dropped off to sleep.

Early in the morning, the ferry docked. Beatrice and her parents were among the crowd of tourists who disembarked. Ernesto noticed a man holding up a sign with the name "Stradivari". He called him over, and the chauffeur helped them with their bags to the waiting car. They drove along the coast road to the Villa Dubrovnik. The hotel's interior pleased Beatrice. The lobby was decorated with local arts and crafts, and floral bouquets were everywhere. Her room, next to her parents' suite, had terrace doors which opened on to the Adriatic. To the right was a splendid view of the old city with its casemated walls and towers. When she looked straight down, she saw a beach and rocks on which to sunbathe.

Beatrice decided to nap before sightseeing. She was already formulating her plans for the day: late breakfast followed by a walk into town; browsing in the shops along the Placa, then guitar practice in one of the hotel's conference rooms. It was Friday, and she was scheduled to perform Monday, the first day of the festival. She was confident she could polish her program over the weekend.

After a siesta, she unpacked her bags and joined her parents for breakfast. Pierina noted how relaxed her daughter appeared. The pinched look was gone.

"Mama, I'm glad you and Papa convinced me to come. It's beautiful."

"I'm happy you chose to listen", her father said with mock sternness, adding: "It's a perfect day for walking. You two explore the city. I intend to swim and do some boating. Pierina, have lunch out. I will meet you both for an aperitif before dinner." He kissed his wife and daughter. "Enjoy the day."

While Ernesto lolled on the beach, Beatrice and her mother strolled about the old town. They had entered through the Pile Gate. The wide street known as the Placa, paved with stone slabs and worn smooth, was thronged with sightseers. The houses on either side, once destroyed by an earthquake, had been rebuilt in baroque style. Their window displays under canopies contributed to the festive atmosphere.

They walked to the far end. Here was Lusa Square, the hub of the city. Both mother and daughter paused at a fountain to splash their faces from the water spouts. A few feet away, musicians and singers were entertaining an audience. Pierina and Beatrice would have stayed, but they were eager to see the Rector's Palace. They crossed the street. On the right, looking toward the harbor, was the palace, its architecture resembling a Venetian façade.

"Mama, let's see if it's open. This is where I'm performing. I'd like to test the acoustics." They passed under the columned portico and tried the front door. It was locked.

"They may be preparing for the festival", her mother suggested. "You will see it soon enough. Your father gave me the name of a cafe called Sebastijan. Can you find it?"

"That must be it, Mama, where the umbrellas and tables are."

They crossed the street and walked over. They had their choice of seats. The waiter came and took their order of cold drinks.

"How do you feel about the recital? You were all nerves when we left."

"How do I look, Mama?"

"Calmer. Happier, too. It's obvious you needed to get away. You know how proud you made us in December. You will make us proud on Monday. But your happiness comes first."

"I'll play well if I can walk on stage and not care about the results."

"Grandfather Stradivari used to say it's the only way a musician should play. With total concentration. Not looking over one's shoulder. Play for yourself, he would say, 'the audience is there to overhear.' She changed the subject.

"Let's order lunch. We will take our time and have a leisurely walk back. Then you can practice."

118

The weekend was a felicitous mix of activities: shopping with her mother, sunning on the beach with her father, having dinners together at the Dubravka or at Sarajevo's, sipping Slivovic so that the plum brandy induced unbroken sleep. Late afternoons, she practiced her recital. Her virtuosity was at its apex, her fingers plucking the strings with perfect clarity. She felt stronger inside, refreshed by the city, and bolstered by her parents' caring. The confidence was so apparent, that when she rehearsed at the Rector's Palace, the technicians, adjusting the equipment, applauded when she finished.

She remained confident throughout the festival's first night of music, though she was last to perform. When finally she was announced, she walked serenely before the assembly. She wore a rose-colored dress, her abundant hair held back by her mother's ivory combs. Her face was ruddy from the sun. Without makeup she glowed from her outdoor life of three days. The filigreed lamp posts illuminated the packed audience. Her parents were in the front row. There had been no introduction. The name, Stradivari, was enough.

Beatrice took her seat before the crowd. She remembered what her grandfather had said: "Play for yourself. The audience is there to overhear." So she played as though alone, cloistered by her concentration. In Cremona the Scarlatti had been hesitant, then slightly driven. Now it was even and creamy smooth in articulation. Again Albéniz's music showed her artistry. This time she combined everything: style and technique, passion and intelligence—all were pressed into the service of Antonio's guitar. Nothing was missing, nothing went amiss. The relentless strumming followed by pauses combined Iberian passion with Asian quietude. When the final bar was played and the last note faded, the audience rose and cheered. She stood up smiling, bowed, and left. She gave no encore. She had played from the cell of herself and shared the solitude.

Her parents waited as she passed through the door. Her mother had tears in her eyes; her father had brushed his away.

"Bea", was all her mother could say as she kissed her.

"My sweet daughter, who would have guessed?" Ernesto said, embracing her.

They slipped out the back to the reception in the town hall. It was a *gahtering of about forty, nothing like the populous scene after her recital in Cremona. Champagne was toasted, and glasses of Slivovic were filled more than once.*

"Beatrice, one more song from Iberia."

So she played Lecuona's "Malagueña" as an accompaniment for someone from Madrid who danced the flamenco. More cheering and applause. Then it happened. Konstantin Boravic, who had organized the festival, walked over. A man in his twenties accompanied him. He had black hair and a moustache. Fair-skinned with coal black eyes, he had a panther's muscular grace.

"Beatrice, I should like to introduce the festival's youngest patron. From Istanbul, Cemil Hasan. Cemil, Beatrice Stradivari."

His dark eyes searched her own. The gaze would have been uncomfortable but for the humor that softened it. He smiled, bowing slightly, and kissed her hand.

"Mademoiselle, I used to think human perfection had its limits. After hearing you tonight, I'm not so sure."

It is best that I end this chapter after introducing my sole rival for Bea's affection. All that I have written is true, though I was not present firsthand for every event and conversation. But as a writer who travels alone, I have learned to observe and extrapolate meaning from inconspicuous things. Here I have been helped by what was told me, not only by Bea in person, but through her letters. All this I have set down so that you, my reader, may have a portrait of this woman. Just as the voice came to the Baptist in the desert crying, "Prepare ye the way of the Lord", so have I prepared her a place in this book, my love the only voice of revelation.

The light of the fire and warmth from the logs had so relaxed Philip, that the book slipped from his fingers. An irresistible heaviness pressured his eyes. He opened them briefly and shut them as consciousness waned and went out.

Chapter Six

"Lisa . . . Lisa!"

She had entered the apartment in the hope of not waking him. She had stepped on carpets so the parquet floors would not creak. Her years in ballet helped her move lightly. She took advantage of the silence by gathering her clothes from the closet and packing them in the suitcase she brought for the occasion. It was six-fifteen and she had been up since five. Leaving Vicki's was easy, but the half hour wait for a taxi had made her edgy.

Once inside the brownstone, she moved with caution. She knew if she woke him there would be an argument. Now, having completed her errand, her effort to leave was being botched because of an oversight. As she maneuvered her suitcase in the opposite direction, she failed to notice the books on the coffee table. Piled precariously high, they had ensnared her.

She stood fixed to the spot and listened again for her name. Silence. Perhaps he had called out from a dream and dropped back to sleep. She waited fifteen seconds and tiptoed to the door.

"Lisa, you can't just walk out."

Startled, she swung around. Philip stood in the bedroom doorway looking pathetic and silly, his eyes red from lack of sleep. His hair was tousled, his expression pained like a dog disciplined after wetting the carpet.

Lisa controlled her sympathy. By remembering the pages of Philip's journal she steeled herself against a show of emotion. Her role as tie breaker had schooled her in the art of detachment.

If she ignored his plea and reached for the doorknob, she might exit gracefully. But here she made her mistake. She reacted by meeting his words with her own and created the opening she had hoped to avoid. Words, she knew, were his artillery, and he would use them to win ground. Her only hope was not to contend.

"There's nothing to keep me, Philip. It's clear your feelings are with her."

"They aren't real feelings because she doesn't exist", he said, adept at pulling her into conversation.

"I can't believe this character came from nowhere. That's how you argued the night we drove from the station. You may have changed her name but the original exists. And she isn't anything like me. You modeled her after someone for whom your feelings are intense. More than you've ever shown me."

"I can't believe you're jealous of a fictional character."

"She's not made up. Whoever Daria is, she's taken you over, and that's what's so galling. While you stand there and speak to me, she's on hold. When I leave, you'll want to be alone with her. You'll want to hold her and make love to her. Do you expect me to stand by and do nothing? Or read about it in installments? I may have been a fool to help your career, Philip, but when it comes to love I won't play second fiddle. Why not admit I caught you in a deception? Why these face-saving lies? That's the exasperating part."

"All right. I met someone at the abbey. But she's not what you think."

"What should I think?"

"She's a cloistered nun."

"She's what?"

"A cloistered nun. I read her love poems and was intrigued. I wanted to meet her."

"What's a nun doing writing love poems? I thought they prayed all day. And why is she cloistered? Is she sick?"

"She wrote the poems before she became a nun. And 'cloistered' doesn't mean 'quarantined', though I see her behind bars."

"Philip, I don't understand. First you say she's a nun who writes love poems but not recently. Then you say she's not ill but behind bars. I don't quite get the picture of an amorous nun who's serving time."

"I didn't grasp it either till she and I took a walk one afternoon."

"Now I'm lost. Did she get time off for good behavior? Is she on parole?"

"You're not listening. She lives the strict Benedictine life. Normally, one speaks to her behind a grille. But she's allowed to leave the enclosure. I think it's because she's older."

"How old?"

"She must be near seventy, but she looks younger."

"The woman in your journal is no nun, and she's not in her seventies. More like her twenties. They're hardly the same."

"That's the point. They aren't the same because the woman in my journal doesn't exist. I imagined her young."

"Then where did you get the name, 'Daria Virtuss'? It's odd enough to be real."

"I took the word 'Stradivarius' and scrambled it. 'Daria Virtuss' is the result. Violins run in Mother Ambrose's family. Her last name is Stradivari."

"Philip, it's too much. I'd say I didn't believe a word, but it sounds too bizarre not to be based on fact. I'd like to visit this Mother Ambrose and satisfy my curiosity. It wouldn't surprise me if she wants to flee the convent but needs a nudge. She'd be happy to know she's in a journal."

"She mustn't know that. She has no idea I've begun a novel. It might upset her. I can't risk losing my story by not seeing her again."

"Now you've said something I can recognize. Whoever she

is, you're using her. That I can relate to. Whenever I get the sense you're playing angles, I feel close to the truth. Still, the whole thing is farfetched. I can't see why you're writing about this nun. What's the fascination? I have no right to screen your choice, but reading about Daria makes me feel you're unfaithful. She's taken possession. I can compete with flesh and blood but not with a fantasy. Why Philip? Why this hankering after someone else? That's what's so ripping. It's a sign I don't matter. You're still looking for I don't know what."

Philip did not reply. Somewhere, in the barrage of words and feelings, Lisa had announced a major truth. He could feel it. Though she had aimed widely, the shaft hit dead center. With his zest for precision, he recognized her bull's-eye. Philip felt for her, but he could only be where he was. Had their roles reversed, would he be jealous? Could he have tolerated a man in her life, however fictitious? He doubted it.

He walked to where she stood to comfort her, to urge her to change her mind. What he wanted was to put his arms around her, to hold and be held. She sensed his need but resisted.

"Don't. It will confuse me. I need time to absorb it all."

"Then you won't stay?"

"It's better for me at Vicki's." Without further explanation, she turned the doorknob and let herself out, placing the door between her hurt and his need.

After Lisa left, time dragged. The day promised to be a series of attempts at distraction. It took the mail to lift Philip's spirits and make him forget himself. Two letters reinstated his well-being. The first was from Miles, assuring him that Albion's writers would respect the text of *Torrid*. The only liberty they would take was overlapping various scenes for brevity. Miles ended the letter: "Congratulations! You stood your ground and got what you wanted."

As pleased as he was with the news, it was the second letter that thrilled him. Mother Ambrose had written. He trembled a little as he carried it to his easy chair and laid it on the arm rest. Before removing the contents, he went to the kitchen and made himself some tea. He returned with his cup and sat down. Reverently, he removed the letter from its envelope. Before reading it, he lifted the Saint Philip medal from under his T-shirt and fingered it in some kind of preparatory rite. He then opened the letter. Written in chancery script, it had been posted three days prior.

3 March 1989

My dear Philip:

For several days, I have been confined to my room with bronchial congestion. Don't be concerned. The worst is over and I'm on the mend. As bad as confinement sounds, it provides an opportunity to carry on the apostolate of writing. Time by oneself is rare for Benedictine nuns. Since the Divine Office and monastic duties divide the day into segments, we frugally collect our quarter hours and minutes the way externs watch their dollars and cents.

Sister Vera just removed my luncheon tray, so I have the afternoon free for correspondence. You have been much on my mind since you left, and I wanted to keep my promise to write. I hope this letter inaugurates a happy exchange of words. Am I anticipating more than you? I think not. Somehow I sense you share my seriousness. You know you are welcome to stay in one of our cabins, but your work in Boston makes residing here unlikely. Letters, Philip, are our only recourse.

I have thought of peering through your imagination as through a window on the world. Will you permit me to see people and places I would otherwise miss? This is a teaching role I would like you to play. Perhaps you have one in mind for me. Let me know so that we are partners in learning.

Confined as I was this week, Philip, I managed to finish your novel. The circumstances for doing so were peculiar. I would wake up in the middle of the night with a wheezing in my chest unable to breathe. It was pointless to try to sleep. You would be amused to learn that I would prop myself on another pillow and read *Torrid* till four in the morning. It's deliciously funny. I see now that it more often strikes the right note than not. I mention this, not to rescind my original criticism, but to say that in the wee hours you made me laugh, and that the laughter relaxed me so I fell back to sleep. In your absence you are still a comfort. Had anyone passed my cell door, it would have sounded strange to hear a nun chortling at such an hour. But I had permission to read you. Reverend Mother suggested that I use whatever was necessary to get a full night's sleep. *Torrid* was not in her mind, but she would approve. I'm passing it on to her since she's a woman of broad sympathy.

What are you working on? Have you found the theme to your novel? You hinted as much when we were together, but you never elaborated. I'm eager to learn how novelists do it. What provokes a book and how does it develop? Where do you draw your characters? Is one person the model, or do you pick and choose from a number? Please explain your method. Of course, I would welcome any chapters of a work in progress, and you can count on me to react. I invite your criticisms to any new poetry I send, though in recent months I have written scant little. The Divine Office is the most demanding poetry of all.

At the beginning of this letter, I said that I would like to see through the window of your imagination. The same holds for your intelligence. How did you respond to our discussion of monasticism? I'm interested in what an outsider thinks. Since you're not a Catholic, your pronouncements are valued more. I'm guided here by what Darius once remarked: "I don't know what I've said until

I know what you've heard." You must know, Philip, how I value the interpretation you put on what you've seen and heard. You are astute, verbal, and enjoy performing—all qualities making for an ideal correspondent. Please send your impressions.

So that this letter does not resemble a series of demands, I'll finish by reflecting on your visit. Providence is my favorite Christian doctrine: that exquisite timing, which, in arranging for people to be in the right place at the right time, compels them to choose what they are free to love. Thus, our meeting. At seventy I have had my life pass before me. (Is this a premonition of death or the daily preparation for it?) I have thought not only of the blessings, among which my Benedictine life is the most precious, but of the losses, too. My husband's death I almost took for granted. It was part and parcel of what happened to those who were fighting the Nazis. When it came it was no surprise. We lived at the edge in those days, and death was at our elbow. But Halil's passing, that was different. Yes, I have accepted God's will, for I know my son and I will be reunited. But that his gifts were lost to the world, cut off in so untimely a manner, I cannot abide. Now you have entered my life, no substitute, I know, for what is irreplaceable, but here to tap energies that have lain dormant for years. You are God's gift to me.

Given the demands of your writing, I do not want our correspondence to be a burden but a joy. So write when the spirit moves you. You are in my thoughts and prayers, Philip. They are often one and the same.

Mother Ambrose, O.S.B.

Philip reread the letter several times and was moved by the contents. His mood swung widely from elation to guilt. At first, he was delighted she had chosen him as confidant by investing their relationship with the quality of friendship. Excited by the prospect of corresponding with this woman, he had to admit her monastic choice eluded him. But he was glad her cloisteredness had made her one of the few stationary objects in his otherwise transient world. He could count on her. Stability and depth characterized her life. After all, had she not grasped the truth? Only when Philip tried to answer that question did guilt enter. He knew he had misrepresented himself by not being candid. Lisa's words made him feel that his effort to fictionalize Mother Ambrose had introduced an ulterior motive which superseded real interest. Was he playing angles? Lisa became prosecutor in a trial without jury. But the writer in him defended his choice. It wasn't just the novel. Mother Ambrose had inspired him. Wasn't he trying to safeguard her life by rescuing it from historical indifference? He was engaging in no more crass functionalism than Dante's use of Beatrice, Petrarch's use of Laura, or any great artist's effort to capture the elusive quality of the beloved. He was not using Mother Ambrose to create literature. He was using literature to recreate Mother Ambrose, to fix her for all time so she would not be cast into the dustbin of history. She would be distributed to the ages when both of them were gone. She would endure, resurrected each time someone's eyes settled on the print, matching words to reality. Then the stone would roll back and the glorified one would step forth. That was hope he could handle. Art would ensure her eternal life. After all, it was the only life he knew: the book as guardian angel, the library as haven. No, Lisa was wrong. There was nothing selfish in the role he made Mother Ambrose play. She was his creative muse.

Philip listened for the rattle of a rationalization, but his defense held steady. He was being authentic, he could feel it. To prove it, he would tell Mother Ambrose about his novel. He was not sure he would send her chapters; he did not want her to become self-conscious. But he would let her know what he was doing. That much candor he owed her. When his tale of Daria was nearing completion, he might send it as a gift. The thought revitalized him, and he felt the urgency to return to his story.

Philip got up from his easy chair and went to his desk drawer where he kept his work in progress. He was reminded, as he removed it, of Lisa and her jealousy. No, he would not take responsibility for her shaky self-esteem. He owed no one an explanation for the source of his story. In his imagination he was free, the master of his craft. He looked at his watch. It was not quite eleven. He decided to go to Milano's and write. He would take along von Galli's memoir to spur him on and Mother Ambrose's letter to strengthen his resolve. During the afternoon, he would write a response to her letter and work on his journal. The double demand infused him with life. To hell with jealousy! He had a novel to write.

"Abbey of Regina Pacis. Pax Christi."

"Good morning. Is this the switchboard?"

"No, I'm the Guest Mistress, Mother Thérèse. May I help you?"

"This is Lisa Roberts calling from Boston. I'm an editor at Little, Brown, a publishing house."

"Perhaps, Miss Roberts, you would prefer speaking to our librarian, Mother Scholastica. She's in charge of books."

"No, I was calling about something else. I received the name of Mother Ambrose from a friend. I was phoning to find out if there's a nun at your abbey by that name."

"Yes, Mother is a member of our community."

"Would it be possible to speak with her?"

"Normally, yes. But she's unavailable now. She's recovering from an illness. I'm instructed to take messages for her. Would you care to leave one?"

"It would be better if I spoke to her in person."

"I think Mother will be taking calls by the weekend. Of course you're welcome to come and visit the abbey."

"I was thinking of Saturday. But I'll call on Friday to set a time. It all depends on whether Mother Ambrose can see me."

"Are you sure, Miss Roberts, you wouldn't like to leave a message? Perhaps Mother could return your call."

"Fine. You can tell her I called from Little, Brown. The number here is 617-227-0730. We're interested in doing an anthology of women poets and wondered if she would participate."

"I've taken it all down, Miss Roberts. I'll deliver your message to Mother shortly."

"Thank you. I'll plan to call Friday. If I drive up Friday evening, I may want to stay overnight rather than return immediately. Is that too short a notice?"

"Not at all. The guest houses will scarcely be in use. People find the cold in March disagreeable."

"That's good to hear . . . I mean, the guest houses not being full. Thank you for your time. I'll phone Friday. Good-bye."

When she put down the receiver, she felt pleased at having fabricated the women's anthology. How else could she meet Mother Ambrose? She had to ease her curiosity by testing Philip's statements against the reality. Luckily, she had made a mental memo about the love poems. Perhaps they were out of print or published privately at the abbey. She could concoct something about Little, Brown's wanting to buy the rights for republication. It didn't matter what she said so long as she met this nun face to face. It was amazing, the lengths to which she would go. But she was not ready to sacrifice a three-year relationship for some alleged sexagenarian. It was the "sex" in the sexagenarian that had her worried. Philip had insisted Mother Ambrose was in her sixties? Was it possible? Was Daria really fictitious? By the weekend she would know. Better to face the competition than do nothing but brood. She was experienced at book auctions and could outbid her closest competitor.

Sitting in Milano's, Philip wrote to Mother Ambrose.

Dear Mother Ambrose:

What a lift to my spirit to hear from you. I had been downcast all morning before the mailman delivered your letter. I was having domestic problems but forgot them all after the first paragraph. I hope this letter finds you entirely mended. No matter how much pleasure you derive from solitude, it pains me to think of you confined to your cell. (The word sounds peculiar to an outsider.) I feel responsible for having kept you by the lake. Wayne explained your susceptibility to colds when I asked about your absence from Compline. But your letter shows so much verve that I cannot see you flat on your back for long. You were meant to stride in the open air.

You didn't presume on my seriousness. I'm keen on writing to you. Because of all the hours at my computer, I don't like to send out letters. I'm part of the Phone Generation. But corresponding seems so right for us. For one thing, I can't have access to you otherwise, so there's a happy compulsion in it. It's very olde worlde to have an ongoing record of what we've said rather than numbers on a phone bill charging long distance. Look for a response. I always return a volley.

About my imagination as tour guide: I would be happy to share whatever I see. At the moment, I'm tied to Boston, but I have a feeling I'll travel to Europe soon. Wherever I go, count on postcards, brochures, and slides giving detailed descriptions. If you peer through my imagination, allow me to see through your wider experience. Though you shared with me at Regina Pacis, there are still gaps in your life which only knowledge can fill. Do speak more of yourself if I'm to avoid guessing.

You can't imagine how pleased I was that *Torrid* made you laugh and then induced sleep. It gives novelists great joy not only to be read but also appreciated. We spend days in unglamorous solitude, cultivating semi-psychosis as we listen to voices and hallucinate events. We balance dozens of characters—male, female, and all the intermediate genders our culture produces. We submit our work to puzzled agents, dim editors, and mercenary publishers, lucky to arrive on the printed page. The reader makes it all tolerable. I may broadcast loud and clear, but without your antenna to pick up the frequency I might as well be talking to myself. My fine tuning is rewarded by your laughter. Dial me any time.

I jumped a little when you said you would give *Torrid* to the Abbess. The erotic scenes, while not clinical, simply are what they are. Is it true Reverend Mother was a gynecologist before becoming a nun? If so, the mechanism of sex cannot come as a surprise. Still, I would like to visit the abbey without being stared at. Here I bow to your Superior Insight.

You asked for my reactions to monasticism. They are less intellectual than emotional. It's hard not to be awed by banks of candles, ghostly statues, and glimmering darkness. Together with chant, the atmosphere is steeped in mystery. Then the quietude. I always thought silence was the absence of noise. At the abbey, it's the fullness of peace.

You must understand that I was raised in the stronghold of Congregationalism where religion had all the complexity of Dick Meets Jane and See Spot Run. Ritual was restricted to bowing low or standing tall, while the teachings of Sunday School were presented as embroidered ways of speaking about humanity. Had I not been so impressionable to poetry, I would have dismissed the mumbo jumbo long ago. My visit to the abbey makes me wonder if I've missed something, like a person who lacks depth perception because of blindness in one eye. Is the monasticism of Regina Pacis a cornea transplant for perceiving that lost dimension? And what about the distortions of our two-dimensional world? Must one rush to the abbey at regular intervals to get refocused? No doubt you will address these questions in subsequent letters.

I have yet to reflect on how I write. One novel does not suffice for a full-blown theory. I can only relay a procedure taken largely from Henry James. It involves answering the question: What if? Take, for example, our recent meeting. Allowing for altered names, it would go something like this. What if a recently successful novelist, stuck for a new premise, were to meet a woman with the surname of Guarneri del Gesù. Her first name is after Petrarch's lover, Laura. She is a composer of chamber music, which she has dedicated to some initialed person. The age difference between Laura and the novelist is notable, and compels him to bridge the gap through fiction. To heighten the difference, let us suppose Laura were a Carmelite nun while he is an avowed agnostic. What would happen? How would they conduct their relationship? Assuming they are drawn to each other, what does each of them want?

Maintaining the momentum of plot is impossible without a burning curiosity. But novelists are by nature snoops, voyeurs, double agents, chameleons, people of fluid identity, like actors looking for self-definition in the characters they portray. What accounts for this? Infantile grief? Separation from the primary nurturer? Are novelists Buddhist by natural affinity? A novel is a search for answers by way of ordering chaotic questions. However bogged down the writer becomes, however lost amid plots and subplots, the personal benefits are considerable: power and satisfaction. I can assure you that finishing *Torrid* was intoxicating. I felt I had fulfilled my errand in the world. Yet, for all the exhilaration, I'm reminded that it's art, not reality, and there's the rub. When it's all said and done, the anxiety remains that the words may grow stale and have no constancy. That's why I read "stylists" for clues to writing well. I'm less interested in content than manner. Rhetoric is the Great Embalmer, and long after the critics have exhumed the plot, the prose will remain fresh and incorruptible. In brief, the question "What if?" triggers the novel and nudges the characters into action. I simply take dictation.

As for my visit to the abbey, it still permeates my days. You have entered In and never Out. Your presence has caused me difficulties with my girlfriend—the domestic problem I referred to. She's convinced my alleged visit to Regina Pacis was a lie; that I fabricated the abbey as an excuse for a liaison with another woman. No amount of oath-taking has gotten me off the hook. Lisa believes I'm in love with someone else. While "in love" is farfetched, "fascinated", "intrigued", and "infatuated" are respectively shallow. I have tried taking sanctuary behind your grille but without success. How do I show her she's mistaken when she's uttered a half-truth?

As for writing, I'm reworking the journal of my stay at the abbey. You can't be surprised to learn you feature strongly in my entries. Do you mind? With a name like Beatrice, you are meant to play the benefactor. When I have something of quality on paper, I'll send it to you.

In one of our discussions, you mentioned that the genius of the Strad depends on the varnish. What happened to the formula? Has anyone duplicated it? I imagine it would be invaluable to any violin maker eager to match Antonio's craftsmanship. I read somewhere it was written in a family Bible. "What if" the formula turned up?

One last request before I leave you. Would you suggest some reading? I've just finished James's *Portrait of a Lady* in an effort to grasp the mind of a woman. Can you recommend other portraits that provide an insider's view of female psychology?

Mother, I'm mailing this letter today. I want you to

have it soon so that there's only a brief pause in our conversation.

I was about to ask when I could visit. It needn't be soon. Your letter was visit enough.

Affectionately,
Philip

P.S. I've been digesting *After Long Silence*. How much trust should I put in von Galli's words? After reading him, I'm more jealous than ever.

Philip scanned the letter. The contents pleased him. He could have made stylistic adjustments but decided to leave it as it was for the sake of spontaneity. He placed the letter in an envelope and addressed it. Laying it aside, he took out his journal and reread his story. By the last line, "Daria paused, smiled, and vanished behind the door", he had picked up the threads of the plot and began writing.

I waited two days before phoning her. I was afraid of scaring Daria off with too much attention. So I tried to hang a balance between indifference and enthusiasm. I finally called the third day but without success. I eased my frustration by telling myself she was in class or at rehearsal. I phoned after dinner at intervals. Still no luck. I tried again at midnight, desperate to hear her voice. Nothing. Was she avoiding me? Was she ill and being hospitalized?

On the fourth day the pattern repeated itself. By the time I went to bed, I tossed the whole night, too distracted to sleep. The only way I could dim my consciousness was to resolve to phone her girlfriend who probably knew Daria's whereabouts. The following morning, I met Bill between classes and asked him for Deborah's number.

"What's up, Philip? Why so hassled?"

"I can't reach Daria. I've tried for two days now. I must've dialed a dozen times. Nobody answers."

"I can help you there. Daria stopped by the cafe three days ago to see Deborah and me. She was on her way to the airport. She got news

her father was critically ill. So she left for London. Deborah can fill in the details."

The information both relieved and saddened me. Daria's hasty departure had nothing to do with me. But I felt cheated in not knowing earlier. I wanted to say, "At least she could have called to say she was leaving." I reminded myself I hardly knew her. Still, the feeling of having been passed over lingered.

"I'd like to phone Deborah. She's probably got Daria's number in London."

"I'm sure she does. Let me give you Deborah's number. Then I have to run. Class is in five minutes."

Bill scribbled something on a slip of paper and handed it to me. "You can call her at four. At five she's at Widener's desk till the library closes."

I was impatient all afternoon and barely heard the lecture on James's last novels. No loss. I dislike them for their twisted diction and bracketed ideas, and the prose is as pleasing as Chinese water torture. When the bell signaled the end of class, I was the first out. I rushed through the corridor to the Yard and ran to the phones in Harvard Square. One was free. Widener put me through without delay.

"Deborah. Bill's friend, Philip. Sorry to bother you, but I've tried for days to reach Daria. Bill gave me the news about her father. How is he?"

"I called this morning about one our time so as not to miss her. The housekeeper got on the phone. Daria's father suffered a massive heart attack and never came out of it. He died two days ago. She got there just in time to see him. She's an only child so she'll have to stay and settle the estate."

"How old was he?"

"Would you believe? Eighty-five. My grandparents never lived that long. There was thirty-five years' difference between her parents. Her mother passed away years ago."

"How so?"

"Daria's mother married her father when she was thirty and he was sixty-five. She died when Daria was born. So her father was all she had." I wanted to say, "She has me now", but added, "Do you have her number in London? I'd like to call her."

"Yes. She'd appreciate it. She mentioned you before she left."

"She did?" My clouds dispersed while the sun shone in an unbroken sky.

"Daria said she enjoyed meeting you Sunday."

Deborah gave me the number and I said good-bye. After I hung up, I was sorry I hadn't asked for the address of the funeral home where Mr. Virtuss was being waked. I wanted to wire flowers. On second thought, I decided the gesture was inappropriate since my introduction to Daria had been so recent. Phoning was best. It meant waiting up till one so I could reach her in the early morning.

The evening dragged on. I tried distracting myself with activities. I went to the Harvard gym, swam twenty-five laps, and had a leisurely dinner at an eatery on Brattle Street. In the Square I saw a movie with enough violence to trigger a world war. Development of character was minimal, while bullets, head bashing, and torture proliferated. When I entered my digs at Apley Court it was almost eleven-thirty. I turned on the TV, heard a stand-up comedian's one-liners for fifteen minutes, and watched him interview the latest hydrocephalic rock star. A blond with black roots, his hair was teased a foot high. I turned off the TV and decided to read Henry James. My assessment still held. He was top-heavy with verbiage. Where was his editor when he submitted the manuscript? Words everywhere like sweet smelling gas. I was gagging on the fumes. I made myself some tea, lay on the couch, and thought of Daria. What was she feeling? Unless she was part of an extended family, she probably felt abandoned. My hunch was that there was no one else. Solitude surrounded her when we first met: the way she walked and talked, as if she were wrapped in silence.

I wondered what her father left her. Obviously he had money. You don't own a townhouse near Grosvenor Square without being wealthy. Did this mean she would return to London and stay? I knew so little about her. Yet in those hours in church and at brunch I sensed a depth I wanted to share.

Since meeting Daria, I couldn't imagine splitting my emotional life from sex. She was bringing them together in a kind of integrity. I was willing to take my time and court her. I looked at my watch. It was after one. I dialed the international code, the London exchange, and her number. It rang three times. I was convinced I was in for another *bout of frustrated calling. On the fifth ring someone answered. I expected the housekeeper.*

"Hello', I said, "Is Daria Virtuss there?"

"This is she."

"Daria, Philip. I received word from Deborah about your father. I had to call to say how sorry I was about his death. I wish I could be there to help."

"I wish you were, too, Philip."

"I'd like to drop everything and fly right over. Does that sound mad?"

"It's very thoughtful, but you mustn't think of disrupting your semester. Things are moving swiftly here. The burial was yesterday and the memorial service is late this morning. We expect people from all over the world. My father was considered one of the great violin makers. The largest group will come from Cremona."

"When will you return to Boston?"

"In about a week. The estate is simple. I found a solicitor, a Mr. Chadwick, who is handling everything including the rentals of the townhouse. I'm keeping the bottom flat for my visits to London. Then there's sorting Mama's jewelry, disassembling Papa's room, and going through his papers. . . . " Her voice faltered. The stiff upper British lip with which she began the conversation gave way to tears. At first I couldn't tell if she was crying until I heard the low sobs. They pierced me like a knife.

"Daria, let me fly over. I had my last class for the week, and I don't have my James seminar till next Thursday. I would gladly come."

"Philip, thank you. But it doesn't make sense right now. There's something you can do. May I send a package to your address? It's mostly memorabilia. I daren't send it to Joy Street. I don't want to risk having it stolen from my lobby floor."

"Yes, of course. I'll take care of anything till you arrive. Shall I call Saturday?"

"No, I'm in and out too much. Let me try to ring you. Thank you, Philip, for your caring. I deeply appreciate it."

"Daria, be well. My thoughts are with you. Good-bye."

I put down the phone. It made no sense to try to sleep immediately. I poured myself a brandy and sat staring into space. I tried to feel what it was like to be alone in the world, to have lost all living relations. A chill gripped me. I would be family to her during her loss.

The next two days I kept myself busy reading for my James seminar. I decided to analyze the character of Isabel Archer in Portrait of a Lady, *but I was still without an approach. Meanwhile, I phoned Deborah out of courtesy to tell her about Daria and her impending return.*

While having breakfast out, I missed Daria's call. When I returned and played my tape machine, her voice registered disappointment, but she insisted that I not call back.

"The package is forthcoming", she said. She asked me to hold it till her arrival the following week. Sunday, I felt a sudden urge to attend Mass at Saint Paul's, to relive again how I followed Daria to church, how I sat behind her and studied her pretty neck and hair. The sermon couldn't have been more apt. The text came from one of Paul's letters to the Corinthians. It analyzed love's qualities: patience, long-suffering, kindness. I sat through the rest of the service distracted by the scriptural message. After Mass I went to the Bistro Français, had croissants and coffee, and thought of Daria's return. I did not know the flight number or airline. I surmised it was deliberate on her part. She preferred returning from Logan without being met.

When I got back from Mass I found still another message: "Philip, I'll need to stay a few more days." (I gasped. I had no idea I would draw on scripture so soon.) "The package should arrive Monday afternoon. Thank you, thank you for being there."

Philip stopped writing and looked at his watch. It was a little after ten. He left his table at Milano's and asked John behind the counter to watch his things while he left the cafe. He picked up the letter to Mother Ambrose, sealed it, and ventured into the cold air. He mailed the letter in the box at the end of the block. When he reentered Milano's, he bought himself a buttered bagel and tea and returned to his corner. The cafe was sparsely populated. He could still count on a murmur of noise. Deeply entrenched in his story, he was pleased it was taking on the accoutrements of a thriller. He knew where it came from. The more he was mystified by Mother Ambrose, the more he would translate her life into a mystery. He decided to write for an hour more. Afterward, von Galli's memoir would regale him. He needed to watch Darius playing with words: serving them hard, hitting them over the net, returning the corner shots—all the oblique give and take of banter.

So, Philip thought, Daria's package arrives by plane followed by her own arrival. Then what? He would have to strengthen the motive for her sending the package to his house. Wouldn't it be more appropriate to have it mailed to Deborah? After all, she was Daria's closest friend. Unless Daria felt this was a way to invite closeness by engaging Philip in an act of trust. He was ready to get on with the story:

I phoned Daria. She had finally arrived from the airport two hours before and was still in the process of unpacking.

"I have your package", I said. "When do I see you?"

"Why not meet me at five. We can have some supper at Ninotchka's on Newbury and talk there."

"That sounds fine."

I arrived early at the cafe. In imitation of Milano's, I chose a corner table. Daria was late fifteen minutes, during which I peered and craned at everyone who entered and left.

"Sorry for the tardiness, Philip. I'm moving slower than usual. Jet lag."

I examined her face. The sadness gave a luster to her eyes. Something in the startled way they looked suggested a person in shock. She still had not comprehended her father's death. Before she sat down, I kissed her lightly on the lips. We ordered two chef's salads and a pot of tea.

"Still in one piece?" I asked.

"Barely. It's been relentless. But the estate is settled, and I can get on with my life. It was wonderful meeting my father's old cronies.

Several plan on coming to my debut at Symphony Hall if I ever get that far. The date makes me anxious. Here it is, October, and I'm scheduled to perform December 9th."

"You'll manage. I'll help."

I looked at her intently and pressed her hand. "How do you feel inside?"

"Like an orphan. It's odd, you know, everyone gone. You walk through life assuming some people will always be there. Then you wake one morning to find the porch empty and you're rocking alone."

"I have a Mission rocker at home. It's a little bulky but it fits a porch. I'll rock alongside."

Smiling for the first time, her face relaxed. At my questioning, she spoke of the funeral service and the eulogy given by her father's closest friend.

"He dates from the time when they both studied in Cremona. Like my father, he had mastered the stages in Stradivari's life. He could repair a violin from any period by producing the style. They were masters of their craft."

I ordered cheesecake with two forks and asked for more tea.

"Philip, would you open the package here? I want to share the contents with you."

From my belt I removed the Swiss army knife that I always carry. I used the smaller blade and slit the corners of the package. Daria leaned over and removed the contents: photos, letters, academic honors, diplomas. "Most of this is memorabilia", she said. She assembled the items in front of her and picked out an envelope which was cut open. She handed it to me.

"One of the last things my father wrote. I'm eager to know what you think."

I reached for the letter and removed the cream-colored stationery. The script was ornate, reminiscent of penmanship around the turn of the century.

My dearest daughter:

As I enter my mid-eighties, I feel obliged to inform you of aspects of your inheritance you might otherwise miss. You will grasp the implications of what I write. You yourself recall the difference between playing on your childhood fiddle and performing on the Guarneri that I gave you for your twentieth birthday. The two are related to each other as the early to the late Rembrandt. I do not wish to exalt craftsmanship over prime spruce and maple. Apart from wood there is nothing on which to build. But the foregoing may all be in vain, for without superior varnish a violin cannot sing.

What the Masters concocted had much in common. All used gum, oil, and colouring matter. But each had his own opinion concerning the proportions, the method of mixing, and the mode of application. Stradivari's genius gave him an insight that produced results far exceeding his rivals'. If it was a challenge to make the varnish, it was another to apply it with finesse. Antonio met the challenge and fashioned legendary instruments that embody what is called "the secret of the Stradivarius".

According to scholars, Antonio's recipe disappeared. The basis for this assumption is a nineteenth-century letter of Giacomo Stradivari to Signor Mandelli. In it, Giacomo confesses to destroying the family Bible in which his illustrious ancestor, in his own hand, had inscribed the incomparable varnish. Giacomo states that he copied the prescription, destroyed the Bible, and hid his copy, resolving never to disclose it. He concluded that if other Stradivaris should master the craft of their celebrated forebear, they should have the advantage of Antonio's formula.

What happened to the copy Giacomo made is the subject of speculation. But no one has come forth to challenge the assertion that he burned the family Bible in its entirety. Despite his avowal, I am convinced he retained the Bible's end paper on which was written the recipe and the manner of application. Yes, he told the truth that, grasping the value of what lay in the Bible, he made a copy and destroyed the book. But the page in Antonio's handwriting he kept. A facsimile of this document, short of the amounts, you will find in the manila envelope. The original is in Cremona in the Banco Ambrosiano. You may use your passport to gain access.

How I came by Antonio's formula need not concern you. I was unable to mix the varnish. The ratio of oil to gum and colouring, and their application require absolute precision. My arthritic fingers could not meet the demands.

Though you are well established, Daria, with ownership of the townhouse and rents from the second and third floor flats, you will need additional funds to further your career. If I cannot be your advocate, let the varnish do in my absence what I may not because of death. I entrust you with this "secret" and ask you not to disclose it lightly. My hope is that you never regret your guilelessness. I love you more than my life. You are always il cuor del mio cuore.

Lovingly,
Papa

Philip looked up from his reading. Daria noticed how flushed he was in the face.

"Philip, you look like you're in shock. What are you thinking?"

"Daria, if what he says is true and the document is authentic, your father is helping you to accomplish all your goals as a violinist. You stand to become a very rich woman."

"What should I do?"

"Nothing for now. Get yourself settled. Begin rehearsals again. It will all have to wait till after your concert."

"I don't understand. What will have to wait?"

"The trip to Cremona."

Philip put his pen down. He had written all he intended. He had left his story at a tantalizing point where, on another day, he could advance the plot, urged on by the mystery. His imagination needed to rest. It was his turn to be fed by someone else's.

Mother Thérèse accompanied Lisa to her room at the top of the stairs.

"I hope you'll be comfortable, Miss Roberts. It's unusual to have only one guest in the house. The weather has kept the others away. It was too late to bring you supper, so I left some food in the refrigerator. There's salad, and the casserole is easily heated in the microwave. You'll find tea, coffee, and hot chocolate in the pantry."

"Thank you, Mother. I appreciate the thoughtfulness. I tried to arrive early, but the snowdrifts made driving impossible. Then there was the usual Friday exodus from the city. It's a miracle I got here. What should have been an hour trip took three. I'm exhausted. I'll have some hot chocolate and go to bed."

"That's a fine idea. Breakfast is at eight in the morning after Mass. You're welcome to join us in the chapel down the road. Mother Ambrose will see you in parlor around nine-thirty. I'll leave you now. The Compline bell will ring shortly."

"Compline?"

"It's the last sung prayer of the day, what we call one of the Hours. I would ask you to join us, but it makes more sense for you to get your rest. Good night."

"Good night."

She heard the nun descend the stairs and the outside door slam shut. The only sounds were the crackle of logs in the fireplace and the steam pipes hissing and snarling at intervals. For a moment, Lisa looked out the window. The snow was voluminous, heaping the roadway with a white silence. She had risked driving to Regina Pacis, even though the forecast had announced a storm alert. She had been lucky to arrive in one piece.

Lisa emptied her bag into a bureau drawer with no concern for order. Her cosmetics and toiletries she left in full view. The room was austere but the bed felt soft. A down coverlet and an extra pillow and blanket ensured her sleeping comfort. So far, she couldn't complain. The abbey had been hospitable beyond her expectations. She went downstairs and entered the kitchen. The teapot was on the stove. She lit the gas jet and waited for the pot to whistle. She emptied a package of hot chocolate into a mug and poured the boiling water over it. She opened the refrigerator, removed the milk, which she added to her drink, and took a generous sip. The sweet warmth gave her a sense of renewed purpose. She could hear the faint sound of chanting from the chapel down the road. Whatever loneliness she felt was dispelled by the nuns' voices singing at close distance. She went into the living room and sat in an easy chair before the fire. She imagined Philip alongside her the way they sat in the apartment, both of them staring into the flames, occasionally looking over to smile, touch, and kiss. She missed him. Yes, she was punishing him because of his deviousness, but she was punishing herself, too. Was she mad to drive all these hours to ease what amounted to jealousy? Would she make a fool of herself before a perfect stranger? She would press her case for an anthology of poets and ask Mother Ambrose to contribute. All she knew was that this nun, as a young woman, had written love poems. Suppose Mother Ambrose asked her how she learned of their existence, what would she say? Would she mention Philip? Somehow she would conduct the interview with Mother Ambrose, though she would have to fake it.

Her thoughts gave way to a yawn. She was exhausted. Staying at Vicki's was not a congenial arrangement, especially sleeping on a futon. She got up from her fireside seat. The fire, the silence, the hot chocolate—all of them drugged her and she felt a heaviness in her limbs. She left the cup on the end table and pulled her legs up the stairs. Somehow she managed to get to her room, slip out of her clothes and into her flannel nightgown. Her last intelligent act was putting the eiderdown on the bed. No sooner had she stretched between the sheets and arranged her head on the pillow than she was asleep.

The hissing of the radiator woke her next morning. She put the pillow over her head and squirmed under the covers. The hissing turned to a rattle. She dropped the pillow onto the floor and kicked off the covers. She picked up her wristwatch to check the time. "Oh, my God, it's after eight." There was no time for a languorous shower. She slipped out of her night-gown into her clothes. She looked for a mirror. The only one was in the corner, scarcely a foot square. So she took her cosmetic bag, brush, and comb to the bathroom where she splashed and dried her face, brushed her hair, and lightly applied some lipstick. As she descended the stairs, she could smell the coffee brewing. Her stomach growled. She had eaten nothing since the afternoon of the previous day. She sat at the dining room table, poured some orange juice, and reached for a muffin. She finished it and had another. Whether it was appetite or the country air or a combination of both, she ate with gusto. She rose from the table and went into the kitchen. The coffee was ready. She poured herself a mug, put oatmeal in a dish, and returned to the table. It was an enormous breakfast in contrast to her usual toast and tea. She had earned the quantity after the fast of half a day. The door opened and Mother Thérèse came in wearing a parka with a hood over her veil.

"I hoped you were up and serving yourself, Miss Roberts."

"I'm grateful for the large breakfast, Mother. I was famished. And I must get the recipe for the muffins. They're delicious. Last night I forgot to ask you. Where do I find Mother Ambrose? You spoke of a parlor."

"Why not finish your breakfast? I'll return at nine-twenty, and we can walk together to the main house. The parlor is at the side entrance."

"And the dishes?"

"You can leave them on the tray. I'll carry them back to the house."

With that, she left. A competent woman, Lisa thought, as she lingered at table; attractive, too, with a crisp style that wasn't rude or pushy. She reminded Lisa of several ballet teachers she had studied with: efficient, clearheaded, and always well intentioned.

About nine-fifteen, she stood waiting outside for Mother Thérèse. She was enjoying the effects of the snowfall. White blanketed everything. Her enjoyment would have been complete except for the nervousness she felt about meeting Mother Ambrose. There wasn't time to cultivate anxiety. Mother Thérèse was walking toward her, her breath smoking in the air. Lisa went to meet her and together they walked to the main house.

"The side door is just ahead." They proceeded another thirty feet. Lisa thanked her again, said good-bye, and mounted the steps to the small foyer. The inner door said Parlor One and opened onto another room with a chair facing the grille. She had barely fifteen seconds to be astonished at the mesh divider when a figure entered and sat down.

"Good morning, Miss Roberts," said Mother Ambrose, "I'm glad you could come despite the weather." She had entered so softly that she seemed to materialize out of thin air. Was she supposed to rise in the presence of a cloistered nun? What was protocol? There was little time to answer. Lisa was too busy examining her rival's appearance. Philip had told the truth. Mother Ambrose was clearly older. But, Lisa saw, Philip was true to his aesthetic sense: she was immensely attractive. She sensed she was in the presence of a writer. She had fraternized with too many not to recognize the intense observation—the eyes assessing, memorizing, and imagining a story from the smallest gesture. Mother Ambrose pulled her shawl tightly around her. However bright and astute the face, Lisa could see she was still convalescing. The face was pale, the eyes magnified because of their violet shadows. Lisa discerned a wheeze in her breathing.

"I appreciate your seeing me, Mother."

"May I call you Lisa? For all the formalities of Benedictine life, we try to treat our guests as part of our family."

"Yes. I prefer it."

"So, Mother Thérèse tells me you're an editor at Little, Brown. Have you been there long?"

"About five years."

"What brought you there?"

Lisa found it difficult to answer, for the transition from dance to print had been a major crisis. How could she explain to this nun that for years she had struggled with diets to keep a ballerina's body? It had been a losing battle. She thickened despite every dietary effort to the contrary. At the time, she refused to admit that her thighs were large, her frame broad, her breasts too full. She had fought these truths courageously, dangerously even. Insight into her unsuitability came when the diet pills failed and anemia became chronic. Hospitalization followed by counseling at a woman's center rescued her. To escape what she knew would be her mother's disappointment, she had left for Boston where she used her background to write for the *Globe* about the local dance scene. Journalism became her entree to Little, Brown. All this she recalled as she sought to answer Mother Ambrose's question. Lisa distilled her reply in generalities:

"At one time I studied ballet," she said, "but I realized it wasn't for me. So I came to Boston and started another career. I went to a publishing house and ascended the ranks. I'm up for an executive editorship. I have a feeling it will happen soon. I need one more commercial success. They give us points in the business. For all the hoop-la about finding new talent, publishing is largely buying and selling."

"Is that why you're interested in women poets?"

Lisa became flustered. For the moment, she had forgotten the anthology.

"It's a recent idea. I hadn't made the connection, but you're right. It's commercially promising, especially while the women's movement is so prominent. To have a nun as a contributor gives a rounded picture."

148

"It's unusual outside monastic circles to know my poems. How did you learn of them?"

The question made her squirm a little; it was too undemocratic in its precision. Did this nun know more than she admitted? Was she playing with her? It was hard to tell, for the voice was sincere. But there was humor in her eyes.

"To be honest, Mother, I haven't read your poems. I heard about them from a friend who praised them. I respect his opinion."

"Ah, yes, Philip."

There was a pause. It was as if this nun were waiting for her to declare herself, to admit what really brought her to the abbey. Lisa remembered how Catholics prized confession.

"Yes. He spoke highly of you when he returned to Boston. His visit here stirred his imagination. You affected him deeply."

"Does that cause you difficulty?"

"It did make me wonder who you were."

"I was once in a similar position. You see, I was married before I became a Benedictine. I had co-authored a book of poems with a man, whose initials did not match my husband's. I took great pains to explain that the feelings in my poems were literary, representing a time gone by, and that they did not compromise what I felt for him."

"Did he believe you?"

"To be frank, Lisa, I don't think he did. In fact, I lost with both men. But the problem had less to do with jealousy than with my attitude."

"What was that?"

"Something I came to call range and concentration. I believe some people can focus their entire emotional interest on another human being. The two proceed, if they're fortunate, as partners all their lives and astonish their friends with each anniversary. Others cannot do that. They are frequently artists and mystics. They need to diffuse their energies over more than one person.

149

My husband, Cemil, I loved dearly, but I realized late I was one of those persons. I needed to love intensely on different levels. Otherwise, I felt suffocated."

"Are you saying Philip is like that?"

"To some extent, yes. I'm reminded of what Browning wrote when he said 'A man's reach should exceed his grasp / Or what's a Heaven for?' That soaring nature is true of the greatest writers. They feel a transcendent itch. It's hard on the lovers of such people. They want to suffice absolutely. It isn't possible. The only reality of which one can speak absolutely is the Absolute. But, then, I'm a religious person. I have a stake in such language."

Silence filled the parlor. Lisa turned her eyes away while her face reddened. This nun had grasped her real intent and was addressing it from a new perspective. It was no longer a question of winning or losing. Mother Ambrose had refused to contend. Lisa looked back at her face. It smiled benignly. There was no gloating at having bested her; just the silence of seeing through her ruse and moving beyond it.

"You know why I came?"

"Yes."

"I had no idea I was so transparent. Do Benedictines always lead people to major truths?"

"We practice on ourselves and develop the knack. We're also committed to being led."

"By what?"

"Truth. Goodness. Since the world is shy of the word 'God', we could say, Reality with a capital 'R'. It sounds abstract but it isn't. It's as concrete as the two of us facing each other. Right now, you and I are the local names for Truth."

Momentarily, Lisa felt like a veil had been lifted. What blew away from the window was a gauzy curtain filtering out the daylight. Now the sun rushed in. Something so basic had been spoken that reality no longer seemed flat and dull. Lisa had recovered, however briefly, a depth perception. The ocular shift was dazzling, and she was blinded by the viewpoint. She had laid to rest words like "God" and "heaven". The bag of supernatural tricks had been emptied years before. She was concerned solely with human relationships, most of all, her own with Philip. That was flesh and blood, measurable and concrete. Religion was wasted on her. It was something the old did with their solitude. She imagined shutting the window and drawing the curtain. She preferred muted light to high noon.

"I'm not used to abstractions, Mother Ambrose. I deal with the nuts and bolts of reality like, 'Should we buy this book? Will it sell? How quickly must we recover our investment?' "

"Do you see your relationship with Philip as an investment?"

Lisa jumped a little. This nun could be blunt. She was certainly not naïve. She had once played for love and knew the stakes.

"In some ways, yes. It's not your approach, Mother, but outside, sex and economics make the world go round. In any situation, if I don't find one I suspect the other."

"I once lived in a world in which sex and economics, as you put it, were reduced to their substrate: power and control. Everyone, everything was expendable. Perhaps Philip is showing you that he's dissatisfied with such a view. By coming here he got an inkling of something more."

"With all due respect, Mother, perhaps all he discovered here was you. You seem to have claimed his imagination, judging from his journal."

"I'm not surprised. The abbey has that effect on people. The chant, the symbols, the silence become agents of a larger purpose."

"But don't you think Philip is using you for his own purpose?"

"I don't mind being used, Lisa. We all function for one another. The question is: Does it serve a higher end? And in the functioning, is our humanity respected? You may call my position benign utilitarianism. You underestimate Philip if you

view him as just self-absorbed. He has the capacity for enormous depth. I'd like to think Regina Pacis has wakened it.
There's nothing to fear, Lisa. I should think that the deeper he
becomes, the more profound your relationship. You can't but
'profit' — to use your language."

"And what, Mother, do you stand to gain? What's in it for
you? Or are Benedictines beyond self-interest?"

"It's a fair question. I like the candor. I lost a son years ago.
He resembled Philip in so many ways. I learned to do without
Halil. But a certain — how do you say in English, hankering?
— for him persisted. I wondered what might have happened
had he lived. The yearning became intolerable. It was the
energy of nurturing with no place to spend it but on fantasy.
After I entered Benedictine life, I spread that energy over
countless people and places. Now Philip is the focus of that
attention because something in him is making an appeal. It's a
providential matching of circumstance. Without straining, Philip
has caught it, too. I sense the romantic fervor. It's not unusual
for artists to enlarge on people's qualities. He will find his
balance. The more he knows me, the more my weakness will
become apparent. It runs deep like the crack in Michelangelo's
marble. I have the defects of my qualities."

"It's hard to believe. You seem so confident. I'd almost say
your certitude is too certain."

"Lisa, that is what attracts Philip. He's not in love with
me — the idea is preposterous. He's in love with permanence.
I'm only a stepping stone. But you needn't be alarmed. He cares
for you deeply. Could we not both, in recognizing his talent,
help him accomplish his goal? I'm not here to compete. I'm a
friend."

"I came here, Mother, with another idea. I was comfortable seeing you as competitor. But you argue the opposite
seductively."

"The truth is enticing. Joined to love, it's irresistible."

Lisa began to notice how much the interview had taken from this woman. She had maintained her straight posture throughout, but the strain showed on her face. Her natural verve struggled with a body that could not keep up. It was clear she should halt the conversation.

"You look tired, Mother. It's best that I leave."

"You're welcome to stay."

"Thank you, but no. It's better for me to go, now that the snow has stopped. I have a pile of manuscripts in my apartment. I need to start on them before Monday."

They both stood up. "I want to thank you for the frank discussion. I have a lot to think about."

"I would like to give you something. A token of our meeting. Please use it." Mother Ambrose opened a panel to the left of the grille and passed her a wrapped gift.

"Thank you, Mother. It's very thoughtful."

"It may help you accumulate points. Good-bye, Lisa. God bless you."

It wasn't till she returned to her room to pack her bag that she decided to open the gift. Inside the blue and gold paper she found an autographed copy of *Poems for Two Violins*.

Chapter Seven

It was Saturday afternoon at Milano's, and Philip was settling in for a long read. He was eager to learn more of Darius, whose moods swung wildly from enthusiasm to wistfulness. An image of an Edwardian dandy flashed in his mind: the velveteen jacket and spats; the rosebud in the lapel; the filigreed walking stick tapping the pavement. He could even smell von Galli's face after the barber had shaved and patted it with eau de cologne. Philip glanced at the heading, "War Years", and began.

It is fitting now to introduce Cemil Hasan, who has had a small but tantalizing role in Beatrice's story. He seemed, at first, insignificant to me, for the war and the plight of the Jews had kept us apart. At the time, I was writing for Travels Unlimited *and sending home stories from the Italian lake district, while he oversaw his vast estate outside Istanbul. Formerly agrarian in his interests, with lands that produced every necessity within their borders—grain, olives, vegetables—he was in the process of shifting to commerce, of importing goods from abroad and wholesaling them for the public. His overseas involvement made him huge profits, and he was envied for his success. With wealth to foster the arts in Dubrovnik, Salzburg, and Vienna, Cemil ranked high among international patrons.*

Bea once remarked that after meeting him in Dubrovnik, she had made a mental memo of him, as when searching a rack for a magazine, a woman has her eye caught by the glossy cover of another, removes it, flips through the glamorous pages and, saying, "Someday I'll subscribe to this", returns it and goes on looking. For Cemil, the response was more focused. At thirty-one, he was being pressed by his parents to marry. As an aristocrat, it was difficult to choose a wife from within his class, for the old Ottoman families were too widely dispersed.

Thus, he was intent on finding a woman outside his circle with a life of her own that did not conflict with his. He had never considered a European, let alone a performing artist, but after meeting Beatrice that opening night, the still small voice of attraction kept urging, "This is it." Or to put it more suavely, "You have just found the woman you were obscurely looking for." It was five years before Cemil could heed that advice.

Shortly before his trip to Dubrovnik in 1938, he had returned from Oxford after taking the prescribed program in business and financing. Though older than his classmates, he was a diligent pupil who finished the degree in two years and won the prize as top student of his graduating class. Gifted but unassuming, he was astute at finding answers to complicated problems. No one would have guessed from his dress or behavior his status as a member of Turkey's most distinguished family. Cosmopolitan in outlook but no pie-eyed radical, he felt little need to criticize Turkey's existing social order or the political reforms of Mustafa Kemal. Having frequented the mosque as a boy, he had passed through the rite of circumcision at the onset of puberty. It was the last Muslim ritual to which he submitted. No longer formally religious, he remained a person of deep piety and could cite text and verse from the Qur'an.

In 1939, at the outbreak of World War II, Cemil was dividing his time between his estate outside Istanbul and his yali or summer residence on the Bosporus. He took advantage of Turkey's shaky neutrality to enjoy the rich city life while he directed his energies to consolidating financial gains. Though intent on multiplying investments at home and abroad, he learned of the Balkan genocide which the Nazis were perpetrating. He heard stories of those struggling to reach the city, how they came in boats torpedoed by submarines, stowed away on trains to Bulgaria, or on commandeered planes from Vienna to Istanbul. Whatever uneasiness he felt, there was enough to distract him at home. In Istanbul, ethnic jealousy had made the Jewish minority scapegoats. It began with hyperinflation. The cost of staples like bread, sugar, coffee, and beer quadrupled. That peasants were warehousing food, that farm products were vastly curtailed, that shipping faltered and machinery collapsed were all blithely dismissed. The government focused blame on Jewish merchants, who were labeled profiteers. The crippling tax of 1942, the Varlik Vergisi, was used to punish them. Jews unable to pay it after their property was sold were sentenced to labor camps. Cemil, whose import and export activities centered on Jews as middlemen, remained under a cloud. The government felt it could discredit him, despite high connections and an aristocratic name, by taxing out of existence those with whom he did business.

"My Jewish friends were decimated", he told Bea later. It was an inevitable consequence, for the tax demanded more than their total wealth. Cemil watched as their businesses and furnishings were sold for a pittance. He observed how merchant signs in Karakoy altered daily. Istanbul's influential citizens and Cemil's closest friends were arrested and herded into military trucks. He pleaded with the authorities for their release but was unable to secure it. So he took matters into his own hands. Together with a group of outraged Americans, Cemil catalogued the infamies for C.D. Sulzberger of the New York Times, who in turn warned the officer for Turkish censorship in Istanbul that if he impeded publication, the articles would be posted from Moscow. Fearful, at first, of going public, Sulzberger received Cemil's support. "The Russians are blasé whether you tell the truth or magnify it", Cemil said. "They hate us Turks." Using Cemil's evidence, Sulzberger penned several blistering columns about the tax's effects. The American public was appalled. The U.S. ambassador to Turkey, Laurence Steinhardt, hinted aid would cease if the policy were not reversed. A cable to Steinhardt from the Secretary of State, Cordell Hull, further admonished the government. Apprized of Hull's cable and stung by the articles, the government canceled the unpaid taxes and the Jews went free. It was Cemil's first victory on their behalf.

Cemil's preoccupation had moved beyond Istanbul's Jews, who had returned home after the government canceled the Varlik Vergisi. As word of the concentration camps arrived, Cemil received a firsthand report from Buchenwald. Concealed under the coats of casualties, an escapee had journeyed through Lithuania, Latvia, and Estonia. Taking refuge on Cemil's estate, he recounted his story to members of the

Istanbul Delegation headed by Chaim Barlas and his colleagues known as "the boys". From them I have reconstructed the interview, which Chaim conducted while Cemil was present.

"What is your name?" Chaim asked him.

"Josef... Schneiders." He was so bewildered by his new surroundings that he paused between name and surname as if groping for information. They gave him a weak soup—the only food he could digest—and he ate it, one laborious spoonful after another. He then changed clothes from the filthy rags he was wearing. When he removed his shirt there was an audible gasp from those who helped him. His rib cage protruded from his chest, while his inhalations alternated between gasping and wheezing. He was suffering from a grave illness, whether pneumonia or tuberculosis they could not say. Chaim waited patiently for answers without pressing him with questions.

"Where did you live before you were interned?"

"The city of Weimar. I was a medical student before being arrested. My family and I were rounded up by the S.S. and herded through the streets with about a hundred others. I learned my parents and sister were sent to Dachau. They were called 'socially unfit'. I was sent to Buchenwald, east of Weimar, where I underwent 'rehabilitation'. My medical background saved me from the gas chamber. For months I assisted the German doctors with what I thought were neutral medical procedures. I found out later I had been duped into helping them determine who should live or die. One day, I was assigned to a group of prisoners who were transporting wheelbarrows of dead bodies from the clinic to the lime pits. First we dug a hole, then we stripped the corpses of shoes, clothes—anything we could salvage for the rail cars. Two of us sorted the garments into piles. We managed to hide under a mound of coats. My friend died in my arms, choking on his vomit so that the guards would not hear." Schneiders began to tremble and would have cried, but no tears came.

"Tell the world what the Nazis are doing. At least twelve thousand a day are being gassed. Do not believe the lies about sequestering political prisoners. The deportations precede mass murder." His impassioned plea made an impact on Cemil.

One incident alone cannot explain his unconditional commitment to the Jewish cause. However unsatisfactory—for who can discern what goes on in another's soul?—I must turn elsewhere for reasons. It was partly because of what the Turkish Jews had suffered, partly because of his identification with ancestry. His maternal great-grandmother had been an Armenian Jew. But Cemil's sister, Sema, explained it another way:

"In December of 1941, Cemil and I had seen a film at the British embassy. It was called Pimpernel Smith, a contemporary rendition of the novel, The Scarlet Pimpernel. The English actor Leslie Howard took the role of a lackadaisical professor who saves countless Jews from arrest by fooling the Nazis. Cemil was impressed with Howard's armchair professor. That Cemil looked like Howard also helped. As we walked home from the embassy, I noticed my brother was lost in thought.

"Did you dislike the film?" I asked. I thought his silence meant we had made a mistake in seeing a whimsical film, especially when the times were desperate.

"Quite the contrary", he replied, "I was riveted."

"I found the premise implausible", I said. "I mean, the Nazis are cleverer than that. I can't imagine someone getting away with so much on such a large scale. The film was a piece of wish fulfillment, that's all. But too bad we don't have a Pimpernel Smith around."

"Perhaps we shall. I'd like to give it a try, Sema. In fact, it's exactly what I want to do."

"Cemil, you can't be serious."

"I'm afraid I am. Someone has got to outsmart the Nazis at their own nasty game."

"And you think you can succeed where others have failed?"

"I won't know unless I try. I want to do more with my life than store olives."

And, indeed, Cemil was summoned to accomplish more.

"Will you help initiate rescue operations for European Jews by establishing a route to Palestine?" Chaim Barlas asked him.

"Yes", Cemil replied immediately. His role was to extend the protection of a neutral Turkey to Jews, who were being victimized by the savagery engulfing Europe. An optimistic estimate showed that the operation would involve eleven million Jews including those of Greece, Italy, Hungary, Romania, and Turkey. Europe was to be searched from East to West for them. Cemil was to contact Jewish communities, send funds, and help smuggle refugees to Slovakia, from there to Hungary and Romania, thence to Istanbul and Palestine. In the execution of this vast operation, he was answerable only to Barlas. It was another peak in his career, a time of exhilaration when his resourcefulness was being tested.

If I were to judge his success on the basis of the people he saved, I would have to say it was modest, for the numbers were limited. A sober estimate has it that ten thousand found freedom via Istanbul, though some have calculated as high as fifty thousand. Whatever the number, Cemil utilized Istanbul's location as the ideal base for reaching into occupied Europe.

"The city offers a way out of what is otherwise a cul-de-sac", he told Bea. Since he lacked official standing, Cemil was vulnerable to harassment by the Turkish secret police. We learned later that the Emniyet, Turkey's National Security Service, knew exactly what he was doing. After the war, hefty folders of reports and photos detailing his activities were uncovered. Despite his unofficial status, Cemil was protected by the Delegation's alliance with British Intelligence. Major Arthur Whittal of the celebrated Anglo-Istanbul family became Cemil's protector. Flashing his ingenuous smile, he explained his terms to Cemil:

"We will get you the 'sources'. But you must get us the information."

"Jews in exchange for espionage?"

"Yes", Whittal said, "It's as simple as that."

Cemil's most ingenious ploy was issuing protective passes to Jews who could show they had links with Turkey. Drawing on his business training, Cemil's use of the Hasan pass was a brilliant stroke. Printed on vellum and embellished with the crescent and star of the Turkish government, it was dotted with stamps, signatures, and countersignatures. Though it claimed no legitimacy in international law, it inspired respect by announcing that the holders were under Turkish protection. Once refugees arrived in Istanbul, they received Hasan passes and were housed and fed for months before they could be put on the Taurus

Express to Palestine. Cemil worked tirelessly in finding money to support their stay. He became a black market wizard by changing gems into cash and foreign money into Turkish currency. He smuggled diamonds in toothpaste, shaving cream, and soap. When he wasn't smuggling, Cemil was setting up hospitals, nurseries, and soup kitchens throughout the city, or buying food, clothing, and medicine with the funds he had accumulated. He coordinated rescue efforts with the Papal Nuncio, Angelo Roncalli, the future John the XXIII, and organized the heads of missions. Cemil worked round the clock, allowing himself no more than a few hours' sleep. He exhibited a resolute zeal even Goebbels might have envied. His intent was unambiguous — not just to rescue Jews, but to get them to Palestine as citizens of a future state. To avoid prying eyes, Cemil turned his estate into a center for unaccompanied refugees. Local volunteers speaking fourteen languages worked there from morning till night, his sprawling house always jammed with people.

While Cemil worked tirelessly for the Jews in Istanbul, Bea struggled to bring Italian Jews across the Swiss frontier. However dangerous the trip, it was her only alternative. Southern options did not exist. Between September 1943 and April 1945, over five thousand entered Switzerland through the Ticino, passing near Lakes Maggiore, Lugano, and Como. Others crossed the mountains from the Valle d'Aosta and the Valtellina, a route which led north along Lake Como. All approaches were hazardous. Towns and villages near the frontier were teeming with soldiers, and all vehicles going north were routinely searched.

Those strong enough to ascend a mountainous section avoided the barbed wire, the police dogs, and the Nazi guards by crossing at a height of over a mile. Once their guide had left, their biggest problem was hiking down the lake without a trail. Invariably, escape across the border involved major problems. These were solved when refugees, staying in villas nearby, had suitable documents and an Italian accent, and they approached the border aided by benefactors. Their odyssey began in a convent. Bea enlisted Benedictine nuns for this purpose. Later, she moved the refugees to private homes, barns, and huts, their mobility a way of reinforcing their safety. Her goal was to reach the end of the Italian line. At fishing villages like Cannobio and Laveno on Lake Maggiore, they met a boat and rowed to an isolated hamlet where they hiked to the border. If they were lucky to get that far, they found electrified wire guarded by Nazis and Dobermann pinschers. This is how Bea described one such incident:

"We had been waiting for hours in the woods. We shivered while a cold rain soaked us, our hands and feet swollen from chilblains. Fascist soldiers patrolled nearby, so no one stirred. There were three couples with two children aged nine and four. It was seven in the morning and I expected the change of border guards to take ten minutes. We were a stone's throw from a gap in the wire, fifty yards from the guard post. It was now or never. The first two couples passed through the narrow opening in the wire. The nine-year-old followed. I waited on the other side as the last couple put the four-year-old through. In an effort to cling to his mother's neck, he grazed the electrified wire and the alarm went off. Terrified by the pulsating siren, the child began to cry. Border guards, heading in our direction, started shooting. We were standing targets. I dove for the mother who clutched her child. It was too late. They were felled by consecutive bullets. The husband began screaming for his wife to get up. In the fracas he did not see they were hit. The others, not knowing whether to turn back and help their companions, were frozen in their tracks. 'Keep going!' I yelled and tried to head off the husband who rushed to his wife and child. He was shot at their side and toppled over them. I raced to the others, barely escaping with my life."

Such scenes were not unusual. But crossing the border could be even more daunting. No refugee proceeded without a knowledgeable guide. Bea knew the obscure trails, the gaps in the wire, the schedule of the border guards, the routine of the patrol boats. She knew, too, those guards who would turn their backs with or without a bribe. But not all guides were as magnanimous as she. Many who escorted Jews were contrabandieri, smugglers, adept in crossing the border. Bea, who was concerned with guiding partisans or political outlaws, worked for the Resistance selflessly, whereas most guides worked for money. Jews often succumbed to the belief that a higher fee assured results. And the payment was dear, often ten thousand lire for each man, woman, and child at a time when the daily wage was less than a hundred. Benefactors who shared their resources by feeding and housing Jews could not meet the cost. Unscrupulous guides took their fee and deserted their clients at the frontier, betrayed them to guards, or stopped at the barbed wire, refusing to go farther unless more money was paid. The luckiest refugees had Bea, who acted not from mercenary gain but from higher motives.

Once across the border, the refugees had to persuade the Swiss guards to issue permits letting them remain. Swiss policy toward the Jews before 1943 was stricter than in 1944, when the category of refugee was broadened. Thus, the guards' behavior was erratic. Bea told me how a group of Venetian Jews whom she guided was ordered to return the way they came; otherwise, they would be arrested at Chiasso.

"One guard", she explained, "respected my family name and felt sympathy for the group."

"Return after midnight", he said, "when I'm alone. I'll see what I can do." Despite the group's gnawing fears, they did as he instructed but not without heated debate.

"It's a trap, I'm sure of it."

"Then why would he ask us to return?"

"We'll be arrested en masse. He'll be promoted for his action."

"But he's Swiss. He's on our side."

"How can we be certain?"

"All I had to go on", Bea continued, "was the Stradivari name, that he had heard me in Lugano five years before. His devotion to music was my sole guarantee."

"We returned at midnight when he was alone, and he let the group cross safely. I gave him a faded picture of myself, which I inscribed on the back: To Ernst, whose love for music set us free. With gratitude, Beatrice Stradivari."

Stories about Bea abound, for she was as resourceful in rescuing Jews in Italy as Cemil was in Istanbul. She accompanied groups of refugees to Milan and found refuge for them in a Benedictine convent on Lake Como, then took them to Cernobbio where they were handed over to guides. If this was not possible, she entrusted them to Madre

Donata at the Istituto Palazzolo. There hundreds of Jews seeking passage to Switzerland found shelter.

Of Bea, one refugee, Eda Lambruzzo, confessed to me: "Meeting Bea Stradivari was the most vivid event of my life. She immediately fed me, gave me her bed to sleep in, and directed me to a convent of nuns." Similar remarks by Vittorio Luzzo, Letizia Purgo, Lodovico and Silvia Contente, and Enzo Modigliani attest to her tireless efforts at rescuing Jews. Little is known of her work staffing shelters or establishing food centers en route to the border. Many stories have vanished with the passage of time. But one truth is incontestable: she would not remain indifferent as desperate human beings struggled to cross into freedom.

Cemil's first contact with Bea since Dubrovnik was a message she sent to Isaac Hertzog, chief Rabbi of Palestine. The rabbi passed it to Barlas who in turn passed it to Cemil. She wrote straight to the point: "Please contact the Papal Nuncio in Turkey, Cardinal Roncalli, to petition His Holiness. The Pope must use his influence to save our brethren from the ovens." Roncalli acted immediately, and the transport of Jews in Turkey was stopped.

Cemil's second contact came during a visit to Greece. He had traveled there because he feared for the lives of the sixty thousand Jews concentrated in Salonika. Having constituted a community for over twenty-five hundred years, their dense numbers left them vulnerable to arrest. Predictably, the Nazi roundup began in 1943; however, the Italian consulate insisted that Germans spare anyone of Italian origin. Bea, who had entered the city with the authority of a consul, broadly defined the word "Italian". She eventually explained her approach to Cemil whom she met at a consulate dinner.

"He was tall and lean", she told me, "his hair showing flecks of gray near the temples. His face had a resolute expression bolstered by smoldering eyes. He was a man fired by a cause. For all the horrors he had witnessed, he kept his feline grace and moved like the born aristocrat he was.

"I was near the refreshment table when I sensed someone observing me. Cemil's eyes continued to stare as they tried to place me. The face was intense until insight made him smile. Though he looked familiar, the memory of where we met escaped me. He walked over.

'Mademoiselle Stradivari. It's a pleasure to see you again.'
'You look familiar. Did we meet after a concert somewhere?'
'Dubrovnik.'
'Ah, yes, the panther.'
'Excuse, please.'
'A musical notation. You needn't worry. It's rather flattering.'
"He smiled without comprehension. Perhaps he realized I was having fun not entirely at his expense. He asked me why I was in Salonika. Since his effort at rescuing Jews through Istanbul was general knowledge, I confided to him my approach for helping them out of the port city. Within twenty-four hours—that is how swiftly the panther moved—we were issuing naturalization papers to Jews married to Italians and to their alleged children, adults in middle age. In fact, Cemil and I capitalized on any connection to Italy."

The two worked closely, presenting the Nazis with daily lists of naturalized Italians awaiting deportation. They even instructed Italian soldiers to visit detention blocks to claim Jews as their wives. The deportees were released. Cemil and Bea arranged for Italian military trains to carry the freed Jews to Athens where they were housed, clothed, and fed. Their freedom continued till the Italian armistice, after which most Greek Jews did not survive. Nearly two thousand in Athens, five thousand from the Greek mainland, and several thousand from Rhodes, Corfu, Crete, and Paros were rounded up. Without the Italians to protect them, there was no one to intervene.

Under the anarchic conditions, it was dangerous for a Muslim Turk to be out in public. Bea pleaded with Cemil to terminate his activities in Salonika and leave with her for Athens and then for Cremona. She had every reason to fear for his life. The death brigades were after him. She recognized his sense of guilt, which arose from the disparity he felt between his life and that of the Salonikan Jews. To compensate for the difference, he took greater risks in his rescue attempts. Even when the bullets were flying around him, he rarely left his car to take cover among the corpses, dead animals, and burning debris. I asked Bea once if Cemil was ever afraid. She replied: "He said it was terrifying but he had no choice." She remembered his words exactly: "Bea, I'm committed to this mission. I could never return to

Cremona without knowing I've tried everything to save as many Jews as possible."

When the Nazis finally captured him, they refused to acknowledge Cemil's identification papers. To prove their suspicions were correct, they stripped him naked and pointed to his genitals. For those who were circumcised (and in this matter Turks resembled Jews) it meant certain death. That is why Cemil Hasan was shot by a firing squad on the island of Paros. He died as a Jew.

Philip looked up from his book. John had called his name from behind the counter and signaled him over.

"Phone call for you."

"For me?"

"Stratton, right?"

"Yes."

"You can take it in the corner."

Philip walked over to the pay phone and picked up the dangling receiver.

"Hello."

"Philip, it's Lisa. Sorry to interrupt, but I had to speak to you."

The voice startled him. During her five days' absence, he had struggled to put her out of his mind. Now she had reawakened the pain. His flustered state made him answer in clipped phrases and monosyllables.

"Were you writing?" she asked.

"No."

"I won't stay long on the phone. I just wanted to say I've thought a lot about what happened Monday. I realize I over-reacted. Separation only makes things worse. So I'm returning to the apartment this afternoon."

"Why?" He still had enough mental presence to search for a motive.

"What a funny thing to ask, Philip. Us, of course. Isn't that reason enough?"

"It wasn't, Monday." He sensed she was withholding something. Her explanation seemed too simple to be sincere.

"Let's not discuss it on the phone. I'm still at Vicki's. I'll pack my things and be back in an hour. Did you eat lunch?"

"No."

"Good. We can eat together. Is there anything in the fridge?"

"Nothing."

"I'll stop at the deli. I'm happy to be coming home. See you later."

He hung up the receiver and stood there, motionless, as if he were waiting for something. John looked over.

"You okay?"

"Yes."

"Anything serious?"

"I don't know."

He went to his table and gathered up his book, paper, pen, and ink. He couldn't deny a large part of him was eager to see her. But the phone call announcing her return had rattled him. Part of him was still lost in the memoir. Though von Galli's recounting of Cemil and Bea's activities had been matter-of-fact, Philip was completely absorbed. Now their story would have to wait. Philip exited into the cold air. Like hearing a conversation that competes with a TV, his mind was crisscrossed with voices. Why had Lisa changed her mind? As he turned onto Mt. Vernon Street, curiosity gained momentum and impelled him up the incline at a rapid pace.

"Philip, I left everything on the kitchen table. I'd appreciate it if you made me a ham and cheese sandwich and started the coffee. The stuff Vicki keeps in her apartment is vile. All those brown pellets — they look like mouse manure. I'm going to take a bath. Her hot water was on and off all week. I want to sit in a tub and soak."

While Lisa spoke from the bathroom, Philip was in the

bedroom. He had moved her suitcase to the corner for her eventual unpacking. Her shoulder bag, bulging with toiletries, lay on the bed. He heard her running the water as he moved to the kitchen to make sandwiches. In just fifteen minutes, everything was back to normal. The sound of bathwater running, a voice making requests from the bathroom, groceries being unpacked in the kitchen—it was an image of connubial bliss. He forgot his original intent, for the restored domesticity had superseded his curiosity. He took out the dishes and set the Danish ham on one, the Jarlsberg on another, and symmetrically arranged the rolls on still another. He ground the mocha beans fine, placed them in the automatic coffeemaker, and set the dial for four cups. While the water, spitting and sputtering, seeped through the grounds, he returned to the living room to tidy up. The *Boston Globe* and the *New York Times,* accumulated over a week, were strewn about the apartment. Dust balls rolled like tumbleweed on the parquet floor where the rug did not reach.

Philip went to the bedroom. He could hear the tub water lapping, could smell the buttermilk soap through the crack in the door. As he imagined Lisa bathing, the soapy water covering her breasts, he had an urge to undress and join her. He had been abstinent for five days, and the desire to be intimate was acute. He noted that his curiosity about her return was receding to the background, for it introduced reluctance, like a driver putting on the brakes and the gas at the same time. What one got was a stalled car while he needed to go full throttle. He laughed at the image which Lisa inspired. Her bath was a sexual signal. She would soak and preen and anoint herself, knowing full well his sensitivity to perfumed skin.

Philip continued staring at the bathroom door. "Lisa, do you want your things unpacked?"

"Stack them on the bureau. I'll put them away later", came the disembodied voice.

He opened her suitcase and removed her undergarments:

bras, body stockings, slips—all had the scent of the perfume she wore, the one choice with which he agreed unequivocally. It was Guerlain's Shalimar. Whenever he shopped where it was sold or passed a woman wearing it on a street, he thought of Lisa. He pressed a slip to his face and inhaled. It summoned up the Taj Mahal, the Mumtaz, the Shah Jahan. He remembered their love story, recalled the tomb the shah had built after her untimely death. "As the white bird of her soul flew from the bough of her body, the emperor was alone"—he had written that line early in his poetic career. He had begun composing a pentameter poem about the legendary couple. But the verses he penned dripped with gems and brocade till he scrapped them as too rich for his blood.

He listened for Lisa. She was drying herself, the towel brushing against her skin. Should he go in and perform the ritual himself? He was on the verge when she stepped from the bathroom wearing her velour robe cinched at the waist. She bent forward, towel drying her hair which hung in polished strings. He followed his impulse. "Let me do it." The ritual had begun. It was a case now of simple progression. She had signaled, he had responded. The escalating intimacy was inevitable.

As he nudged Lisa down on the bed and put his arms around her, her shoulder bag fell to the floor, the contents spilling on the rug. Kneeling upright, Philip saw a blue book with its title barely in view. He registered the letters from the corner of his eye, while his mind assembled them half consciously. He leaned over, shoving the bag a little, and the book's title came into view. He opened the cover and read the inscription: "For Lisa Roberts from Mother M. Ambrose, O.S.B., Abbey of Regina Pacis, 11 March." He jumped to his feet, turning his back on Lisa, who hunched up on her elbows.

"Philip, what is it?"

He did not reply but walked to the living room where he sat

169

down, his back to the door. Lisa entered, barefoot, dressed in her robe.

"What's wrong?"

"Lisa," he said, "do you want to say anything about your five days away?"

He looked at her squarely. Her face blanched as surprise and guilt lay prominently across it.

"I don't understand what you're asking." She paused, trying to deflect his interest: "Don't be ridiculous. I didn't meet anyone else."

"So you met no one. What about this morning?"

"Philip, what are you asking?" Her look had turned to alarm.

"You went to the abbey to see Mother Ambrose, didn't you? You were checking up on me, weren't you? You've proven you're in sole possession, haven't you?"

"How could you think that? . . . "

"Don't insult my intelligence. If you'll examine the floor by the side of our bed, you'll discover that when your bag fell, a book of poetry slipped out. It's clear why you're back. Having visited the abbey, you're withdrawing the charges."

"All right", she admitted, "so I went. I had to meet her. Yes, she's everything you said she was. I even liked her in the end. What's wrong with helping myself feel safe? Your diary made me think you were cheating on me. Daria sounded real. I had to know if she existed."

"To think you checked on me with a cloistered nun. God, what must she think? Your behavior shows a basic lack of trust. I just don't feel comfortable in your company. There'll always be the sense that you were suspicious of my characters, that you'd want to know who was behind them. Suppose I wrote about a lesbian? Would you hire a detective to see if it was a smoke screen for a male lover? You've taught me something about yourself. It's better I found out now."

He walked into the bedroom, took out a duffle bag, and threw in some clothes. She followed after him.

"Philip, my fears got the better of me. I'm sorry. But don't walk out."

"I'm not walking out. I'm leaving." He moved to the front door as she continued to follow. He turned to her.

"I'll tell you something, Lisa. My threshold for pain is high. But mistrust, never. Next time you get involved, do it with someone you can control. It will free you from making an act of faith." He opened the door and left.

An hour later Philip was settled in his agent's apartment on Commonwealth. He had phoned Miles' secretary and learned he was in L.A. for the next month. Philip had a standing arrangement to use the studio whenever Miles was out of town. It was another hideaway for escaping into his work. It now provided distance from Lisa.

Philip had thrown his bag onto the love seat, hung up his parka, hat, and scarf, and sat down to review the letters he had removed on the way out of Lisa's building. He had exercised enough mental presence to collect his mail. He now sat at the butcher block table, sorting it out: a sale at Louis, Boston; a bill from Shreeve, Crump & Lowe; an advertisement for tickets to Symphony Hall; a brochure for a deluxe edition of Yeats' poetry. Among the personal letters was an invitation to do a reading of *Torrid* at M.I.T. The honorarium was a thousand dollars; he would probably accept. Finally, the prize: a letter with the address of Regina Pacis. His fingers tingled as he cut the envelope open. There it was, the calligraphic script, precise and self-assured, on watermarked paper. The sheets crackled like fresh minted money. Did he discern a perfume rising from the stationery? Had she scented it? Something of the abbey's odor seemed to come from the folded sheets. Perhaps she had added lavender to the ink before filling her fountain pen. He smiled at his imagination.

Philip turned up the dimmer lights so he could read with ease. He had forgotten everything—Lisa, their argument, his anger—in the wake of this woman's letter. That she cared enough to write mattered preeminently. Suddenly he remembered. Would the letter mention Lisa's impending trip? Though penned before her visit, Mother Ambrose would have known of it at her writing.

9 March 1989

My dear Philip:

If I was oscillating between "ill" and "much improved", your letter nudged me toward "fully recovered". There is wisdom in the assertion that deep caring lifts the immune system. I cannot prove a cause-effect relationship, but I felt decidedly post-convalescent after hearing from you. Thank you kindly for your swiftness in answering. I'm happy that you find our correspondence an agreeable addition to your busy life. Now that I'm back into the Benedictine rhythm, I shall be penning my letters in fits and starts. If you notice that the ink color changes, or that my penmanship has lost its flourish, you will know why. Still, there are advantages to these interruptions. It means that when I write you, if I am halted mid-sentence to attend meals, choir, or Mass, I must put the letter aside. It also means I will bring you wherever I go. A complex way of saying you are not now, nor will you be, far from my thoughts.

Your letter bristled with ideas, gave replies to my questions, and made inquiries of your own. It's difficult to know where to begin. So I'll plunge ahead, knowing you are clever at picking up the thread.

First, I must tell you that Reverend Mother thoroughly enjoyed *Torrid.* Her reaction confirms the tolerance and mental flexibility of the woman. A devoted humanist, she was also a woman of letters before she entered the order. She agreed with me that you came dangerously close to

172

irreverence. She also admitted that the fanaticism you lampoon warranted the full force of satire, one extreme correcting the other. During a visit to my sickbed, she added: "You know, Mother, he reminds me of Saki who chose flagrantly outrageous ideas to make very moral points." You may cite her in future blurbs if you think an abbess can boost sales.

While on the subject of books, I enjoyed your comments about how you generate a novel. Your brief treatment of a Carmelite nun, surnamed Guarneri, who meets an aspiring young novelist, made me grin. But isn't it premature to translate our friendship into fiction? Do what you like with what transpires between us, Philip. I trust you completely. Of course, I cannot hide my interest in your diary notes, but you will pass them on when you feel comfortable in doing so.

You asked for some book titles. I offer you two. The first is Gertrude von Le Fort's *The Eternal Woman;* the second, Helene Deutsch's *The Psychology of Women.* They should enhance your grasp of the feminine psyche no matter how attuned you are to bipolar relationships.

I'm surprised you are reading von Galli's memoir. I had no idea it was still available. My guess is that you found it at Harvard. *After Long Silence* has been out of print for years. You ask how much you can trust Darius. While I cannot deny his experience, I beg to differ with him on the sequence of events. Darius was prone to all the distortions of those who fall in love without reciprocity of feeling. His emotional outbursts were stormy. They resembled those squalls that blacken the sky over Como with thunder and lightning, deluge for ten minutes, then vanish. Had I married him after Cemil's death, he would have kept me as a curio for his display case. There I would have gathered dust like a jewel in the Topkapi. Most of my life I refused the pedestal, for there is little room to maneuver in such a cramped space. But that is where Darius wanted me. I value him for what he was, a loyal friend and a magnanimous man, but misguided in his affections, who till his death pursued me to satisfy some insatiable longing. Another time I will share with you the version I call the truth—my own.

You speak of a trip to Europe. Will you be passing through Italy? Rome, perhaps? If so, I would be grateful if I could engage you on a delicate, diplomatic mission. During our first conversation, Philip, you asked me about my family. I replied that I had one living relative, my sister, Daniela. I lost contact with her over the past year because of a misunderstanding that developed into an insurmountable rift. I have sent countless letters of reconciliation but without response. Since my letters are not returned, I must surmise that someone is receiving them. But who? Would there be an opportunity for you to call on her? Frankly, I'm anxious. It pains me to think that her last words to me amounted to thwarted rage. Daniela has no phone, so I give you her address:

> Daniela Stradivari
> 50 Via Quinto Miglia
> Rome, Italy

While visiting her, you may find the answer to another question. About the varnish. Daniela was knowledgeable concerning our family's history. It was she who established a complete genealogy. Through her I learned that our father, Ernesto, was illegitimate, a fact confirmed by Daniela's probing into the municipal records. When my parents died within months of each other, I had already moved to the States and entered the order. As the only living Stradivari able to inherit, Daniela became sole heir. She sold the villa in Cremona but kept some of the antique furniture and tapestries together with memorabilia dating back to our forebear, Antonio. The strife between us was a consequence of her intent to auction family letters and heirlooms. The formula for the varnish may be among them. I doubt if Daniela considers it significant, but you may impress on her its value.

I forgive you the flippant remarks about your religious upbringing. This is not to deny your criticism of shallowness. You are also right about the mystery you found at Regina Pacis. All our chanting and ritual, all the liturgies with their incense, flowers, and banks of candles are meant to promote one goal, namely, lifting the human spirit to God. If that does not happen, ceremony is reduced to pageantry. One might as well visit the nearest museum where heightened aesthetics offer a profound insight into what is beautiful. That is not the depth Benedictines seek. You received an inkling of this other dimension, Philip. You would not question what you did not implicitly know. Do not rush this perception. It comes in its own time as a completely free event. It is best described in Wordsworth's words, "surprised by joy".

I must leave you, for bells are summoning me to Vespers. I eagerly await your letter, but be at ease in answering. I look forward, too, to my meeting with Lisa, who phoned in advance of her visit tomorrow. When she sees my garb and assesses my age, her feelings for you will be properly reinstated.

You are in my prayers, Philip. You know you have an abiding place in my heart.

Mother M. Ambrose, O.S.B.

The same day he received her letter, Philip made travel arrangements to fly to Europe. He booked his customary flight to Zurich with a connection to Rome. Rather than answer Mother Ambrose immediately, Philip decided to write her from Rome after meeting with Daniela. The letter would come as a surprise and sweep away anxiety about her sister.

Learning that Eric was in town, Philip arranged for supper at Cincìn. They now sat at a corner table under a poster of the Piazza Navona. They had shared an antipasto and were eating pasta. The Chianti was particularly warming.

"It's been awhile", Eric began.

"Almost a month. But you and I have a rhythm. We don't see each other for weeks. Then we settle for a marathon conversation covering everything. Before I relate my saga, what have you been up to?"

"Mostly painting at the Cape. I have a show in May at the Copley Gallery. So I'm working to finish two canvases. That'll bring the number to twenty, which is about right for an exhibition. As for Vicki, we still get together. We're on speaking, not sleeping terms. It's comfortable so far. She became antagonistic once when she raised the subject of moving. She's still fixed on the coast. I'm as firm about staying in Boston. Now with my show coming up, no way. We met at Ninotchka's for coffee when I got back from the Cape. She said Lisa was staying with her. What happened?"

"Lisa read my diary, the one I keep of a novel in progress. She was convinced I was seeing someone else. I tried explaining and got nowhere. She walked out and had the gall to check up on me with Mother Ambrose. She was satisfied with the evidence because she returned to the apartment on Saturday. I found out by accident about her trip to the abbey. I can't stand anyone monitoring me. It's such an insult. It shows basic mistrust. Lisa will always feel insecure if I write about anyone who isn't based on her. I won't let what she calls love hold my imagination captive. I have to feel free when I write. I'm not an artist in a Fascist state."

"Any basis for her fears?"

"None now. She met Mother Ambrose. It was obvious she was dealing with an older woman. But Lisa can still insist my Daria character is based on someone else. That may have been the next stage. I decided not to wait around."

"So no grounds for her mistrust?"

"None. Eric, what are you getting at?"

"In a way, you are involved with someone else."

"You, too? I didn't ask you to dinner to be accused."

"Hear me out, Philip. It's not unusual for someone we live with to wonder who our subjects are. I mean, if Vicki and I were together, she'd certainly question who the women were in my paintings. They're not Vicki. Right now, I don't have to face that."

"What are you saying?"

"Nothing new. Just thinking aloud. Even if you had nobody real in mind, that you've taken someone else as your model shows a certain distraction. Lisa must sense it. Frankly, I wonder if you were looking to get away from Lisa and used your imagination to do it. It's safer to focus on a fantasy than on flesh and blood. I haven't read your diary, but I have a hunch it's incurably romantic. Eventually, we come up against the limits of a real woman, no matter how expansive she is. Love makes us willing to live within limits. I know. I'm facing them with Vicki."

"I'm not afraid of limits, but I resist constraints. Since you introduced the word, I think some are tolerable and some are not. With Lisa, everything has to be negotiated. There's no laissez-faire. I'm tired of explaining myself. I just received a letter from Mother Ambrose yesterday. She accepts me unconditionally. It's nice not to have to earn it."

"Sounds like the love mothers give their infants. Your favorite, Yeats, wrote, 'Hearts are not given as a gift, but hearts are earned.'"

"That's not what I'm saying. I just want to be accepted for who I am. No more trying to change me."

"But all living involves growth, and growth means change. That's one reason for sharing with someone: to be challenged to grow."

"The issue isn't growth but trust. If Lisa felt secure about herself, my characters wouldn't threaten her."

The waiter removed their plates and handed them a dessert menu.

"Cheesecake for me and a double espresso", Eric said.

"Signore?"

"Anisette toasts and a cappuccino. . . . Eric, the reason I asked you out was not to discuss Lisa but to let a friend know where I'll be. I already left word with Miles' secretary and gave my parents a ring. I'm leaving town. I fly to Rome from Zurich tomorrow. I'll be there several days, then take a plane to Milan. My final destination is Como. I want to visit a villa there, the home of a writer, Darius von Galli."

"Why now?"

"To advance my story. To do a favor for Mother Ambrose by visiting her sister. I need more facts if my novel is to have the ring of realism. You know how I rely on local color."

"Where are you staying?"

"I'll probably rent a room on Monte Mario. As for Como, I'm not sure. I'll visit Bellagio and do some touring. The small villages along the lake are charming. I'll let Miles' secretary know what my itinerary is as I go along. You can ring her if you need to find me."

"How long will you be away?"

"Two weeks."

"Should I tell Lisa if she calls?"

"No. She'll think I'm with someone and she'll put out a tracer."

"Another cappuccino?"

"No, thanks, Eric. I'd appreciate it if we made it a short evening. I need to make some phone calls early in the morning and do last-minute packing."

Eric stood up. "Up and at 'em."

"What?"

"Just wishing you zest on your journey."

Chapter Eight

Philip had finished the vegetarian meal in the upper deck and was sitting in the last row where he could ignore the film. It was time to continue Daria's story. He removed his portable computer from its case and set it on his lap. Philip was pleased the aisle seats on both sides were vacant. Someone's annoyance at the muffled click of keys would have proved an impediment. To focus his mood, he adjusted his Sony Walkman and played Beethoven's *Violin Concerto*. The music filled his ears as if he were sitting in Symphony Hall. With the people in his cabin imagined as audience, he began describing Daria's concert:

She seemed so fragile on stage. Dressed in a gown of black velvet, she wore a diamond heart that sparkled at her neck. Her hair swept back in a French twist was as I remembered it that first Sunday in Cambridge. Her pale skin looked like alabaster against funereal black. At the opening strains of the concerto, she lifted the Guarneri, holding the bow like a wand, and waited till the orchestra announced the major theme.

Imperceptibly at first, then rising above the orchestra with a strength matched by the accompaniment, the violin emerged in the first movement. Steadiness of pulse characterized her playing as the music poured over me. The aesthetic chills came with a regularity that made me hug myself for warmth. I was no impartial judge of how she played. I was disposed to calling the performance poignantly lyrical and stupefyingly beautiful. I was subject to all the distortions of lovers who magnify the simplest quality.

The music flowed from her like a woman giving birth. It was something only she could do, no matter how supported by maestro or audience. I no longer wanted to rescue her, for her confidence set me at

179

ease. She had become the music to which I was joined in an auditory rapture.

Her playing balanced lyricism and strength. The first movement's cadenza was nimble in articulation while I had rarely heard the slow movement with such purity of intention. When she made the link with the finale, she managed it with an exuberance charged with excitement. The drama of the reading was unforgettable. The bond forged between Daria and Maestro Morelli appeared as an alliance between two inspired artists at their peak.

When the final note sounded, and the audience rose to applaud and throw bouquets, she took three curtain calls. I succeeded in escorting her out a side door past jostling crowds to the Cafe Budapest. After drinks and dinner, the waiter brought us the first review, and I read aloud from Aubrey Chanler's column. Her face beamed with pride, only once clouding over as if to say, "I wish Papa were here."

"Rarely has Beethoven's Violin Concerto been played with such tenderness and strength as it was tonight at Symphony Hall. Imbued throughout with classical serenity, Daria Virtuss' debut performance was notable for fullness and resonance. She adapted to speed but never once sounded rushed, finding time for poignancy in every phrase. For some, her thoughtful reading may have lacked the drive one comes to expect in this concerto, but the soloist's electricity more than compensated. The finale's minor key episode, which justifies a slow tempo, was wonderfully limpid. Miss Virtuss moved easily between lyricism and aggressivity. She produced a tone that was round and singing but avoided lushness that undercuts the work's raw energy.

"The orchestral control Zino Morelli exhibited was evident in the polished, full-bodied performance. It was conspicuous in the last movement, which was a curtain raiser. Any effort to heighten the drama was unnecessary, for the tension between orchestra and solo violin never waned. In a sentence, this joint appearance of Virtuss and Morelli was memorable and must be counted a final statement on a masterpiece."

"Your career is set", I said. "You'll be receiving invitations to perform everywhere. What Chanler says is true, but it's an understatement. I *had no idea that notes could be so laceratingly beautiful. You drew the line between joy and pain so close. The human spirit can take just so much ecstasy. How does it feel to exert such power?"*

"You overestimate me."

"Maybe it's because I'm falling in love. I already imagine a life with you."

"Philip, please."

"Don't you feel the same way? What's the matter?"

"Do you know what you're saying? Don't use words loosely."

"I'm not. It's just that being with you is like a religious feeling. A sense of humility and gratitude. It's new to me and I want it to continue.... I have an idea, Daria, why not travel together? You've finished the concert. You've been practicing hard for months. I have a week off for spring vacation. We can go to Cremona and see what your father left you. After, we could go back to Milan and take a train to the Italian Lakes. I've saved enough money. We'll visit Bellagio and stay for a few days. What do you say?"

"Young man, would you help me? I need a blanket from the overhead compartment."

After the movie, the lights had dimmed and people were settling down to four hours of sleep. The compartment was uncomfortably cool.

"Of course", Philip answered. Reaching overhead, he handed the woman a blanket. She thanked him, and he retrieved the remaining pillows and the cashmere sweater, with which he invariably traveled, for warmth. He was feeling sleepy but pleased that he had managed to advance his story. He would continue it after his trip to Como once he had more firsthand experience. For now, he would just dream about it.

It was dark when the Swissair jet landed in Zurich. Philip found his way to the gate where he waited for the 7:25 A.M. flight to Rome. He was about to take out his laptop to continue his story, but he had only an hour, and writing prose was difficult with people encircling him. He started fiddling with a poem about Daria. She seemed so real. Had he encountered her in some other life and now the residue of cause and effect was surfacing in this one? What was it about her that set him at ease? He scribbled some lines in pentameter. Then began the process of cutting, shaping, ploughing through, with words arranged in tiers, till one word was victor and established the end rhyme. By the time he was ready to board, Philip had salvaged the following lines:

> As infants lulled by noon's full light
> Soon yield to sleep, I also yield where
> Slumber holds my limbs in warm esteem;
> I cannot tell what heart my heart has met.
> I only know that, were this love a dream,
> O let me dream on, and do not wake me yet.

It was a smooth flight over the Alps. Philip skipped breakfast. He had had his fill of thick espresso and flaky croissants. It was an hour before they deplaned at the airport. For a March day the sky was clear, the weather temperate, the sun brilliant. The terminal was jammed with people searching for cabs, and Philip despaired of finding one to take him to his hotel. After an hour of trying, he found a taxi.

"*Signore, vorrei andare a Monte Mario, per piacere. Via Massimi cento quindici.*"

In a half hour, the cabbie was turning up a long driveway to the Villa Mosconi. Philip knew he was taking his chances. He had not called ahead, but he was counting on the availability of a room. As the cab pulled in front of the red-tiled house, he paid the exorbitant fare and carried his bag to the foyer. The man at the desk spoke English.

"*Si, Signore.* We have two rooms overlooking the back garden. The bath and toilet are in the hall. The rooms are scarcely used because of the location, but they are spacious and quiet."

"I'll take the one closest to the bath."

"How long will you stay?"

"Overnight. I'm traveling to Como tomorrow."

"*Grazie, Signore.* Would you fill out the registration?"

At a signal from the concierge, a young man appeared and carried Philip's bags to his room. Philip entered, tipped him at the door, and looked around. The room had a high ceiling with old furniture and a huge window that overlooked the garden. The silence was broken by twittering birds and the sound of a hose watering the lawn. Philip unpacked his bags. Before taking a bath, he returned to the man at the desk.

"Signore, would you check in your Rome directory for a Daniela Stradivari?" Philip gave him the address. "I would like to have her phone number."

He took out the book and flipped through it, found the letter "s", and examined the minute entries.

"I'm sorry, Signor Stratton. There is no one by that name. Perhaps the phone is unlisted or under another name."

"How long is the trip from here to Via Quinto Miglia?"

"About the same as from the airport. I would suggest you take the autobus near the Via Bitossi. It will leave you near the Piazza Risorgimento. You may walk from there or take a taxi."

"Thank you."

Philip walked back to his room and lay down for a few minutes. He swore he would not sleep, though his body clock was at four in the morning. He picked up the poem he had reworked in the airline lounge. The last thing he recalled was reciting the line, "O let me dream on, and do not wake me yet."

Philip woke after a two-hour nap, took a quick shower, dressed, and left the villa. He walked up the long roadway to the front gate and turned right to the Via Massimi. Once on the bus, after several twists and turns, he descended at the Piazza Risorgimento and walked to the Borgo section to Armando's. There he had a salad, a half liter of wine, and a pasta with prosciutto and peas. The food was delicious and had not changed since his last visit two years before. While drinking a cappuccino, he took out Mother Ambrose's letter and reread the contents. Did he discern a suppressed anxiety in her words? There was something disquieting in the tone. He put the letter away and checked his watch. If he wanted to see Daniela, he could leave now. He paid his bill, hailed a cab near the restaurant, and ten minutes later stopped at the Via Quinto Miglia. He found the door and looked for Daniela's name. There were two on the bronze plate: Kuan/Stradivari. It was odd. Mother Ambrose had not mentioned a second person. Philip rang the bell and waited. After a minute or two he heard steps coming toward him. The door opened. An oriental of Korean or Chinese descent stood there. Full-chested with broad shoulders, he seemed an expert in Karate or boxing.

"Scusami," Philip said, *"ma parla inglese?"*

"Yes, I speak English a little. What is it that you want?"

"Perhaps I rang the wrong bell. I'm looking for Signora Stradivari. Does she live here?"

"Why do you seek her?"

"I'm a friend of her sister. She asked me to find her."

"What is the message?"

"I prefer to give it to Signora Stradivari in person. Is she in?"

"How do you mean 'in'?"

"Is she at home? I prefer speaking with her in person."

"Always she is at home, but she sleeps for the moment. Come back within the half hour. I will inquire whether she wishes to see you."

"May I ask who you are?"

"It is of no importance."

He shut the gate behind the front door. Philip walked onto the street puzzled by the conversation. Should he chalk it up to rudeness, a protectionist impulse, or just poor English? It was probably a little of each.

He was beginning to feel the time difference despite his earlier nap. He needed coffee to stay awake. He saw a small cafe at the end of the via and walked toward it. He sat at an outdoor table and ordered an espresso. As he did at Milano's, he stared into space, wondering who Daniela's companion was. He seemed young to be her lover. Perhaps he was a guardian, but what did he mean she was always at home? Was she ill? But from what? If so, why didn't she tell her sister of her condition? That she might be asleep was nothing strange. Daniela would be doing what Italians did, resting to refresh the mind now that the body was satisfied.

Philip motioned the waiter over, paid for the coffee, and walked back to the house. In the interim, he had acquired a case of jitters similar to the churning he felt before walking with Mother Ambrose at the abbey. He rang the bell. At the sound of Kuan on the speaker, Philip announced himself. Immediately, the first door opened, then the second. Philip walked a few steps to the lift which was waiting and pressed five. He watched it inch to the proper landing. When he arrived, the elevator clicked open. He entered a hallway but did not need to search. The opposite door was marked Kuan/Stradivari. He pressed the buzzer, saw the peephole open and close, heard the locks unbolt and the door swing wide.

Philip passed from a small foyer into a large living room. It was difficult knowing where to move because every corner was cluttered with furniture: overstuffed couches, end tables, credenzas, armoires, and at least two marble coffee tables. The walls were covered with portraits, paintings, and tapestries, while shelves were crowded with bric-a-brac. There were Taoist figurines and ivory Buddhas, silver Crucifixes, and statues of saints carrying instruments of martyrdom in one hand, a palm leaf in the other. Candles were in sconces on the walls and in holders on the lacquered tables. Threadbare rugs in odd sizes were scattered everywhere. The drapes and shades were lowered, and the sun slanting into the room made the light take on a granular brilliance. The room looked as if it belonged to a silent film star, whose career had ended with the advent of sound, but who clung to the vestiges of celebrity.

He looked for a chair. Finding one, he sat waiting for movement in this living tableau. The room was still, the only activity the grainy sunlight whirling near the windows. Suddenly, Philip heard murmuring. The door of the inside room opened, and a wheelchair pushed by Kuan came toward him.

"Kuan, over there near the fireplace, out of the light."

Only when Daniela was settled did Philip receive a full view. She was dressed in Chinese silk pajamas and matching robe, the red silk shirt monogrammed with her initials. She was heavily made up, her hair dyed chocolate brown. The penciled eyebrows, chalk-white skin dabbed with rouge, and painted lips made her look clownish. Kuan, who waited for instructions, was dismissed with a wave of the hand.

Philip stood up when Daniela entered. Once Kuan left, he sat down and observed her closer. For all the garish makeup, she was clearly Mother Ambrose's sister. Her almond-shaped eyes and high cheek bones, together with her dramatic entrance, suggested similar qualities of personality, but they were arranged with a different intent.

"So," she began, "you are here on an errand for my sister." Her voice had the same lilt with no distinctive country of origin. The register of the voice was lower, almost husky, but with a trace of irony. "What is it she wants?"

"Nothing in particular," Philip replied, "except to know you're alive and well."

"Is that what she told you?"

"Not exactly. She was concerned because she had written

186

you and received no answer. None of her letters were returned. She didn't know what that meant."

"For a cloistered nun, she has trouble interpreting silence."

"I don't understand, Signora. A silence meaning what?"

"Indifference. But that is to put it mildly. It is contempt tempered by illness producing boredom. Does that shock you, or are you under her spell?" Before Philip could react, she asked:

"What is your name?"

"Philip Stratton, Signora." He added: "Are you over your illness?"

"Not in the least. My doctor says I'm living—as you say in English—on borrowed time. The cancer is erupting everywhere. It is lava burning whatever is in its way. A scorched earth policy. An intense image, but were you where I am, watching each organ surrender, you would know no image meets the reality. Since there is scant time to do what must be done, I conserve my energy. Empty correspondence saps my reserves."

"Then your sister doesn't know?"

"She would be here in a flash arranging things her way. Now it is my turn. Anyway, she does not care."

The antagonism with which she spoke shocked Philip. Were they speaking of the same person?

"I don't understand, Signora. I can't imagine your sister not caring about your health. She expressed concern about what was happening to you. Otherwise, she wouldn't have asked me to find you. The urgency was there last time we spoke."

Daniela smiled. There was bitterness in her voice.

"So," she continued, "it is as I thought. You are on her side. She has duped you into believing she is concerned. She does not care if I live or die. It is not for me she is anxious but for . . ."

She pulled herself up from the wheelchair and pointed. "Open that drawer . . . yes, there, the middle one."

187

Philip did as she asked. It was filled with letters in small bundles, all tied with ribbons.

"Now the one beneath." There were more neat bundles.

"Hundreds of family letters," she continued, "some dating back to Antonio's time. Relics of a family dying off without issue. They are the sole progeny together with Antonio's instruments. Also, furniture, tapestries, and her guitar in that corner. But most of all the letters. Add to them those written by my father to Bea—they, Signor Stratton, are what she would protect from the cancer of time. She cares not a whit for me. Only her heirlooms, her precious history."

Pleased to have a captive audience, Daniela paused to study his reaction. He had blanched and was trembling a little. For the first time the object of his esteem was under attack by belligerent words. Huns were at the gates armed with pickaxes ready to shatter the sculpture beyond restoration.

"So, you belong to her troupe of dazzled admirers. You have not grasped her resemblance to a tree that chokes out all vegetation by its luxuriance. She entices by her shade and entangles, only to suffocate."

"Excuse me, Signora," Philip protested, "I can't believe we're speaking of the same person. The sister you describe is not the Mother Ambrose I know."

"Mother Ambrose! Mother Ambrose! Bea hides under the veil. How fragile she must look behind the cloister walls—like an endangered species in a sanctuary. She relishes the attention in the way she did when she stood in front of the curtain, tantalizing the audience with encores, and vanishing. Her timing was perfect. And our parents beaming in the front, my father especially. Always Bea this, Bea that. Bea the star, who gave luster to the family, while I sat behind, biding my time.

"It pains her to see me control the family assets. With her solemn vow of poverty she can inherit nothing, can dispose of nothing. She is canonically dead. I am free to disperse the inheritance in whatever way I wish. That Kuan will inherit the estate—that the bastard son of a peasant gets everything—will rankle her. If there's any message for her, it's this: a Chinese coolie gets all.

"Why should she make claims? She took enough in her life. Darius, then Cemil. Growing up alongside, I did without. Now I am in possession, and she must abstain. It will teach her poverty of spirit. She will imitate her crucified God. Her need for detachment coincides with my desire to strip her—an agreeable match. My intent and her Rule vindicated."

"Frankly, Signora, I'm speechless, no small admission for a writer. Your version doesn't tally with my experience. What I've read in von Galli contradicts your words."

At the mention of his name, Daniela flushed with anger.

"Von Galli. Another bewitched disciple. He spent his life in an amorous stupor over someone who treated him like dirt. Playing one man against the other, that's what she did, for she could not commit to either. And to think, I could have loved him, given him what he needed. He held out for the unattainable, as if the one who withheld herself were more valuable. Because I was within reach, he dismissed me. She was always an arm's length away: a fruit bending low enough to tease, yet high enough to cling to the bough. She cannot give herself. Best that she pursues her unseen God. It is easier to love a God whom she cannot see than someone whom she can. She has chosen her calling well."

"But you're wrong. She risked her life for countless Jews."

"Ah, yes, the heroine who courted death. It is true. She took every risk to silence the guilt. It is not easy to live with having destroyed a husband. Even von Galli did not guess the stakes for which she played. His memoir is another distortion." Pausing, she continued:

"Have you seen the portrait of Bea? The one at the Villa Galliano, his estate on Como? It all depends on the light. She used chiaroscuro to her advantage. Now she has chosen the nun's funereal garb. Its darkness hides a multitude of sins. . . . "

Daniela shut her eyes, pausing to catch her breath. "It is late, Signor Stratton. For all the satisfaction contempt brings, it is wearying."

She reached over and pressed a button on the wall. Kuan appeared, ready to wheel her out.

"May I visit again?"

"To what end? You have heard it all."

"Since I will not be returning, I have one request." He knew what he would ask might sound self-serving, but it was his last chance. "It involves the formula for Antonio's varnish. It's critical to a book I'm writing. I've read it was in a Bible which your great-grandfather destroyed. Is it true he made a copy before burning it?"

"Do you ask only for yourself? It doesn't matter. Open the second drawer. The bottom envelope. Remove it."

Philip did as he was told. The envelope was sealed.

"It is of no use to anyone. Kuan, see the gentleman out."

Philip rose, bowing slightly, and waited for Kuan to wheel Daniela away. When he returned, he opened the door without speaking and let Philip out.

He returned to Villa Mosconi exhausted from his visit, his mind a whirlwind of confusion. What did it mean, the assertion that Bea had destroyed Cemil? When he got back to his room, he collapsed on the bed and slept through the remainder of the day and night, awakening the next morning after fourteen hours. He had tossed and turned, Daniela's needling voice pricking his memory, while the inscrutable Kuan stood in the background. A sister dying of cancer, a Chinese expatriate inheriting everything—it was too much to absorb. Mother Ambrose had sent him on a mission of inquiry; his answer, that she would be left empty-handed.

Philip dismissed the dismal thoughts as he showered, shaved, and dressed. He resolved while having breakfast that he would leave for Como that morning. The decision made him move with dispatch. He would visit von Galli's villa and see the portrait, convinced it would clear the air of Daniela's lies. She had introduced a doubt—that despite Bea's faceted brilliance, a flaw existed vitiating everything.

Travel arrangements through the hotel proved easy. He took a flight to Malpensa airport, from there a train to Como; finally, a ferry and a boat to the villa. It took three hours to make good his resolve.

Beyond Lenno was the Tremezzina, the Azalean Riviera. Here the soil gave birth to a profusion of shrubs and trees, and where magnolias and laurels did not cover the hills, azaleas bloomed in red luxuriance.

Von Galli's estate was situated on a point jutting into the lake. The villa, built in the eighteenth century to take advantage of the panoramic views across to the Bellagio spur, was the summer home of the Paravicinis. Famous for the statue of Saint Michael with sword in hand and Lucifer at his feet, the villa promised security to lakeborne visitors. To the left of the landing stage and peering through an explosion of color, the statue's pedestal was the most photographed spot on the lake.

To reach the villa, Philip took one of the steamers that plied the length of Como. He was awed by von Galli's unique estate inching into view halfway up the western shore. From the boat one glimpsed the manicured grounds and box gardens, while the building set upon rock embodied all the intrigue one expected of an Italian villa. Living alone on this promontory, known as Punta di Galliano, von Galli had been pleased by the astonishment of occasional guests over the views looking in all directions. The villa, open to the public on Wednesdays, was accessible by boat from Sala Comacina. Set in a landscape, Mediterranean and Alpine, the ambience combined both worlds: palm trees lining the shore, snowcapped mountains in the distance.

Philip had chosen a glorious day when Como, nestled by hills, was awash in green and terra-cotta tones. As a passing cloud shifted the light, the trees along the banks took on an indigo hue. Disembarking from the ferry at Sala Comacina, Philip hired a *motoscafo* which left him at the villa's dock near the striped mooring pole. He climbed the stone stairway and ambled along a walkway lined with Roman statues. Triumphs of style over nature, the gardens were filled with topiary, rhododendrons, and azaleas. At the villa's front door, he purchased his ticket allowing entry into the first-floor rooms. They contained von Galli's priceless collection of pre-Columbian art. A hybrid style characterized the villa's interior: ceiling frescoes, mosaic flooring, stucco fireplaces.

It was not till Philip walked into the panelled drawing room that he saw it. He stood before the portrait as though he were in the nave of a church looking toward the high altar. Staring back was a woman with high cheekbones, a sensual mouth, a nose slightly narrow in the bridge. He decided there was nothing in her face to indicate the mystery Cemil and Darius had found. But as he gazed at the painting, he saw that here was a woman ineffably attractive on the verge of declaring something that would change one's life. The portrait did what the viewer asked. It riveted. Under the spell of that gaze, he decided the source of her enigmatic smile was serenity. He was viewing a woman who claimed the most precious insight of all: self-awareness. She seemed to be saying: "Nothing compares to the peace that comes when you know yourself as you are. I know. I approve and I am thus resigned."

But as he gazed at the brow and easy smile, he began to doubt. Was it serenity or the complacency of a woman who had fooled her public? Was the painter duped into fabricating an image no less idealized than the one Daniela said he falsely entertained? If so, this was a Dorian Gray in reverse, the portrait retaining innocence while its subject was rank with lies. It was a terrifying thought, yet he was thinking it. Daniela's words, "another bewitched disciple", taunted him. If only he could peel away the paint and discern the real Bea underneath. But what was real when you dealt with people? Weren't they an anthill full of tendencies moving in all directions?

He shut his eyes, opened them, and looked again. As his questions shifted, so did the face. At first benign, it became ironic, the gaze an indifferent stare. Was the glint in her eyes the victor's triumph at suborning the viewer? He had a flashback of Mother Ambrose that first night at the abbey, her face in darkness and light. Here was the same chiaroscuro teasing him. What did he know of her? Bits and pieces forming an image. But was it true to reality, or the result of yearning and unresolved wishes? He was feeling victimized. Anger welled up inside. Had he stood there longer, he might have done something irreparable: cut the portrait to pieces. The violence frightened him. Shutting his eyes, he prayed to be wrong. Presently, he looked up. She had returned with her benevolence intact. The chiaroscuro was there, but light preempted the shadow. His perception of her was through a glass darkly, but he knew her, nonetheless. Faith bolstered by love had secured him in truth.

The steamer that Philip took back to Bellagio's pier docked a few yards from the Hotel Villa Serbelloni. It was an imposing old-world palace offering respite in a lakeside setting. Faded but retaining its opulence, the hotel overwhelmed with its ceilings, chandeliers, and sweeping staircase. Philip threaded his way through rooms proliferating with mirrors and columns, rugs and gilded chairs. Having registered at the desk and settled his bags, he lunched on the terrace. Lake Como's fjord-like beauty was enchanting. He imagined himself on a steamer gliding by hamlets or maneuvering in and out of harbors. He took out a sheet of hotel stationery and began writing.

Dear Mother Ambrose:

This sunny afternoon, it is baptism by desire. I have christened myself a Borgia for the day. I'm sitting on the terrace of the Hotel Villa Serbelloni, looking out on mountains surrounding a crystalline lake. My back presses against a padded chair set under an awning. A stone balustrade sweeps down past hedges to the heated pool where, at the shallow end, children chirp with delight as they splash one another. The warmth of Benedictine diffuses within me while my eyes rove left and right to encompass the lake. Terra-cotta roofs punctuate the shoreline together with cedar, pine, and olive trees.

Having just had a lunch cooked with sacramental respect for the local produce, I sit observing a body of water unchanged since Pliny the Younger heard the waves lapping at his window. Stendahl wrote here; Henry James, too. I'm in a long line of scriveners.

Who were the owners who cultivated these gardens and filled them with lemon trees and wild rosemary? Who planted the wisteria climbing the walls and encircling the trees? Whoever they were, their ashes have mixed with the roses. The blooming continues.

It is pleasurable to surrender my senses to a hotel rivalled only by Cernobbio's Villa d'Este. I'm part of baroque art.

The twilight falls as I sample a raspberry tart with melon ice.

Philip reread what he had written. He knew it was escapist, for it made no mention of Kuan, Daniela, or their conversation. He had translated his turbulence into a rapture meant to hide his agitation. He felt like ripping up the letter and starting again. But what should he write? If he mentioned Daniela in any detail he would need to repeat what was said. Neutrality was impossible. She would sense the evasiveness. Philip decided the best course was to write nonchalantly and hope she would question nothing. But how to sound casual about cancer? He picked up his pen.

> I met Daniela this morning. She has been ill but is currently holding her own. Since she is convalescing, my stay was brief. She has domestic help at her beck and call, so you needn't worry. I'll give you details when I return.
> I visited the Villa Galliano and saw the portrait. It shares one of your qualities: it's riveting.
> If you wish to write, please do. It would gratify me to have your letter when I return.
>
> > Affectionately,
> > Philip

"It sounds impetuous. Whatever possessed you to go at such short notice?" Eric asked, when, at their favorite restaurant, Philip described the last segment of his trip. It was a week after Philip had returned from abroad.

"That's what I would have asked. The best explanation I can give, Eric, is that the doubts returned. They woke me at night, needling me with my misplaced trust. I felt I'd been taken in. Call it humiliation, call it a passion for truth, I had to know more."

"So you flew to Istanbul to find Cemil's sister? But all you had was the episode in von Galli's diary. You weren't even sure Sema was alive."

"You're right. It was pure hunch. I arrived at Ataturk Airport and taxied through the traffic to the Byzantine walls and the city's congestion. Istanbul has over six million people. If you arrive by air and take a cab, you'll drive past half of them.

"First, I thought of staying in Üskudar on the Asian side. But it's reached by bridge or ferry, so it was out of the question. Then I considered the old quarter near the mosques and monuments. But it's densely populated and noisy. So I settled on the new city across the Golden Horn.

"I checked in at the Hilton, the only hotel I knew. It has superb management, and it's almost large enough to guarantee a room if you're walking in off the street. I was lucky the day I arrived. A travel group had cancelled the Turkish portion of their tour."

"But how did you know where to find her?"

"I had little to go on except some cursory reading and the Hilton's directory, which confirmed my hunch. I learned that during the eighteenth and nineteenth centuries, it was fashionable for Ottoman society to retire to the Bosporus for the summer. A new style of architecture sprang up called the *yali*. It's a wooden structure with sloping eaves and balconies. My reading indicated that the Bosporus fostered a lifestyle of European manners and Oriental calm. It sounded like something Cemil's family would have enjoyed.

"The best way to get there is by ferry. It leaves Sirkeci at odd hours and acts as a shuttle between villages. At the suggestion of the Hilton's tour desk, I got off at Bebek, a community known for its elegant shops and cafes. Since the Bosporus gets congested on weekends, I went mid-week."

"Did you reach her?"

"Yes. I telephoned and she was at home. The success of making contact astonished me, but sometimes it's a bull's-eye the first time. Initially, she was slow in responding. I mentioned that I was a friend of Mother Ambrose. I then corrected myself, using the name Bea Stradivari. I said I was working on a book about the violin family, and that I needed help in sifting certain facts concerning her brother. There was a pause that went on longer than was comfortable. For a moment, Eric, I thought we'd been cut off. Finally, she spoke and asked me to meet her at a pastry shop called the Bebek Badem Ezmesi. It's supposed to make the best marzipan in the world. It was easy to find. We met there."

"What was she like?"

"She was a woman in her seventies, slender and graceful, with erect posture as if she'd been a dancer. Her hair was streaked with gray, her face still unlined. She was fair complexioned with heavy-lidded eyes made prominent by shadows and startling blue irises. She resembled a Renaissance Madonna, the dead Christ on her lap, the face expressing shock, loss, and resignation. She wore a knit skirt and jacket with a silk blouse and a double strand of pearls.

"I stood up to greet her, and she responded with a faint smile. All the while, her eyes focused my attention. They appeared not to belong to her face. One thinks of Turks as dark-eyed and swarthy, but some are so ethnically mixed anything is possible.

"Sema spoke English well, but her diction was somewhat stilted. I gathered it was a language she used, but not daily. She spoke slowly, pausing from time to time for the right word. Her hands were folded on her lap. She wore no marriage band, only a man's signet ring fitted to her marital finger. I had a feeling that she'd never married, that Cemil had been central to her life. I addressed her throughout as Madame Hasan, and never once did she correct me. Neither did she soften the formality by allowing me to call her Sema. I introduced myself and was frank about my reasons for coming. I told her how I'd returned from Rome after visiting Bea's sister.

" 'Mr. Stratton,' she began, 'what is it you wish to know? You said that it concerned my brother. Would you explain further?'

" 'Madame Hasan, I was hoping you could rid me of my confusion. My visit with Daniela was disruptive. Her words were hostile toward her sister. My turmoil comes, not so much from her attitude, though that was disturbing enough, but from remarks she made about Bea's dealings with Cemil. Daniela said Bea destroyed her husband. Such an assertion is unthinkable and completely at odds with the woman I know. Of course, whatever happened was decades ago, and people change over time. But during the visit, it was difficult to believe we were even remotely speaking of the same person. Our points of view were completely opposed.'

"We asked for Turkish coffee, Eric, and two pieces of marzipan. I was happy when the waiter came with our order. I was feeling a little uneasy. Sema was listening intently, her face lost in thought. She seemed to be hearing something inaudible to my ears. The coffee and sweets interrupted her reflection, and she finally spoke.

" 'So you have come to seek clarity and thus rescue your feelings for another. It is obvious you value friendship, Mr. Stratton. I am impressed by your loyalty.'

" 'I wish it were just loyalty.'

" 'You are a little in love with her, are you not? I mean, in your imagination where love thrives. She is, doubtless, still intriguing. She was for my brother when they met in Dubrovnik. For days, I heard nothing else after that encounter. The combination of a beautiful, unmarried woman and a gifted artist was irresistible. But the war intervened. Only years later did that meeting ripen into a relationship. Again Cemil fell in love. This time it was not just beauty and artistry, but a shared commitment to the Jews. Nothing is more likely to cement a union, Mr. Stratton, than a shared passion for justice. The two became inseparable as they waged war against the Nazis. When Cemil proposed, he did not tell her immediately the personal limits she would be accepting.'

" 'Surely Bea knew the risks he took of an early death. They were both endangering their lives, she in Italy; he in Istanbul — it was nothing new.'

" 'I do not mean that. It is clear you do not know.'

" 'Not know what?'

" 'That my brother was injured in a bomb blast in Salonika

before Bea arrived. It was during the early roundup of Jews. He and members of the Greek resistance had tried to stop a convoy from transferring its live cargo to the railway. Cemil was hospitalized in Athens for secondary burns to the pelvic region and post-traumatic shock. The burns damaged tissue with little hope of regeneration. He recuperated but learned there would be bouts of impotence with sterility as a side effect. Like the countless Jews, whose children were incinerated, Cemil was told he would share their childlessness. When he met Bea in Salonika, he had been discharged two weeks from the hospital. Earlier, I had come down from Istanbul for his convalescence. When I returned home, a letter was waiting in which Cemil spoke of meeting Bea, of how he had fallen in love with her for the second time. He contemplated marriage but recoiled from telling her they would have no conjugal life. It was a cruel fate. His honor was at stake as well as the family name.'

" 'I don't understand. Bea had a son, Halil.'

"At this point in our conversation, Eric, her face showed so much pain, I was reluctant to continue my questioning. She turned and said:

" 'I should like to share something with you. Do you have time to accompany me home? Afterward, Yusuf, my driver, will take you to the Hilton. Our *yali* is but a brief drive from here.'

" 'Of course', I said.

"I was baffled, Eric, by the new information. I couldn't connect the pieces of the puzzle so that a central image formed. I paid the cafe's bill and escorted Sema to her car. In fifteen minutes we were at her waterfront home. She did not invite me into the main house. It was a striking piece of architecture with a Palladian portico. It resembled a Venetian villa on the Brenta canal.

"I waited in a garden just beginning to bloom. I sat in an arbor with a stunning view across the Bosporus. A maid served tea and biscuits while I tried to calm my nerves. I distracted myself by watching the ferries in the distance, pulling in and out of the harbors and belching smoke into the air. When she returned, she had removed her jacket and wore an Angora sweater. The sun was bright, but there was a chill near the water. She sat to my left. In her hand was a letter.

"'This is the last Cemil wrote from Salonika. I shall translate.'

Dearest Sema:

The atmosphere in Salonika is tense. I do not know how long Bea and I can continue forging passports and passing off Jewish nationals as Italians. But the community is sixty thousand strong. We must do what we can to save as many as possible.

My healing is almost complete, and I rise and sit without difficulty. The major scar is to my psyche. How much can my conscience conceal without deception? You know how deeply in love I am. The spark ignited by Bea years ago has become a constant warmth. How could it be otherwise when I am daily exposed to her radiance. She gives so much. The musician, the patriot, the companion— it is like loving three women. The other night, we declared ourselves to each other. The aftermath for me was mental pain. I had said nothing about my condition. But if marriage is imminent, and that is the next step, I must tell her soon so she is free to look elsewhere.

To what kind of bondage do I invite her, Sema? To what kind of life? I may be asking a vital, passionate woman to enter marriage as one enters a cloister, to live her life like a nun. My fear is not her negative answer, but the yes she might give from pity. With the urgency of youth, she might hold out for a medical procedure, some protocol, that will reverse the doubtful prognosis and signal a full marital life. More doctors, more consultations, more dashed hopes. Do I dare invite them? I look at her and know there is no one else. Bea and I are one, however, I am closed off from a union of body and spirit.

The desire for an heir is strong. It is another repudiation. At times, Sema, I feel like a Jew, my past and future wiped clean with nothing but Allah's memory to assure me I have lived on the earth.

Soon Bea leaves for northern Italy on a dangerous mission. She will guide across the border a group of Venetian Jews together with a photo journalist. He is smuggling pictures back to the west to expose the Nazis' tactics for securing the Jewish Solution. So much depends on the success of this mission. I pray for her safety. She has insisted that we marry before she leaves. We would have two weeks on Paros out of the Nazi mainstream. But I dread the fruitless passion. Were it not for the thousands who need me, were it not for Bea's commitment, I might have capitulated to the death squads with the words, "Take me also. Like your Jews, I am worthless." It was a fleeting thought, Sema, which the needs of others thwarted.

I miss you terribly. How I wish I were with you in Bebek, hearing the ferry's plaintive whistle and the muezzin calling the faithful to prayer. Sweet Istanbul, mother of empires, you are the one I have consummated in my heart.

I embrace you, dear Sema. We shall see each other soon, if Allah wills.

Cemil

"After she finished reading, Eric, she replaced the letter in its envelope. I had the sense she had done this many times before. The letter was her access to a brother who no longer lived. I was so absorbed by her ritual folding and replacing, I nearly missed seeing that her eyes were moist. She wasn't crying — the tears were past — but the sorrow was there."

"Did you question Sema about the contents?" Eric asked.

"Yes. I'll do my best to reconstruct our discussion. It hid as much as it revealed.

" 'Did Cemil finally tell Bea about his physical debility?' I asked her.

" 'Yes, but as Cemil had anticipated, it mattered nothing. Bea was in love and full of optimism. She was convinced his condition would reverse itself. It did not. Meanwhile, they worked together forging passports and marrying Greek Jews to Italian soldiers. Tension crept into his relationship with her which no amount of understanding could alleviate. Cemil would have loathed to admit it, but Bea was the occasion for his humiliation. When she finally received word from northern Italy to guide a Venetian group, Cemil saw it as an opportunity to put some distance between them and their problem. He remained in Greece, taking more risks, occasionally going to Athens for treatments that promised much but delivered nothing.

" 'When Bea returned to Salonika to rejoin Cemil, she was exhausted from her northern experience. She had nearly lost her life trying to escape the Fascist patrols on Como. Her flirtation with death brought the two of them closer. A spiritual intimacy replaced the physical one to which they still aspired. But Bea's health appeared to be undermined. In the early morning, she began having dizzy spells and nausea during which she would throw up her food. When she joined Cemil on a trip to Athens for his checkup, she took a battery of tests, learning what she already surmised. She was pregnant.'

"Eric, when Sema said those words, which I could feel approaching, I winced. I sat there gaping at her with shock on my face. Questions assaulted my mind. How could it have happened? With whom? Was it an accident? I needed to ask Sema nothing. She translated my bewilderment. She turned and said:

" 'You are white in the face, Mr. Stratton. You have grasped the situation.'

" 'Yes. But why? Bea must have realized Cemil would know the child wasn't his. Why did she risk it?'

" 'At the time, I too struggled with what I thought Bea had done. She was young, I told myself, and may have believed that offering Cemil a child at any cost was better than doing without. Perhaps someone had reached out who could love her as a woman. It may have been a moment of weakness when she was confined with someone who wanted her completely. That is how I debated, Mr. Stratton, until years later when I learned the truth. What was clear was that her pregnancy broke his spirit. Whatever was growing in her, as she swelled week after week, was like a festering tumor. It was torture for him. Cemil who had risked his life saving children now wanted this child obliterated. I can only guess the suffering it cost him. Bea insisted the child was his. There were some grounds for her contention, for Cemil had slowly recovered from his impotence. But his sterility seemed beyond doubt. Whatever her insistence, it called attention to his lack. He fought his depression by working day and night to save the Jews, outsmarting the death brigades that were after him. She pleaded with him to return to Cremona, for she was now eight months pregnant. He was persuaded and promised to meet her later in Athens. He never arrived. She got news that he had been ambushed in Paros and executed. She returned to Cremona alone."

" 'Did you ever recover Cemil's body?'

" 'No. But after the war I went to the place where he died and built a memorial to his name. You may see it if you visit there. It is near the windmill on the hill."

" 'And Bea? Did you stay in touch over the years?'

" 'No. I took my brother's side against her, accusing her of destroying him. So we lost contact. I never saw Halil until the week of his accident. He flew to Istanbul to visit me. I was his only Turkish relative. His plans were to see me, visit the Italian lake district, and take the Swiss train to Zermatt, where he would indulge his passion for mountains."

" 'Did Halil phone you?"

" 'He never phoned. He did what the young often do. He appeared on my doorstep. When my maid, Fatima, announced there was a youth from the States eager to see me, I was curious. When I walked into the front parlor and saw him, I was shocked. I babbled through the introduction. I am sure Halil thought it was the reaction of meeting a lost relative who had suddenly appeared. That was not it."

" 'What was it?'

" 'Mr. Stratton, I was looking at my brother. The resemblance was uncanny. The dark eyes, the radiant smile, the intelligence and humor—it was Cemil resurrected. I started to weep. "If only," I kept moaning, "if only." Halil came and sat beside me, holding my hand and stroking it as he comforted me. All those lost years, Mr. Stratton, of misplaced anger, of secretly hating her. To have it all swept away by the arrival of a nephew calling me Aunt Sema. And then to have that finding become, in just a week, a tragedy. I lost Cemil twice, Mr. Stratton, twice.'

"Eric, she started to cry. Not convulsively, but a steady, rhythmic crying. It was the Madonna weeping for her son. I watched her while my own eyes filled. She gained control and spoke."

" 'Will you be seeing her?' Sema asked.

" 'Yes. Mother Ambrose and I are in contact by letter. But I plan to bring her word of her sister."

"With some effort, Sema nudged the ring from her finger.

" 'Give this to Bea. It was her engagement ring to him. It belonged to her great-grandfather. The crest of the Stradivaris. Tell her I send it with love. My message will counter the bitterness from Rome.'

"She stood up and put the ring in an embroidered handkerchief. She tied the ends and handed it to me. I clasped her hand and thanked her for the gift."

" 'It is good", she said, 'that a writer has the truth. I am

204

assured it will not die. Yusuf is waiting outside to drive you, Mr. Stratton. One request, please. When you complete your book, send me a copy, will you?'

"I assured her I would and left. I had dinner alone that night at the Hilton and decided to fly back the next day. My trip to Istanbul had achieved its goal. I arrived early evening yesterday and called you immediately. After all, Eric, you were the one who started it all. If I hadn't made that first trip to the abbey, none of this would have happened."

"It wasn't your visit to the abbey that sparked it. It was *Poems for Two Violins.* The poetry isn't ended. You have enough now for an anthology."

The waiter came over, and they ordered espressos.

"Now that you're back," Eric said, "what are your plans?"

"There's a stack of mail I have to sort out. I'm hoping for a letter from Mother Ambrose. If I haven't heard from her, I'll call and plan a visit. I owe her some communication about her sister."

"And what about Lisa? You know, while you were away she phoned several times. I kept my promise and never rang back. As far as Lisa is concerned, I was on the road painting more canvases for the exhibition. But it doesn't seem right to avoid the relationship. You can't let it trail off indefinitely. She's a little frantic. It's almost two weeks since you two last spoke."

"You're right, but something in me resists. I feel a hardening in my mind, a calcified judgment. It won't budge."

"You mean you won't. You're just not ready to resolve things. It's only fair to let Lisa know if there's a future with you or not. She's entitled to get on with her life."

"Wasn't my moving to Commonwealth a signal to her?"

"She'll see it as a separation, not a divorce. It's not clear you know what it means."

"At some point, I'll call her. Maybe there's a message from her in that pile of letters."

"You haven't gone through them? That's not like you. It's the first thing you do when you get home—even before unpacking. Obviously, you weren't eager to know."

Philip smiled. He had no idea he was so transparent.

"That's what I like about your friendship. Your truth-telling corners me, Eric, but it doesn't make me squirm. I'm glad you're on my side."

"I'm on both sides. It's late. Let's pay and go."

As soon as Philip arrived back at his apartment, he went over to the mail and discarded what was irrelevant. As he neared the bottom, he found her letter. Her handwriting pulsed like a neon sign. He held it for several minutes. Opening it meant inviting her back into his life. It was also an invitation to reciprocate. Should he or shouldn't he? He recalled Daniela's unfairness at not answering Mother Ambrose. It acted as a lever clearing his mental block. He slit the envelope open.

March 12, 1989

Philip:

I acted wrongly and hurt your feelings. I'm very sorry. You were right. I do have a problem with trust. I can't promise I'll get over it. All I can say is I'll try. If I make any progress, it will be with you. I've never gone as deeply with another man. If there's any trust in me at all, it's in our intimacy to heal me.

I have no idea where you are. I addressed the envelope care of Miles, hoping he would forward it. If you stay away, I understand. Please don't. I miss you and want you home.

Lisa

The letter's candor touched him, and he let the words sink in. They were inviting him to examine his own conscience and discern where he was at fault. The night before he left for Europe, Eric had said he was trying to escape from Lisa by pursuing a fantasy. Did his fear of closeness trigger Lisa's mistrust? Who should forgive whom? "Two to tango" might be a cliché, but there was truth in it as a principle of mutuality.

He recalled his interview with Sema. For all Cemil's heroic activity, he had hurt Bea through mistrust. That was the insight of his Turkish visit. Was he to repeat Cemil's error? He felt the wind of reality clearing his mind. Only one person could help him sort it through, one person who had earned the right: Mother Ambrose. It was too late to call the abbey. He would do so in the morning. If, as a writer, he felt the plot thickening, he sensed, too, the movement toward a climax. He pulled down the Murphy bed, undressed, and slipped under the covers. Whatever the cost, he thought, insight was all. It made him sleep soundly.

Chapter Nine

Philip woke the next morning after ten. It was rare that he slept so late, but his body was still adjusting to jet lag. He brewed some tea and took a mugful to the terrace overlooking the garden. When he slid back the door, he expected a chill March wind. Instead, the day was mild with a forecast of spring. He could smell the earth as if it had been turned for planting. The sun was making its morning ascent, and as he lounged in a deck chair, it warmed his face. The aroma of tea and the fragrant garden set him at ease, pressuring him to do nothing. It was too early to call the abbey—he would phone later and arrange to see Mother Ambrose—and his Daria story could wait. The only dark spot on the cloudless horizon was Daniela. Philip did not want to cause Mother Ambrose pain, but she had to know about her sister.

He recalled his meeting with Sema. Eric was right. It had been impetuous to fly to Istanbul for an afternoon with a total stranger. But he needed to appease his burning curiosity. He smiled at the word, "burning". The description was apt, the inflammatory questions fueling the mind until doused by the facts. He did not regret the expense of his journey; it was a truth stipend well spent.

Suddenly Philip jumped up. Where was it? Had he packed it? He rushed inside to check the pocket of his suitcase. Cemil's ring was still there. He undid the handkerchief, removed it, and returned to the terrace. He sat down and turned it on his marital finger. He nudged it a little and found it fit perfectly. Sliding the ring off, he studied the heraldic design. Oval-shaped, the crest was horizontally engrailed in equal parts, the top half displaying a gold dolphin against a red background, the lower half, a red dolphin against a gold background. Both were leaping from an invisible sea. Carved under the crest in bold letters was the name, STRADIVARI. Though the crest sufficed in identifying the family, the name was appended as clear confirmation. Rather than return the ring to his suitcase, Philip decided temporarily to wear it. He nudged the ring down on his fourth finger. In Mother Ambrose's absence, her escutcheon would do.

Despite his late rising, he yawned at intervals. The sun had made him so groggy he could not resist shutting his eyes. He struggled but conceded defeat. In his comatose state, Philip began to dream.

He saw himself in a sailboat fifty yards from a tropical beach: palm trees, white sand, lapping waves—all the paraphernalia of a paradisal setting. The boat was drifting on calm waters. He was lying full length, astern, his head cushioned by a pillow on the back seat, his left hand furrowing the water. Suddenly, he heard splashing in the distance. He sat upright, scanned the horizon but saw nothing. All at once, something leapt from the water and vanished into the depths. He waited and watched. It leapt again, a silver-blue dolphin now only feet away, its arched back, slender snout, and silvery fins in full view. Smiling benignly, it dove once more and just as swiftly shot into the air only to dive again, appearing and disappearing in a parabola of light. Soon it was alongside the boat, which unaccountably followed the dolphin's lead. During its leaping and diving, the dolphin cocked its head to the left, staring at him, and with its fins beckoned him in. At first, the invitation terrified, but the attraction to follow became irresistible. Again the dolphin hovered midair and beckoned. This time Philip threw caution to the wind and dove. Together, he and the dolphin leapt from the water at equal heights and plummeted into the sea, the two of them enacting an aquatic ballet. Each airborne splash left behind a rainbow.

He gazed at the dolphin's face. Its features kept altering. At first he saw what resembled Bea, then Daria, finally Lisa. The ambiguity perplexed him, enticing him to follow. The two continued to leap and dive, splash and play while she alternated faces. But whom was he following? As he looked through the shimmering depths, he realized his female companion had vanished. Had she intuited his question and fled? He looked again. All he could see was a coral reef and marine flora swaying. Swimming to the surface, he found himself back at the side of the boat and hoisted himself over. Bereft of his companion, he sat there, forlorn, scanning the cloudless horizon. Suddenly, and for the last time, he saw her leap from the water. She soared upwards to a prodigious height, her body arched, the argentine fins flashing, as she hung suspended above the placid sea. Though he could not discern who it was, he knew the dolphin gazed at him with benevolence. Swiftly she had pursued, with constancy she would abide. Under the sign of the dolphin, he had found love in the companionable sea.

Philip awoke. Wind was flapping the canopy above the terrace. The canvas lapped like waves near a shoreline. He looked at his watch. It was after eleven. He knew that if he was to call Mother Ambrose, it had to be now. Lunch was served midday at the guest house, and it was conceivable she would be assigned to the retreatants. Reentering the studio, he put Cemil's ring in the handkerchief, replacing it in the suitcase, and returned to the terrace with Miles' cordless phone. He resumed his seat and dialed the number which he knew by heart. As he awaited a response, he played with his Saint Philip medal. Finally he heard Mother Thérèse at the other end.

"Abbey of Regina Pacis. *Pax Christi.*"

"Hello, Mother. It's Philip Stratton. How are you?"

"Fine, Philip. It's good to hear your voice."

"I know I'm calling close to lunch time, so I won't hold you. I recently returned from Europe, and I thought I'd arrange a visit. I'm eager to see Mother Ambrose."

"You're always welcome to come, Philip, but for the time being, Mother isn't seeing anyone. A week and a half ago—it was after you left—she had a relapse. The weather turned nasty, and you know how sensitive she is to the cold. Her condition went from bad to worse. The infection became bacterial. It was touch and go, but the doctor gave her antibiotics just in time. They can't always be relied on if the infection has spread through the body. But they bought Mother precious time so her natural defenses could work. She was in the intensive care unit at the hospital. Now she's in the abbey's infirmary. It will be awhile before she's allowed visitors."

Philip listened in a state of shock as he registered the guarded prognosis. All he could do was express his concern.

"Mother Thérèse, your news is very upsetting. Please tell Mother Ambrose I called. I hope she's received my letter from Italy to cheer her up."

"She has, Philip, and it helped. I read it to her when she was still confined to bed. She was quite ill. She was even anointed as a precaution."

"I'm not a Catholic, but it sounds awfully serious."

"It is, Philip. She's gaining strength now, but slowly. Is there anything you want me to say? I could pass on the message."

Philip hesitated. This was not the time to relate his meeting with an embittered sister. He put the best face on his reply.

"Tell her everything went accordingly. I even have a surprise for her. May I call in a few days to ask about her condition?"

"Of course. Meanwhile, I'll tell her you phoned. Do say a prayer for her recovery."

"Yes, Mother, I shall", he answered, not certain about what he was agreeing to.

"God bless you."

He put the receiver down and sat stupefied in the deck chair. He had imagined a different scenario: visiting Mother Ambrose within forty-eight hours; giving her an edited version of Daniela's conversation; and then, the crowning touch, returning Cemil's engagement ring. Now all of it would wait.

Restless and upset, he could idle on the terrace no longer. He reentered the studio, locking the door behind him. He needed to be outside, feeling the affirmation of spring. As he grabbed his jacket and book, he formulated his plans. He locked the apartment door and skipped waiting for the elevator, taking the stairs in twos. When he got outside, he walked down Commonwealth Avenue to Charles Street where he took the train to Harvard. Once out of the station, he headed toward Saint Paul's Church where his Daria story had taken shape. Across from the church was the Cafe Pamplona. The outside of the cafe was still vacant of tables and would be till late April, so he settled for a table within. He ordered a double espresso. He needed something strong to clear his head. He had brought von Galli's memoir, having decided to read the last section before returning the book to Widener. As he turned to the title page, his eyes descended to the citation from Yeats, "Bodily decrepitude is wisdom." It was true, he thought. Something in him, too, had become older and wiser. He knew it had nothing to do with age or intelligence but with an attitude toward himself and the world. He had yet to articulate it. That was why he turned to von Galli: to gain clarity. He opened to the last chapter, "Odds and Ends", and began reading.

I have just returned from a long morning walk, my only exercise of the day. The peculiar mix of climate drew me outside. The temperature had dipped so sharply during the night, that by sunrise the red horizon, steaming lake, and spectral trees resembled the dawn of creation. I felt I had returned to some primeval world before the separation of sea from dry land. For half an hour, I stood transfixed by the phantasmagoric fog. When it lifted, I ambled up the walkway past the statues of the ancient philosophers. On a walk such as this, they greet me like genial neighbors. I acquired them thirty years ago when I was half their age, but I have since caught up. Their faces are as rutted as my own, their torsos scarred by the gales not untypical of this allegedly tranquil region. Como resembles a well-behaved child who throws a tantrum from time to time, pummeling everything in sight. Through it all, the statues have maintained their stoical calm.

Villa Galliano has become a principality, and I, the sole ruler of a population composed of four gardeners, three servants, two cooks, and one valet. It is as if this promontory had seceded from the motherland, had declared its independence by imprinting money and stamps, and were governed by its own laws. The grounds comprise an estate surrounded almost entirely by this moat of a lake. No drawbridge lets down to the mainland, no consuls or financiers claim access. I reign alone. From one end of the gardens to the other, I walk a distance of two miles, sometimes circling back, at others cutting through the pine grove to the roadway.

I know every boulder, every bush, every tree. I have memorized this property as a lover does a woman with whom he has lived, day in, day out; who knows the scent of her hair and the pulse points to which her perfume clings; who admires the varnish of her nails and the finger ritual of fluttering them dry; who on bad days endures her rage and punitive silence, and on good, the reconciliation and ensuing joy. Thus, to this villa am I conjugally joined by an indissoluble bond.

This morning, I have chosen to sit in the groin-vaulted loggia near the stone balustrades. Above hangs the crest of the Martell family, whose hammers, triangularly arranged, are barely perceptible under the choking ivy. Alone on this elevated terrace, I encompass the whole of Como. On the table lie the remains of breakfast, which Rico will clear away. Each morning the menu is unvaried: black coffee, toast with jam, a boiled egg. There is little room for improvisation, though Rico entices me with seasonal fruit or biscotti from the local bakery. I disappoint him by leaving these foods untouched. Breakfast moves in a *fixed orbit. My life has become a series of gestures as strict as Kabuki. It is the result of domiciling alone, each day a replica of the last. For all the serenity of this villa, I am held prisoner. In bondage to the rules of myself, I have no one to free me from the shackles of habit. I cherish predictability yet loathe it, turn to routine for solace yet welcome any surprise that proves my life is not circular but is moving irreversibly forward. I look to my end as a source of innovation. Since I do not subscribe to theories of rebirth, I applaud being human once. Death remains an estimable curiosity. In my mind's eye, it resembles the journeys I took to the tops of mountains or the depths of oceans. Himalayas or Pacific, rain forest or sandy desert, the goal was compelling and I felt alive. I am as expectant about death, its terrain filled with promise. It cannot be very far off.*

The other morning, after I had bathed and was drying myself with a voluminous towel, I caught sight of myself in the mirror. In recent years, I have avoided such full-length examinations, but this time I gave a hard stare. The adage, Mirrors Do Not Lie, became a lacerating truth, for the shock was unbearable. My skin was sallow and dry, the upper torso flabby. My arms and spidery legs were mottled with age spots and arthritis protruded my bones. A face notable for its hangdog expression topped this wreck of a man. I was aghast. How did this happen? I asked. Who could have been so cruel? In my mind's eye, I am still the young man, agile in gait and swift in execution, my chest rippled with muscle from scaling mountains or scrambling into ravines. At what point did I transmogrify into this caricature? The impression was so disturbing that I had Rico remove every mirror. I could not repeat the horror. Already, the image keeps me from sleep, for under these lineaments lurks the death mask.

I know why I began this book. When a man has lost all zest for life, it is time to inscribe his memoir. With Bea, it would have been otherwise. I still recall how, in Capri, she wrote her poetry under the trellis after a dessert of figs and wine:

> *Four hours we spoke, oblivious that time*
> *Had ticked the evening past in offbeat rhyme;*
> *But in short space, you bought my spirit free*
> *To counter you in poetry:*

> Like some Bach fugue, whose bland, thematic start
> Compounds itself while it employs
> Impassioned poise and counterpoise,
> So by this rivalry you earned my art.

Since she had denied me physical love, I, too, had swerved my desire into verse. Poetry supplanted the merger of bodies. I had to wait for a farmhouse in Sorico, the Fascists in hot pursuit, to take possession. O union of flesh, whose memory leaves me embittered. I anticipated the brevity when I wrote:

> The passion kindled once with hands grown bold
> So dwindles to estrangement time foretold,
> That now when limbs become the artifice
> Of each embrace, I die upon our kiss.

Despite this disavowal, had we married and together grown old, our love would have introduced novelty, and life might have kept its savor. "Would have", "might have", — how I loathe the subjunctive mood. Whenever I hear the Italian verb form with its peculiar hissing following the word, magari, "if only", I go stone deaf till the speaker is finished. It reminds me too much of my losses. So I avoid the villagers with their babble of wishing and yearning. I prefer the moaning of wind, the susurration of trees, the gurgle of water over pebbles. Nature's sounds have no tense; the mood is eternal.

I leave no heirs. What survive temporarily are my books moldering on library shelves. I had hoped that words were stronger than decay; that style would fix my thoughts for eternity. Now I am not sure. I have offered no comprehensive vision like the great authors; presented no systematic insights like the philosophers. My works give an idiosyncratic assessment of the world which was of interest to the reading public. All of it has passed. At moments, I regret not seeing a son's son carry on the von Galli name. That, too, may be a vain hope, for there is no guarantee that an ancestor, christened Darius, would not exhibit a mind as twisted as a Roman emperor's.

Only once did I think of passing the mantle to a young man who might have been my spiritual heir. His intelligence and physical bearing reminded me so much of myself that I was awed by the *likeness. It was Bea's son from Istanbul. He met me in Bellagio and squired me about in his car; took me to cafes which I might have selected had I known them, and showed me his hotel which I would have frequented had I been aware of it. His gestures, his manner of speech—they were mine. I think we were both disquieted by the overlap. It was uncanny that a romantic friendship should spring up between my rival's son and me. Bea was in the States looking for a home near her sister in Massachusetts. I had invited Halil to move to my villa and stay as long as he wished. The relationship was Greek, the older man eager to memorialize himself in the younger man by replicating himself; the younger man seeking to absorb the savoir faire of the master and thus model himself on the father he never had. It was narcissism, pure and simple. Knowing its name did not make it less compelling. When he left me that summer, the aftermath was wrenching. It was as if I had been separated from my own flesh and blood, cut off from my solitary heir. When, weeks later, Halil died in a climbing accident, I never again allowed such intimacy to develop. I grew into the revered icon people made of me. I became my persona.*

Since I belong to the public, I have made them my sole heirs. I have bequeathed this villa to the Fund for the Italian Environment. All the treasures within, the portrait of Bea preeminently, are gifts to posterity. I have asked Rico to supervise my cremation. No doubt he will be punctilious in scattering my ashes on the lake. No embalming, no sarcophagus or mausoleum. Just the freedom of being airborne, the residue of myself carried by the wind to mix with the lake. The waters will lap my ashes onto the land where I will mingle with the earth. It pleases me to feed the vegetation along the shore.

On the terrace, I have erected a cenotaph upon which the following inscription is struck:

> *Left with the odds and ends*
> *Of dreams, he could only say*
> *As in love, he fell into dying*
> *In the same astonished way.*

I am becoming drowsy. I can feel the volume of sleep pressing down. My eyes are heavy while my fingers struggle to finish this page.

Presently, I will release the pen and my head will nod to one side.
What pleasure I take in dreamless sleep. It is a state of abeyance, of
placid emptiness. How sweet to feel the self grow dim, awareness
flicker, then go out.

Philip closed the memoir, knowing it was for the last time. He
had absorbed more than enough classical resignation. He was
not unfamiliar with von Galli's wistful mood, which struck
him, too, when he was experiencing writer's block. But to end
one's life in a state of acute stoicism repelled him. Such an
attitude was death to resilience, and he needed to retain what
little he had. Mother Ambrose's near miss with death had
troubled him deeply. To continue reading meant being flattened
by Darius' ponderous spirit.

Philip looked around. He was alone in this cafe below street
level. The dimly lit room, the feeling he had tunneled to some
impregnable depth, made him feel cramped and imprisoned.
He had to get out. He paid for his coffee and mounted the few
steps to street level. The air had turned colder, the wind off the
Charles River buffeting his face. He stood for a moment, deter-
mining in which direction to walk. Should he go to Widener
and return the memoir, or not? He was about to decide when
the sound of voices distracted him. Music appeared to be coming from Saint Paul's. He stood and listened again. Yes, he was
right, it was from the church, which had featured so prominently
in his diary about Daria. The music beckoned him forward. He
crossed the street, climbed the front steps, and entered the
warm interior. As he walked down the nave, he heard a voice in
the loft giving directions. Philip stopped midway and turned
around. A fully assembled choir was practicing for an imminent event. In the front pew, the parish bulletin explained,
giving dates and hours for the Holy Week services. Philip sat
down as the singing recommenced. The organ remained silent
while the choir proceeded *a cappella*. What he heard was

Gregorian chant echoing through the vaulted church. As he listened, he recognized single words: *redemptio, crux, resurrectio.* The choral voices rose and fell in arsis and thesis, as the music returned his memory to that night at the abbey when he visited the chapel for Compline. He could see the nuns in their black habits, the long shadows wavering from the flicker of light coming from the candles on the altar. He closed his eyes and saw Mother Ambrose's face. Her gaze was fixed on the hymnal, unaware he was watching from his dark corner. As he visualized her, the thought that death had nearly claimed her agitated him. He heard Mother Thérèse's appeal, "Do say a prayer for her recovery, Philip", and his reply, "Yes, Mother, I shall." So here he was, cherishing a woman in church while his thoughts were accompanied by voices that extolled a crucified but risen God. The music embraced his shifting moods: the pain and yearning, the loss and hope, what von Galli himself had portrayed at the end of his memoir without the final resilience.

"Yes, Mother, I shall." The promise seemed to resonate in the cavernous church and repeat itself like a mantra. The words drew him to his knees, and a petition, stiff from disuse and drawn from a past almost past remembering, was spoken: "Help her." It was finished. Once said, he could not rescind the words without recalling he had said them. He had uttered a plea so simple in its acknowledgment, that an image came back from his childhood of a stone rolled away and an angel guarding the tomb.

He continued to kneel while the words, "Help her", permeated him like the chant filling the church. They became an incantation till he no longer spoke them but was the one spoken through. It was new, this gaping into another kind of space. All his prior sitting in cafes waiting for inspiration, all his search for words seemed like preparation for this gracious moment. He felt filled with possibility, though he had abandoned everything and grasped nothing. It was the upright posture, not of resignation, but of openness.

Philip looked up. To the left of the altar, he observed the Virgin with her arms outstretched in a gesture of acceptance; then Christ with one hand extended, the other pointing to his exposed heart. Both faces had looked on joy and sorrow without demeaning anyone or anything. For the defensive person, Philip thought, such porousness to life seemed incomprehensible. While he gazed at their tranquil features, the chanting finished. As the choir rehearsed the Hallelujah Chorus and approached the terminal climax, Philip was suddenly wrenched out of his boundaried perception of things, and a brilliance, pouring from the statues, washed over him. He sat there in blissful immobility, buoyed on a sea of goodness, feeling profoundly loved: his family, Eric, Mother Ambrose, Lisa—even Daria, whose existence was fictional—all had cherished him. The intensity of this insight was barely supportable, and his eyes began to fill. It was the first time he had ever cried for joy. As the mood subsided and his reflective powers returned, he had to admit he did not know when he had ever felt such freedom and self-affirmation coalescing in one illumination. Here in this Cambridge church, a petition had wedged a door open and a light had so flooded in, that he knew more clearly what he had been seeking. The chorus ended, the choir dispersed, and Philip returned to the linear present from the margin of things.

A half hour later, Philip was crossing the Charles River on his way back to Miles' apartment. Empty-handed, he had returned *After Long Silence* to Widener. As he looked out the window and watched the marina glide by, he imagined seeing von Galli's book shelved in its customary place. Even in that haven of ventilation and cooling, geared to optimal conditions, time would yet have its way. The pages would go from white to yellow to brown as moisture was squeezed from the fibers and the first cracks appeared. Then the flaking, crumbling, and return to dust. Still, he had to admit the book had made its impact. He had read some passages so many times he knew them by heart. Not the stoicism, but the overriding spirit of the prose: the passion, the yearning, the effort to reach beyond the printed word to immortalize, all this Philip had absorbed together with von Galli's need to cherish. The book had, indeed, accomplished its goal. It was right and just to relinquish it like a raft that had reached the other shore. Philip knew he had crossed over in some inexplicable way, the book the means of transit. Even if it never again left its place, he was taking it to Boston. From now on it was his *vade mecum.* Philip had become the book.

The thought eased the sadness at returning home alone. His mood had lightened by the time he unlocked the building's front door. He checked for mail in the inner foyer. Instead of letters, he found a manila envelope with his name on it. The return address had Albion in the corner. It was the film script that Miles had promised weeks ago. As Philip mounted the stairs, he tore at the seal and removed the contents. A note was clipped to the first page.

Philip:

I hope this meets with your approval. Albion has kept its bargain by not tampering with the story. It's virtually verbatim. They simply overlapped scenes for brevity with no softening of the satire. They're nervous about libel, but I assured them you would keep it in mind.

I hope you enjoyed your trip. Let's meet Friday evening for dinner at the usual place. Would you bring along the text with your *final* recommendations?

Miles

P.S. My number in L.A. is (213) 464-6766. Phone if you have any problems.

Two days later at six o'clock, Philip was sitting in Ninotchka's, trying to make up his mind. Miles was expected at six-thirty.

For three hours, Philip had watched the late luncheon crowd come and go. Now the room was half-filled with locals having afternoon tea. Philip was not at home with this overcosmeticized crowd. He preferred the denim look of Milano's.

Heavily penciled in red, the script of *Torrid* lay open before him. Philip had made major cuts, excising dialogue and even dropping one character. In the space of forty-eight hours, he had probed the text surgically as if he were looking to excise something from himself. He was amazed at his censoriousness, especially when he recalled his last conversation with Miles. This time, he had no gripe with Albion. They did what they had been enjoined to do, namely, left the text intact. It was Philip now who needed to intervene. As he read through the manuscript, he found the premise farfetched and its enactment improbable. But it was the articulation that caused him problems. He was appalled at his words, which had a way of sniping at the reader. Yes, the book was funny—but at everyone's expense. The meanspiritedness he rejected, which amounted to disowning what he had written. But could he reject a story that had capped the charts for weeks? And here was a chance to make another killing. Nonetheless, the prospect of wider exposure embarrassed him. Something impeded him from within but he could not say what. Why, all of a sudden, was he plagued by high seriousness? After all, *Torrid* was a diatribe against fake religion, and like the book, the film's satire would clear the air. But none of these arguments worked. All Philip knew, as he stared into space, was that he recoiled at having to tell Miles he wanted to drop the project. The time for reflection was over. Miles was being directed to his corner.

"You're looking well, no worse for all the running around. I heard you were in Rome, Como, then Istanbul. That's an odd sequence."

"How did you find out? I didn't write any postcards, and Istanbul was a last-minute decision."

"Your friend, Eric, told me. He called me in L.A."

"You two know each other?"

"He was looking for an agent to represent him at his first gallery show. He thought I might know someone who wants to work with new talent. I have a name in mind, but I plan to call him first before telling Eric. Why did you go to Istanbul?"

Before Philip could reply, the waiter came over to take their orders. He rattled off the specials—at least five with prices for each—and waited for a choice.

"Miles, I'm not up for a full meal. A burger will do, but I could use some wine. I'm in a drinking mood."

"Sounds fine to me. I'd like my burger well done, and bring a bottle of the Cabernet Sauvignon."

"Waiter, make mine rare but not a blood donor. And lots of relish."

The conversation ranged from L.A. to the East Coast, then back again. Miles was in a garrulous mood. He went through a book list, citing what titles pended at auction for film rights till he finally got around to the question that brought them together. He posed it as their meal was served.

"What do you think of the manuscript?" Philip swallowed some wine.

"I suppose I should be satisfied with the text. Weeks ago, I would have been delighted. It's all I might have hoped for."

"You're not."

"No."

"Why?"

Philip's reaction had caught Miles off guard. He was on the verge of pouring some wine but laid the bottle on the table. Interlacing his fingers on his lap, he awaited Philip's response. Miles' patient, intense gaze was disconcerting. In a conversation, he never backed off from an issue but waited. This time his face showed strain heightened by irritation. What he had hoped would be an easy exchange might turn into a round of negotiations.

"What I'm going to say will sound contradictory, especially when Albion did what I asked."

"What's the problem?"

"I'm not happy with the text."

"But you just said Albion gave you what you wanted. Naturally, they dropped the narrator—the scenario takes care of that—but the dialogue's a carbon copy of the original."

"I know. When I say I'm not happy, I mean the manuscript as I wrote it. From my new perception, I don't like what I see. Consequently, I don't look forward to *Torrid's* going from book to film."

"But why?" Miles asked with exasperation. It was rare that he raised his voice, but Philip was describing his feelings as if they were an explanation when they weren't. Miles sensed something was being omitted.

"Frankly," Philip said, "I think the text is . . . is irreverent."

"Philip, did I hear you correctly? I always said you had a way with words. But never, since I've known you, has 'irreverent' been one of them."

"It is now."

"And what accounts for this enlarged vocabulary?"

"It's hard to explain. I'm not sure I understand it myself. But something happened two days ago in Cambridge, something unexpected."

"Did you run into some street evangelists? There's still a remnant in Harvard Square."

"No, it may have happened in church. Or maybe earlier at the abbey. Or perhaps this evening before I met you. It sounds confused, I know, but I'm not used to carrying around something more than my own creations. I mean, I go about my daily tasks encountering what's in front of me, while my characters engage me at the corner of my eye. For instance, Daria, who's in my new novel. I can see her, hear her, smell her, even. But that's all at the surface. What I'm trying to get at feels like it's coming from way down, a depth that won't remain silent." Philip began tugging at the medal round his neck. Miles noticed his agitation.

"I don't know what to say, Philip. I mean, are you hallucinating? Hearing voices? Perhaps you need professional help."

"I'm not losing my grip on reality. And, yes, I'm having visions and hearing voices. That's what novelists are supposed to do. We're always in a state of psychosis. What I'm talking about is different. It doesn't seem to be coming from me. I mean it is, but I'm not entirely responsible. God, I never thought I'd be at a loss for words. Whatever is happening, I prefer it to the way things were. That's why I'm unhappy about *Torrid.* The story's at odds with me."

The burgers lay half eaten on their plates, but neither of them noticed. Finally, Miles broke the silence.

"I have to be honest. I don't grasp your situation. I'm an agent, not a priest or an analyst. This much is clear. You're disturbed, and it's clouding your judgment. I ask you not to act precipitously. At this late stage, the penalties for breach of contract are enormous. You're young in the field. You don't want to get a reputation. I suggest you take time to focus on what's bothering you. Speak to someone who knows you, or see a professional. We all do at some time or other. You're just backed up a little. Meanwhile, I'll stall Albion. Since we're being frank, I must say I'm not prepared to accept a no from you, not in your confused state. . . . Look, I have to go. I'm flying to New York in two hours, and you know what it's like getting to Logan. Stay put at my apartment as long as you want. At least I know where to reach you. I'll ring you in a few days and check in."

As a result of a call from Eric two days later, Philip found himself sharing another dinner. They were repeating a pasta and wine ritual at La Dolce Vita. Despite Philip's abstracted air, Eric chatted on amiably about the canvas he was painting. When he shifted to the subject of the forthcoming show, he said:

"By the way, Philip, I found Miles Gannen very helpful. I needed an agent's name, and Miles called and suggested William Brewster, the best in the business. I have an appointment with him in a few days. He'll visit my loft and if he likes the paintings, he'll represent me. I wouldn't have come this far without Miles."

"Yes," Philip added, "he's a considerate man. He's not ruled by the dollar sign. He's proved that in my dealings with him over *Torrid.*"

It was just the opening Eric had hoped for. He had something he wanted to say to Philip that had to be introduced diplomatically.

"How is that going? I gather from Miles you got the script and weren't pleased."

Philip became alert.

"You didn't invite me out to learn my reasons, did you?"

"We've been friends for a long time. I don't have to stand on ceremony with you. Your reaction to the script was discussed. Miles was upset. It seemed like such an about-face to get the text you wanted and then reject it. He asked me if I could explain what was happening. I had to admit I was baffled. As for dinner out, you can't blame a friend for being concerned. After all, I've lived through every stage of the book. Forget *Torrid,* you're the one who matters."

"Sorry for jumping at you. I have as few reasons to give you as I had for Miles. All I know is that the book repels me where formerly it pleased. It's irreverent even if Mother Ambrose says it often strikes the right note. She was indulging me. Her first reaction was more to the point. *Torrid* is abusive."

"So that's it. Do you think by squelching the book you'll please a cloistered nun? I happen to agree with her second assessment. The book strikes home when it's being ferocious. It barks, Philip, it rarely bites. And none of the reviewers accused you, outright, of blasphemy. You've never been that close to religion to need getting nasty. Try reading something by an ousted charismatic. Now that's rage. Anyway, you're very far from it all."

"Not that far. In the past, I paid no attention to religion until I met Mother Ambrose. I never guessed that all those quaint doctrines and rituals added up to a coherent way of life. I always thought religion was for the weak or muddled. I'd read Freud and felt he'd settled the issue. But then to meet this sophisticated woman in such an unlikely setting. To talk with her and correspond with her; to read about her and learn of her past. She's penetrated my imagination so deeply I can't get her out. The cliché of blowing one's mind is putting it mildly. Knowing her has been a series of controlled explosions, the way condemned buildings are detonated, and the debris cleared away for something new. *Torrid* needs to be cleared away. It's rubble. Maybe I'm wrong, but I don't think so."

"Why not test if you are or not?"

"How do you mean?"

"Miles told me he thinks you could use some help. Why not go and see Mother Ambrose? She'll help you sort it out. Her name isn't Beatrice for nothing."

"You're right. I've been meaning to."

"Anyway, she started the whole thing."

"You know, I said that to her once—I can't remember if it was in person or by letter. But she corrected me. She said, 'Philip, I'm not the cause of what happens to you, just the occasion.' Can you make sense out of that?"

"Not really. But I'm getting a whiff of the High Middle Ages. On second thought, it's something you'd say after your fourth B&B."

"You mean babble?"

"Intelligent babble."

It was over two weeks since Lisa had written her note to Philip. While her message included a disclaimer, that she would understand if he kept his distance, still, she had hoped he would let bygones be bygones, show a generosity of spirit by phoning her, and return to reinstate their relationship. Nothing happened. She would take her lunch break early each day, check her answering machine or scavenge through her mailbox in search of a message. Each day she was disappointed. Angry at first that Philip had not seen fit to answer, she felt incensed at having made herself abject to him. But when she reflected on the events that had preceded his departure, she turned the rage against herself, transmuting it first into guilt, then into mourning and depression. She desperately missed him and rued the moment she had decided to check Philip's story at the abbey and prove him a liar. If only she had trusted him, she told herself, and had not let anxiety destroy the most precious thing in her life. Now she was left with the intensity of her love and no Philip on whom to bestow it.

With her appetite for food diminished, Lisa lost ten pounds in two weeks. When she returned home after a taxing day, she felt no desire to eat dinner while staring opposite at an empty seat. Her restless nights reaching for an empty pillow, her fruitless reliance on pills to help her sleep made her during the day alternately listless and edgy. If she could see him just for a moment or at least learn where he was. She had phoned Eric, but he had already left town to paint at the Cape. Before leaving, he had returned her call, saying that Philip was in Europe but had left no itinerary. She had been tempted to interrogate Eric, asking, 'Did he go alone?" but salvaged her pride by stifling the question. The only one who phoned regularly was Eric's girlfriend, Vicki. Alarmed at what she saw when she visited the Mt. Vernon apartment, she said:

"You're as thin as a rail. You've got to put him out of your mind and take control. He'll come back, they all do. If he sees you looking anorexic, you'll be at a disadvantage. He'll know that without him you fall to pieces."

"I'm already in pieces."

"Then pick them up and put them together. I went through the same thing with Eric. Believe me, Lisa, nothing good happens till you get your house in order." The strong advice was heeded for a day, weakened, and died.

Lisa's editorial work suffered also. She was supposed to cast her ballot for or against a pricey manuscript, but she could not concentrate on the text, let alone gather the data to formulate her judgment. In a moment of desperation, she phoned Regina Pacis, hoping that Mother Ambrose, who had been Philip's confidante, might disclose his whereabouts. But Mother Thérèse relayed to her the message she gave to all callers, that Mother Ambrose had been gravely ill and, although on the mend, was still incommunicado.

"I will tell Mother you phoned. Shall I say you were asking for Mr. Stratton?"

"No. Yes. I mean . . . "

"I'm not sure I know what you want, Miss Roberts."

"Mother Thérèse, I wish I knew. Just say I'll call in a few days to find out how she's doing. Please send my best wishes for her recovery. And tell her I'm grateful for our last conversation."

Her call to the abbey reminded her of Mother Ambrose's counsel to respect Philip's freedom. Lisa remembered how, faking her reasons for her visit, the ruse of an anthology of poetry had been exposed. Poetry—the word reverberated in her psyche. Suddenly, she jumped up. Where was it? Frantically, she searched her file cabinets and closet, then her desk drawers till, opening the bottom one, she retrieved the slim volume in its blue wrapper. She clutched *Poems for Two Violins* as if it were a lifesaver tossed to her on a stormy sea. She had kept the book for days and, except for the inscription, had not bothered to read it. Now, pressured to secure help from any quarter, she pored through the contents in the way Philip had weeks before.

Similarly, the poems gripped her. For the first time in days, she forgot her romantic obsession and focused her energy on something beyond her relationship. Setting aside the manuscript she was supposed to evaluate, she read page after page of poetry, completely riveted. What helped her retrieve Mother Ambrose's image was one stanza attributed to the mysterious D.V.G.:

> This evening, Bea, inward vision sees
> Your form advance with calm, intrepid grace.
> My questioning mind has asked, what could appease
> The passion and compassion of your face
> Or set that high-born, brooding soul at ease,
> Whose common anguish is what's commonplace.
> The vagrant poor, the undistinguished dead
> Become your gracious wine and altered bread.

For split seconds, in between verses, she imagined a deluxe edition; or perhaps a text like Dante's *Vita Nuova,* where poetry alternated with prose written about Mother Ambrose by relatives and friends. Lisa felt an idea summoning her. She would forget the anthology. It had been a ploy. Here was something that mattered preeminently. That night, for the first time in days, with the poems bedside, Lisa slept soundly.

Chapter Ten

1 April, 1989

Dear Philip:

    With the arrival this afternoon of your surprise parcel, I wanted to take the first opportunity to thank you for the astonishing contents. If my convalescence needed a boost, your package achieved it. How thoughtful of Daniela and Sema to part with such precious items. Though I knew of the Stradivari formula, I had not seen it for years. As for the engagement ring, I thought it was irretrievable, either because the Nazis had stolen it or because Cemil, in an effort to send it from Paros, lost it in the mails. The reception of both gifts was like having limbs, formerly severed, surgically rejoined. If your intent was to enhance my recuperative powers, you have succeeded. Before the grand opening, I was advancing steadily. Now I speed to recovery.

    When shall I see you? Mother Thérèse tells me you telephoned, so perhaps I'm anticipating what you already plan. The doctor assures me I can have visitors. Do come. I cannot disguise my eagerness for news. That you are the source heightens my interest. Your vivid imagination, proven by the letter from Como, takes me where I cannot go. Most of all, Philip, your presence is the best gift of all.

Affectionately yours,
M. Ambrose, O.S.B.

If his express mail gift had astonished Mother Ambrose, her letter equally thrilled him. The chancery script on the envelope's face was indubitably hers. Considering the gravity of her recent illness, he noted the fluency of her penmanship, neither hurried nor labored. She was clearly on the mend. The same morning her letter arrived, he phoned Regina Pacis, spoke with the Guest Mistress, and arranged to visit the next day. Rather than take the train to Springfield, a tedious ride in uncomfortable seats, he dallied with renting a car. The climate was still volatile as the mild April days alternated with raw ones. For the moment, Boston was enjoying a spate of spring-like weather. He decided to drive.

The trip proved agreeable. Philip left Boston around seven, the light traffic easing his exit from the city. While driving, he reached to turn on some music but decided on silence. He needed to think. Since receiving Mother Ambrose's letter the day before, he was plagued by serious questions. He asked himself repeatedly if his petition in a church had anything to do with her return to good health. Did she feel the effects right after he had pleaded, "Help her"? His request had been granted, but how could he verify the source? Since learning of her recovery, an urgency arose in him to say, "Thank you." But to whom or what, he wasn't sure.

Philip was pleased by her convalescence, but he wondered if his prayer had altered the nature of things. Could he, Philip Stratton, be cosmically that important? And what if Mother Ambrose's condition had worsened? Wouldn't he have had to acquiesce to the Larger Scheme of things? Religious faith, he thought, always had it both ways. All would be well, no matter what. Though the questions disturbed him, they did not churn him up. At a deeper level, he felt at peace and did not, for the life of him, regret having prayed. But would he do it again? He recalled how once, in France, he had taken the train to Monte Carlo. While at the gaming tables in the Hôtel de Paris, he kept coming up with sevens. Was prayer like that, a favorable roll of the dice against the odds? Though he was no theologian, the comparison seemed odious. Still, he had to admit he had acted in a way that suggested a religious point of view. But Philip was hard pressed at the moment to say what it implied. Here was another catacomb through which Mother Ambrose might guide him.

Philip's attention shifted to the contents of her letter. He wondered if he should correct the misapprehension about her sister's generosity. After all, Daniela had parted with the parchment contemptuously, and only because he had requested it. And what of Sema? Should he inform Mother Ambrose of the conversation which occasioned the ring's return? Mother Ambrose wanted news, but how much should he reveal? It would be difficult to edit his remarks since she was counting on him for details. And what of Halil and the nettling question about whose son he was? Philip had to know if the portrait of Bea were to be complete. Somehow it meant entering her cloister and moving behind grilles and screens. Had a prayer in a church earned him the right to probe her inner sanctum? The questions crisscrossed as he drove. They were like a tortuous road running past detours toward a precipitous drop. He longed for conversation with her, yet feared the turns it might take, which were so much riskier than the highway outside his windshield. And Lisa, what of her? He had still made no effort to call and reestablish contact.

Momentarily distracted, he looked ahead a hundred yards and saw a rabbit hop onto the highway. Cars moving in the second lane caused it to freeze in its tracks. Since no vehicles were behind him, Philip drove off the road to avoid hitting it. As he watched it leap across the highway into the underbrush, something about its movement reminded him of his dream: of the dolphin leaping and diving into the sea. He shut his eyes and was back in his reverie, the dolphin beckoning to him. As if in control of a video cassette, he pressed "pause", freezing the frame, and examined the face. It was Lisa's. No ambiguity this time, nor did the features alternate with others. It was Lisa who had leapt into the depths. It was she who had lost and found him. Like the dolphins on the crest, she was his constant companion; her life paralleled his. Emotion surged within him and his eyes moistened. He longed to see her, to touch her and be touched. Opening his eyes, he managed enough alertness to drive back onto the highway. If he had not been so close to the abbey, if he hadn't already glimpsed the turnoff to Springfield, he would have veered the car around at the next intersection and returned home to call her. It was true all along, his dream confirmed it. Her fidelity was stronger than his resistance, his yearning stronger than her fears. He would abide her anxiety if she could live with his yen for privacy. Perhaps, he told himself, if he were more communicative, she would fear losing him less. It was clear he had to adjust his ways if they were to stay together. The insight filled him with purpose. As he took the road to Windsor, he wondered if, at the time he had said "Help her" in a Cambridge church, Mother Ambrose was saying "Help him" in her abbey room. He smiled at the thought that prayer might be a benevolent conspiracy.

After leaving his car in the abbey's parking lot, Philip went to Saint Thomas More House. He climbed the creaking steps to the second floor and opened the door, noting again the plaque and the saint's name to whom the room was dedicated: Saint John the Evangelist. "Another writer"—that was Sister Ursula's way of telling him he was in good company. He was eager to walk through the house and see if anything had changed. He descended the stairs and looked around. Everything was just as he had left it. The fireplace had been emptied of ash and a pile of wood was stacked to the side. The rocker was there standing at an angle to the hearth and the front door. As he moved to the dining area, he noted the table set for two. Place cards announced the lunch guests. His own name was on one, Father Stewart's on the other. There would be no Wayne Johnson to share the responsibility of conversation. Philip didn't dislike Father Stewart, but he would have welcomed a third to relieve the parochial talk.

As he looked more closely at the table, he noticed a message on his plate.

April 6, 1989

Philip:
Welcome back to Regina Pacis. We are happy to have you as a guest again. By now, you know your way around, so I needn't instruct you. Mother Ambrose looks forward to seeing you this afternoon. She will be waiting for you at the gazebo at one. She will be free until Vespers. If you have any problem finding your way, check with Father Stewart. He will be at lunch. Have a fruitful stay.

M. Thérèse, O.S.B.

He looked at his watch and noted he had two hours before lunch. Suddenly it occurred to him that he had forgotten his Daria story. Why had it slipped his mind? He had promised to give Mother Ambrose a copy. It was still undeveloped. Perhaps it was better to wait till the story was finished. Though he had forgotten his novel, he did pack the map of the grounds which Father Stewart had given him on his last visit.

Philip went out the door. The April day was mild, the sun not quite overhead. He inhaled deeply and enjoyed the air's freshness. A downpour had soaked the ground during the night. He could see the dark earth supersaturated in spots with water. Purple hibiscus were opening in clusters everywhere. He remembered e. e. cummings' description of spring, how it was "mud-luscious" and "puddle-wonderful", both apt descriptions of the abbey grounds.

Where to walk. He thought of the gazebo but chose to keep the lake and ducks for later that afternoon. He decided to amble up the hill. He took out the map and studied it. He recalled

Father Stewart's remarks about the pine forest. Reverend Mother had first arrived there, and it had already been laid with boulders in preparation for a new abbey. "It will be a marked contrast to the house the community lives in", Father Stewart had said.

Using the map, Philip followed the road past the barns. The hill was just beyond. He had always been interested in architecture, but had never seen the beginnings of a new monastery. His walk would while away the time and satisfy his curiosity.

The road up the hill was paved. In sections, it was strenuous going, the incline steep. Philip enjoyed the effort, for it slowed him down and allowed him to enjoy the scenery and the clement weather. The effort felt good after being stationary in a car for two hours. He checked the map again. According to the line drawing, the pine forest was just ahead. He left the road and turned to his right where he entered a large, shaded area filled with towering trees. They had covered the ground with droppings of reddish brown needles. The pungent odor of pine freighted the air and combined with the smell of dank, overturned soil. For a moment, Philip thought he caught a rose scent from somewhere in the vicinity. The pine reserve would have been silent were it not for the robins and blue jays vying for attention under the canopy of trees. Whoever had planted the trees spaced them generously. There was ample room to move around their thick trunks. Twigs snapped in the underbrush as squirrels zigzagged up trees and rabbits scampered into bushes. At a distance, he could hear a woodpecker hammering away at the porous wood. Philip stood still and listened to the chorus of sounds like someone sorting out motifs in a Bach fugue. He was enjoying his time alone with Nature, knowing, too, that the person he most admired was close, and that her company would shortly be his.

He stepped slowly, almost reverently, as if he were on holy ground. He saw the skeletal foundation up ahead. As he quickened his pace, he noticed to his right some slabs of stone. It wasn't till he approached that he realized it was the abbey's cemetery. Smaller stones that enclosed the area, while they could not forbid access, acted as boundary. Several tombstones were already showing signs of erosion. He looked at the names: Scholastica, Cecilia, Clare, Helena, and as he checked their dates and calculated their ages, he realized all of them had died in their eighties and one in her nineties. After each date, there followed the Latin words, *Requiescat in Pace.* The scent of tuberoses he had detected earlier was here particularly strong.

He walked ahead and finally stood on the periphery of the building site, a large area where walls of stone were partially erected. Large rocks and some boulders stood ready to be incorporated into the architectural scheme. Only the massive fireplace was complete. For all the promise the building offered, it resembled a medieval abbey in ruins. It made him think of his friendship with Mother Ambrose. It, too, had a recent foundation. Would it prove to be a false start given her age and chronic illness? Her bronchial weakness suggested as much. If he could have his way, he would whisk her off to some climate like Capri's where she would do more than prevail. She would flourish.

They seated themselves after Father Stewart had said grace. The priest greeted him warmly and asked, "What time did you get here, Philip?"

"Two hours ago. I took a pleasant walk around the grounds. I finally used the map you gave me. I took the road up to the pine forest. It's a poignant spot. The cemetery took me by surprise, not to mention all those tuberoses. It's quite a juxtaposition: towering pines, tombstones, and roses."

"It's very special. The place has a hallowed feel to it. Once a year in May, I say Mass for the whole community on the spot where Reverend Mother arrived. The scent of the tuberoses is everywhere. You know, Philip, you can take them back with you in a vial. The abbey produces a perfume called Attar of Peace. The nuns received the formula from one of their most famous guests, Michael Valerius. He's the Brother Distiller of the Chartreuse liqueurs in Voiron. He lived with us before he joined the Carthusians. The perfume Valerius gave the abbey is a blend of moss, gardenia, and jasmine, but the dominant note is the tuberose growing wild near the pine forest."

"Why didn't I receive a vial the last time I was here?"

"It's given to a guest who returns a second time. Then the community knows the person is serious about keeping in contact. The perfume seals the relationship. No doubt, you'll receive some before you leave. When you're home, you can remove the stopper, smell it, and allow your nose to take you back to the pine grove where the tuberoses bloom. No matter where I go, I always take a little with me. It keeps me close to the community. The perfume, as we have it, we owe to Mother Scholastica who prepared it according to the formula. She died last year. Maybe you saw her tombstone. Ninety-five. She would have gone on living, but I think she was eager for eternal life. I anointed her with holy oil and then touched her forehead with the perfume she had produced. She was in pain but the Attar of Peace made her serene, as if she'd been given a sedative. She died smiling."

Father Stewart's description of Mother Scholastica's death, however cheerful, disturbed Philip. He controlled his agitation and asked:

"Father, how serious was Mother Ambrose's illness? I gather she was also, as you say, anointed. Mother Thérèse mentioned the ritual to me. I remember reading something about it years ago in an Evelyn Waugh novel."

"It was more than serious, Philip. It was critical. For awhile, we thought she would die. The doctor feared her lungs might collapse. We had round-the-clock prayers in chapel. We needed all we could get."

Philip was hesitating, but he said it anyway.

"I said a prayer for Mother, too. I'm sure I was very clumsy. It was the first time in years. I was hoping against hope. I did it anyway."

"Thank you, Philip. Yours was the one that probably got listened to the most. I'm sure it was the loudest. Like Abraham's. If anyone hoped, it was that old man."

"Excuse my blunt question, Father, but how can you be so sure our prayers did anything? Could one ever establish a clear connection between my muttering in church and Mother's recovery? It sounds wildly disproportionate. I mean, why should God be obliged to listen? Doesn't God have better things to do?"

"God isn't obliged. The reason we pray is that we've been told to. It's conversation. And that's how intimates deal with each other. When we're close to someone, we speak up. We let our desires be known. All the saints knew how to speak up. Some had very strong voices. The Bible is studded with prayers who were do-ers. They were power brokers for humanity. Unfortunately, we're losing our capacity for prayer. So we're losing a power to influence ourselves and our environment. Without it, some humanitarian institutions would come to a dead halt. I know an entire hospital that's run on prayer."

"You can't be serious."

"Yes, I am. I was as skeptical as you till I saw it. I arrived in Canada to do some priestly work during my first summer after ordination. I was living at a rectory in Montreal. A young lawyer, Jean Lumière, invited me to visit a famous medical establishment. We took his car and went. The hospital was remarkable for both light and cleanliness. The feeling I had while sitting in the foyer was of a soft wind blowing through the place. While I waited for Jean, I got up and walked around. I noticed a blackboard on which I read in French, *'Nous avons besoin de.'* What followed was an enormous list of food, vegetables, medicines, even medical specialists. The list outlined the needs of that day. And you know, Philip, everything came through. It happens like that every day. What's more remarkable is that they don't keep anything in excess of their needs. What's superfluous is given away. Each day a new list is posted, each day the requests are met. Once, they were tested. They needed money for a new wing costing thousands. A millionaire happened to be driving through, read the bulletin board, and donated the money on the spot. Providence runs that hospital. It's alive with warmth. It's not for nothing it's called the *Foyer de Charité.*"

"But you can't run a hospital that way."

"That's what I told Jean. He said to me—and I was just ordained—'Father, the problem with Americans is that you want to do everything. How do you say it? You want it "all sewn up"? You leave nothing to God. This hospital is different. It gives Providence room to act.' I never forgot that visit or Jean's retort. He wasn't preaching passivity. He was one of the best civil rights lawyers in the city. He never denied we have to act as if we depended on ourselves. But praying, that's different. It's letting go and trusting. Or, at least, desiring to let go and trust. Some people never get much farther. It seems to me that's what you did in church. Mother Ambrose will be happy to know you were part of the chorus pleading for her health. When are you two getting together?"

"I'm meeting Mother at the gazebo at one o'clock. Is there any reason for being there rather than indoors?"

"The doctor wanted her up and about. The weather has been beautiful. He suggested she relax on the lawn and take the sun. She's been doing that for the last two days. She made me laugh yesterday. She said, 'The doctor was right. It's about time I got some color. A chalk-faced Italian is a contradiction in terms.'"

Father Stewart looked at his watch. "It's a quarter to one

Philip. I'm sure you want to get to your meeting on time. Mother is eager to see you." They both stood for the prayer of thanksgiving.

"Philip", the priest asked, "would you like to lead us in grace after meals?"

"What do I say?"

"Some form of thank you."

Taking his cue from Father Stewart, Philip lowered his head: "We are grateful for the food we have received, but mostly for Mother's recovery. Amen."

"Amen."

After the intervening weeks, his first sighting of her made his heart jump. She was sitting on the lawn in a deck chair near the gazebo, where she overlooked the entire lake. Her back was to him. As he approached the still figure, he noticed that, for all the warmth of the day—and it had risen into the seventies—she had her black shawl wrapped around her. From where he was standing, he could not tell if she was asleep, praying, or simply gazing at the tranquil scene before her. Ducks and ducklings glided on the lake at their leisure, disturbing the mirrored surface with widening ripples. The air, sweet with the odor of grass, promised the advent of a new season. The stately junipers bordering one side of the lake cast perpendicular shadows, now that the sun was overhead. The whole scene was a composition for an impressionist painter. Philip imagined the finished painting in some gallery: a huge, pointillist canvas entitled, *Lake View with Nun.* In the painting's absence, he let his mind's eye snap the picture. He would retain it in the album of memory to be extracted at some future time. For now, he turned his focus on the motionless figure. He did not want to startle her. Five feet away, he called:

"Mother Ambrose."

Her head lifted a little as Philip's voice alerted her to his presence. With some effort, she moved her torso to the right in his direction. He walked around till he was in full view.

"Philip, my dear boy!"

She rose and, for the first time, embraced him. The affectionate gesture was so timely yet so spontaneous, that a deep happiness took root in him.

"Philip, the chair leaning against the gazebo. I had a workman bring it out for you."

He went over and placed it to her right. As he set it down, he had a chance to observe her. Clearly, she had aged, for the illness had taken its toll. The face seemed more lined, her movements less vital. The expressive eyes and smile — these had not changed. They were landmarks on a worn landscape. It was like coming on a building that had been spared destruction after an earthquake. It was not in ruins, the structure proudly standing, but the cracks in the façade were apparent. Philip brought his chair up close to where she was and sat down. Reaching for his hand, she clasped and released it. She put her own with the other, concealing them both in her habit's broad sleeve.

"I've thought of nothing but seeing you", he began. "When I called and Mother Thérèse told me you had been sick, I felt guilty at not being here to support you."

"But you did support me", she said, her diction still touched by her Mediterranean lilt. "If it had not been for your letter, I might not have rallied at all. When it came I had Mother Thérèse read it to me. It was beautiful, Philip, and puckish, too. I could see Como from the veranda of that elegant hotel. I could smell the flowers. Soon after, my fever broke and I began to convalesce. Your words restored my will to live. What pleasure it gives me to have you seated beside me. I want to enjoy every moment. I am only permitted small periods outside even when the sun is strong. Then I must lie down. So tell me of your trip. How is Daniela?"

242

The question was inevitable. Philip had dreaded it for weeks, but like a plane in a holding pattern running out of fuel, it had to land. He exhaled slowly to calm himself.

"I had no trouble finding her, but I had to wait to see her. She doesn't live alone. There's a Chinese gentleman who shares her quarters. He combines the roles of nurse and house attendant. His name is Kuan. He asked me to return when I first asked to see your sister. She was asleep, so he didn't want to disturb her. As I found out later, she needs her rest."

"But why?"

"She's also been sick, Mother. The prognosis of her illness is not encouraging. Daniela has cancer and doesn't have long to live. I asked her why she didn't answer your letters and . . . "

"You needn't pause, Philip. I can cope with what you say."

"Well, she questioned your interest in her, saying that the family heirlooms were what really mattered to you. I protested, but she went off into a tirade about . . . "

"Darius?"

"Yes, and Cemil. It was awful. Because she was so ill, I controlled my anger. I can't bear the thought of anyone abusing you. I knew what she said was the ranting of a jealous sister who never came to terms with life. She sees herself as deprived and betrayed."

"It isn't untrue."

"Mother, you can't mean that. Please don't defend her against yourself because her life is terminal."

"Every life is, Philip. It's a matter of time. No, I could never deny her anger. I guessed it might be the case, but I was hoping it had softened. No, her outburst doesn't surprise me."

"But why did you send me if you knew she might react that way? I hated every moment of it. I can't tolerate anyone maligning you."

"I sent you because I suspected she might have an outburst. You had to hear it. It was important for you to know

243

that, though you esteem me, someone like my sister despises me."

"Mother, I don't understand. If you knew my faith in you would be tested, why did you jeopardize it by having me meet her?"

"So you would know my weakness. So you would have your fantasies altered and your idolizing modulated. So you would be challenged to love me despite my past and whatever darkness Daniela cast on it. I wanted you to accept me in the way I did you. I did not reject you after reading *Torrid*. I took much of the novel as part of your shadow side, the darkness your light cast. But it was the light that mattered. I sent you to Rome so you would not forget I have my dark and light sides, too. I had been self-centered as a young woman before the suffering of the Jews converted me. You see, Philip, I am a mix. At best, I am like Michelangelo's marble before the sculpting of David. There was a flaw in it, a crack in the marble. To produce his statue, he made the crack work for him. God has fashioned me into what I am, using the crack so it doesn't show. It is still there, only transformed. It is the paradox of flesh and spirit, dust and splendor. Despite the truth in Daniela's words, do you love me still? Without your acceptance, Philip, I am a dead woman."

"Mother, of course I accept you. And I'm not the only one. Another person esteems you as much. Sema. Her affection is stronger than any doubts she ever had."

"About Halil?"

"Yes."

"And yourself, Philip, do you entertain any doubts?"

"Not doubts, Mother, confusion. I can't seem to get the full picture. Daniela's version, Sema's account, von Galli's memoir. The pieces don't add up. I feel I'm missing something. It's all right. I can learn to do without. But as a writer, I can't help but wonder."

"About what?"

"About Halil. Sema is convinced that despite Cemil's sterility, Halil was Cemil's son. It was his obvious physical resemblance. But in the last part of his memoir, Darius hints at a resemblance between Halil and himself. That Halil went to visit Sema and Darius may suggest he was trying to clarify his identity."

"He was."

"And did he?"

"I do not think so. Not in this life."

"I don't understand."

"You have heard Sema's account. It is true that Cemil had bouts of impotence. They tested our marriage since we both wanted children. The strain was eased when I went to the north to guide Italian Jews across the border. There I met Darius. I had not seen him for many years. It was obvious after all that time he had not forgotten me. He was still in love. I enlisted his help as a photo journalist to keep a record of the German atrocities. It was important for the Allies to see the horrors. We worked together for two months near the Swiss border. Did you read where we nearly capsized on Lake Como and he almost drowned?"

"Yes."

"And how we escaped the patrols by putting up in a farm-house?"

"Yes."

"It happened there, Philip. And what is the truth? That he had his will with me? That I gave myself to console him? I cannot tell you if Darius took advantage, or if it was pity that broke my resolve. It happened once in a farmhouse. The next day, when we slipped past the patrols, I proceeded to Lugano to screen a guide for some Jewish refugees. Darius wanted to accompany me, but he needed to see his family in the Grissons. He was the only son, and communications with his parents had been cut off. He was sure they thought he was dead. We left

245

each other and the war intervened. I never saw him again till the twenty-fifth anniversary of my vows.

"When I returned to Salonika, Cemil and I began to enjoy a full marital relationship. His treatments at the hospital were successful, but there was still the question of sterility. Later, when it became clear I was pregnant, he was certain he was not responsible. I tried convincing him otherwise, but my admission of the episode in the farmhouse shattered him. It is possible he volunteered for Paros as a way of exposing himself to danger. His Turkish honor had been compromised. To this day, I cannot say what his last feelings were. Did he send his engagement ring as an act of severing, or did he intend that it be worn with my scarab ring, two keepsakes eliminating all uncertainty? I hold to the second despite evidence for the first.

"As for Halil, as the years passed, though he never knew his father, he enshrined his father's image. He so resembled Cemil that I never once doubted he was his son. But after Halil's visit with Darius on Lake Como, I believe the doubts came again, this time to disquiet my son. They are reflected in a last postcard from him in Zermatt. Like portions of the Gospel, I have it memorized:

> Dearest Mother:
>   I need to be alone to think things through. So I've come to these mountains. The light at this altitude wraps me in clarity. What I feel without, I seek within.
>   They say to understand all is to forgive all. I'm still groping.
>
>   Halil

"That was all, Philip, the words of a dead son. I cling to the salutation he used, 'Dearest Mother.' But sometimes I have thought it was written with irony. At others, I say, 'No, never Halil. It was not his way.' More shadow amid the light, Philip. More chiaroscuro. Now you know my version. The portrait is

246

finished except for God's version. It is the only complete one. I look to that Presence for the final truth. Saint Paul helps. Here, we see darkly, but there, face to face. And that other limpid line: I shall know even as I am known. These promises are not yet fulfilled. I try to be patient and do without.

"It is true what Daniela says. It pains me to let go of heirlooms: Antonio's parchment and my father's letters, the Stradivari guitar and the family furniture. I hunger for continuity. I cling to my family tree when I should cling to the Tree of the Cross. I have taken a vow of poverty. But it is hard, Philip, to be dispossessed. In my heart, I do believe that when all is taken, it comes back in another form. That is why I risked sending you to Europe. So you would come back and know me for the first time. Do you love me still?"

"Yes, Mother. Unconditionally. It will not change."

"Thank you, my dear boy. I feel born again. The burden is lifted." She removed a handkerchief from her sleeve and wiped the tears from her eyes. Reaching for Philip's hand, she clasped it and began again.

"I have something else to share with you which touches on the present. It is difficult to say."

"What is it?"

"The abbey is beginning a foundation in New Mexico. Three choir sisters and I have been chosen to go. My strength is returning and I should be ready to leave at the end of April. I will be Superior, and the overflow of postulants from Regina Pacis will join us there. Reverend Mother says she has chosen me for this work after consulting with our house physician. He has indicated that if I stay here another winter, I may not survive, whereas the climate of the Southwest is exactly what I need. It will be like returning to Capri. It also means, Philip, we shall be separated. Once we have established ourselves in New Mexico, you know you are welcome. You must come and visit."

"I'm happy for you and the community. It's a sensible decision. But it will feel empty with you gone."

"We have the mails, Philip. We will channel our communication in letters. In my absence, you will not be alone. Lisa will be there to support you. She cares deeply."

"Yes, I know that now. I hope it's not too late. We haven't been in touch. It was a silly misunderstanding, and my stubbornness didn't help. While I was driving here, I had this desire to be with her. If it hadn't been for seeing you, I would have gone back to Boston. Perhaps I can pick up the pieces after I return."

"You do not have to wait."

"Why?"

"She phoned several days ago to say she had given up the idea of an anthology of poetry. Instead, she has convinced Little, Brown to reprint *Poems for Two Violins* in a deluxe edition with poems I have written over the years. She spoke of a memoir, but I told her it would be best to discuss it in person. It is now two-thirty. She arrives at three."

"Mother, you're amazing."

"Not amazing, Philip, resourceful. I think we had better walk back if you're to be there when she arrives."

"Mother, before we go, I have one last question."

"What is it?'

"The parchment that Daniela sent you. Is it of any value? You know I kept notes for a novel based on your life. Antonio's varnish might be an interesting detail to use."

"The parchment is real, Philip, and the recipe it gives is the one Antonio used. But what is missing is essential: how the varnish is applied to the violin parts. I had to smile when I read it. My thoughts turned to the image of grace, how it is the same for all but varies in its application. It produces vastly different saints like Bruno and Ignatius, Joan and Teresa. They differ as much as an early Strad violin from a late one. Yet all have that unmistakable sonority.

"I have suggested to Reverend Mother that we auction the parchment and that the proceeds go for the new foundation. She found the idea most agreeable."

Philip helped her to her feet, and they took the incline toward the house. As they walked, he did something he had never done before. He offered her his arm. She took it, interlocking her own with his.

"Does Lisa know I'm here?"

"Yes. We've had enough jolts for one day."

"I agree. Too many turns in the catacombs. You've proved an excellent guide."

"Is that what they were? From now on, you've surfaced into the light of day."

It was a little after three when they reached the abbey. He walked Mother Ambrose to the door. Before leaving, she kissed him in the European way on both cheeks.

"Philip, I shall write you from New Mexico. Meanwhile, God bless and keep you. You had better go to the parking lot. If my eyes are not playing tricks, I think Lisa is waiting by the car." He embraced her and she disappeared into that other world.

Philip ran toward the car, and as he did so he noticed Lisa was coming toward him. When they met he swept her up in his arms and hugged her tightly.

"I've been foolish", he said. "It mustn't happen again."

"I know, Philip. We would have lost something precious if it hadn't been for Mother Ambrose. I must see her. I need to leave this contract and explain our plans for a new edition."

"She's probably in the parlor. You go ahead. I have one last thing to do. I'll meet you later." Alarmed, she looked at him as if she were going to lose him.

"It's all right. I'm just going to the chapel."

Leaving her, he walked the short distance. The chapel was

exactly as he remembered it: fresh flowers in vases, banks of candles flickering, the sanctuary lamp burning at the side altar. He moved down the nave toward the statue of the Virgin. Standing before her, Philip was startled by what he saw brightening her figure in the afternoon light. He went to his knees and in a barely perceptible voice said, "Thank you." He knelt for several minutes, rose, and left. Once outside, he took the path leading to the main house. Pausing to look back at the chapel, he thought:

The names of Hasan and Stradivari are hardly remembered in daily conversation. Yet whoever enters the chapel of Regina Pacis, which its Benedictine foundress never saw, will note how the afternoon light, filtering through the stained glass windows, illumines a chain around the Virgin's neck. On it hang pendants of contrasting origin: a scarab and a crest of dolphins, conjugal remnants of another age — the Rings.

Renewing his pace, Philip reached the abbey where Lisa had just left Mother Ambrose. As they walked to the parking lot, hand in hand, she said:

"She's an elegant woman. Finesse in her words and everything done with grace."

"I agree", he replied, as he moved more buoyantly. "Everything."

Epilogue

Dear Mother Ambrose:

I thought I would initiate this correspondence, since your move may find you still getting settled. Though I wrote you before at the abbey, it seems odd mailing a letter to New Mexico. I've never visited that state and would be hard pressed to say where it is. The name conjures up another culture.

I've wondered what it's like to start a monastery, and at what point it becomes an abbey? Is the climate salutary, and do you feel the benefits already? I'll be bristling with questions till I hear from you or visit you in person. Lisa and I plan a trip in September when the sunsets are awesome and display all the signs of a theophany. No doubt, the best plan is a visit at six-month intervals. I would like to see the Southwest in February when the desert begins to bloom. The conjunction of cactus, flowers, and limitless sand must be breathtaking.

Lisa is hard at work on *Poems for Two Violins.* She is collaborating with an accomplished artist of musical instruments. Having seen the first drafts, I can say that his eye for detail is microscopic, especially his rendition of Antonio's instruments on the facing page.

The special edition, comprising fifty copies, will be printed on paper handmade from the Portinari Mill in Florence. The crest of dolphins, embossed in gold, will adorn a crimson cover. Your own copy, Mother, will be bound in morocco. Presently, Little, Brown will send you a shipment of books that you will have to inscribe. *Poems* is being published under "Bea Stradivari." Will you need a Vatican permit to use your secular name?

You see how curious I am about the Church. As a result of my probing, Lisa has dusted off her convent school catechism. At my nudging, she's taken me to High Mass. While she fidgets through the service, I remain riveted. We both feel your benign influence even at a prohibitive distance. Three months ago, I might have said I felt your prohibitive influence at a benign distance. See what you've done.

At our last visit, I forgot to give you a copy of my novel in progress. Early in our meetings, I spoke of composing a biography based on your recollections. In their absence, I've written a fictionalized version, which is nearing its close. I'll mail it when Lisa sends you your poems. I've disguised the facts by making the protagonist an English girl studying violin at the Boston Conservatory. Since returning home, I've made some changes in coloration. The Daria character now has blond hair and green eyes instead of auburn and blue. The blonding and greening happened as if they had always belonged. Intuition tells me the changes are fixed.

As for *Torrid,* I finally approved a script. The last one from Albion was substantially the book I'd written; however, my altered perception found it irreverent, and I was preparing to drop the whole project. My agent was apoplectic even as I remained unbudgeable. A conversation with Eric and a review of your letters eased my repugnance. Here and there a nip and tuck tightened the dialogue, removed the abrasiveness, and strengthened the satire. While hypocrisy is hung, drawn, and quartered, piety goes unscathed.

Recently, I reread Dante's *New Life* and was so entranced with Beatrice that I let her lead me through *Paradise.* She's quite a lady, and though a distant object of awe in the first book, is rather social in the second. She exercises perfect tact, knowing when to appear and vanish, leaving Dante in capable Hands. You can imagine how strong was my déjà vu, after being guided this year by my more local Beatrice.

Mother, I miss knowing you're a car ride away. When the desire to see you becomes intolerable, I find my vial of perfume, remove the stopper, and take a whiff. The scent summons up the abbey grounds and the tranquil paths where we walked. Olfactory memory helps but it doesn't suffice. I want the real presence. Nonetheless, I accept the medical and monastic reasons that have taken you away, for I know the climate and your new office ensure your flourishing for years to come. I have to smile at a vow of stability that has you straying thousands of miles. If you were a missionary, would we lose you to another galaxy?

Several weeks ago, Lisa and I had dinner with Eric and Vicki. We took the occasion to tell our two best friends we were engaged and planned a church wedding in September. In fact, we've arranged things so that our honeymoon coincides with our trip to visit you in New Mexico. I have a hunch it won't be long before Eric also proposes. My premarital happiness is getting contagious.

Since our engagement, we all go out in a foursome once a week. After dessert, I've introduced a little ritual. It entails raising glasses of Benedictine to toast your incomparable Order without which, dear Mother, I would have enjoyed neither your golden liqueur nor you.

Yours,
Philip